KATRIANA
gripping the
"Ander, pleas

"Oh, we're past the point of begging," I told her, sliding my belt through the loops. "Spread your legs, Omega."

She didn't, her instinct to rebel too strong.

Breaking her of that habit was going to take time.

Fortunately for us both, patience came naturally to me.

I dropped the leather to the ground and flicked open the button on my pants. "You'll find that I do not enjoy repeating myself, Katriana." Her eyes followed my movements as I slid the zipper down. "You're also about to learn what happens when an Omega misbehaves."

Wolves maintained a hierarchy for a reason. Alphas at the top, Betas in the middle, and Omegas at the bottom, though they were cherished treasures owned and protected by their Alpha mates.

Katriana was mine.

To punish.

To fuck.

To impregnate.

To protect.

And I couldn't proceed with the latter if she was hell-bent on ignoring my commands.

I toed off my boots and socks, followed by my pants, leaving me clad in a pair of boxers that were far too tight for my growing arousal.

Katriana's eyes grew wide. "*No,*" she breathed.

"It'll fit," I promised her. Despite their petite forms, Omegas were built to accommodate Alpha cock.

But she shook her head in the negative and pulled her knees up to her chest. "*No,*" she repeated on a snarl.

My lips twitched.

She wasn't the only one who could make those sounds.

I returned her rumble with one of my own. However, mine held special properties. A call of sorts that an Omega couldn't deny.

She convulsed violently in response, the hairs along her arms dancing in appreciation. "*Oh God.*"

X-CLAN SERIES
ANDORRA SECTOR

ANDORRA SECTOR

AN X-CLAN NOVEL

USA TODAY BESTSELLING AUTHOR
LEXI C. FOSS

Andorra Sector

Editing by: Outthink Editing, LLC

Proofreading by: Joy Giachino & Tracey Morrow

Cover Design: Krys Janae, TakeCover Design Fiends

Cover Photography: CJC Photography

Models: Riley Rebecca & Taylor Scott

Published by: Ninja Newt Publishing, LLC

Print Edition

ISBN: 978-1-950694-42-6

To Katie, for all the long talks, brainstorming, keeping me company on long car rides to Florida, and for being an amazing friend. I'm so glad fate introduced us and I'm looking forward to many years ahead. Oh, and thank you for letting me borrow a variant of your name. This one is for you.

<3

ANDORRA SECTOR

SECTOR

AN X-CLAN NOVEL

A NOTE FROM THE AUTHOR

Every series I write is dictated and crafted by the voices in my head. This one came to me on a snowy hill in the middle of Andorra.

The voice started whispering about a world in the future plagued by a human disease that turned 90 percent of the population into zombie-like creatures. *She* called them the Infected. I walked around, listening as her story unfolded in my mind. She was a human surviving in the mountain caves, hiding from the Infected and all the supernaturals of the world. Until a wolf found her and changed everything.

Her story grew overnight into Andorra Sector. Which blossomed into a whole new world for my mind to play within.

Right now, I have three books planned, scattered across the globe. All featuring wolves and their survival in this cruel dystopian universe.

It's darker as a result. Sexy as fuck. And not for the faint of heart.

If dubious consent makes you uncomfortable, consider skipping this world. Because my wolves believe in full power exchange. The Alphas make the laws. I'm just the vessel for their voices, and this is their story come to life...

Enjoy.

PROLOGUE

ANDER

Dear Human,

My society is different from yours. We have rules. Alphas lead. Omegas submit. Betas are lucky to survive. If power exchange isn't your thing, I'd stop reading. But if you want to read the story about how I brought my little kitten to heel, continue and turn the page. I dare you.

Don't worry—she gives as good as she gets.

Ander Cain

CHAPTER ONE

KAT

"What the hell were you thinking?" I demanded, ducking behind a fir tree.

We were so utterly and completely fucked.

"Just shut up and move!" Maxim snapped, taking off down the snowy hill.

With a curse under my breath, I sprinted after him with Molly and Peter at my side. They were as angry as I was, their fury at our leader a heat wave that did little to dispel the chill in the afternoon air.

We'd already lost Jack and Serif a mile back, where the ambush went down.

Attacking a food transport destined for Andorra Sector, I thought. *He's lost his fucking mind.* When Maxim had claimed to have found a food source, I'd jumped at the opportunity to help, thinking we were going *hunting.* Not stealing from a damn wolf clan.

If we made it through this, I was going to kick—

A shot rang through the air, whizzing over my shoulder. I tucked and rolled, the next bullet landing far too close to my head.

Then a giant wolf landed in front of Maxim, effectively boxing us in.

Oh, shit...

I immediately bowed my head, knowing better than to challenge the shifter before us. He was probably just a Beta, but it wouldn't matter. A human—like me—stood no chance against the wolves of Andorra Sector.

Which was exactly why Maxim possessed a death wish. Had I realized what he'd intended to do, I never would have followed him here. Too late to regret it now.

Molly fell to the ground by my side, Peter at my back. While Maxim remained standing, his posture rigid. *Idiot.*

Snow shuffled around us, more shifters in wolf and human form spilling in from the trees. I kept my gaze affixed to the snow, not wanting to challenge them.

We needed an excuse. A plan. Something that explained why we'd jumped on that truck. Other than the obvious—we wanted the food inside.

Winter was always the worst for foraging, and living in the mountains meant being buried in snow. We couldn't risk the cities—too many Infected wandering around—and residing near Andorra had always provided us with a semblance of security. The wolves scared off the other predators of the world. Except they were predators themselves and they didn't take kindly to lowly humans drifting about. And the current season diminished our food supply.

Hence our desperation.

"Well, well, what do we have here?" a deep voice drawled.

I swallowed as a pair of boots appeared in the snow, leading upward into black jeans clinging to thick, muscular legs.

Definitely an Alpha.

No question.

I just hoped he wasn't *the* Alpha—Ander Cain. Simply

thinking his name sent a shudder through me. I'd never seen him, nor did I want to. His reputation for cruelty and leading under an iron fist was well known, even to those of us humans who lived outside of the dome.

The air prickled with power as the pack began to circle us, their intentions underlined in malice.

I swallowed. *Don't react,* I told myself. *Don't run. Don't—*

Maxim moved, a flash of silver blinking in the sunlight peeking through the trees, and the sound of growls ensued.

Molly screamed as our former leader fell to the ground beneath the weight of several wolves. Blood splattered across the snow, along with a revolver that landed near the Alpha's shoe.

The moron had tried to shoot one of them.

I suppressed an eye roll, forcing myself to remain still as carnage unfolded not five feet from me. Molly grabbed me, only to be yanked away by a snarling male telling her to shut up.

Which provoked Peter.

And more ripping, snarling, and gnashing began.

I remained on my knees, head bowed, doing my best not to flinch at the violence spilling around me. Yes, these were my friends. But I hadn't survived this long just to become wolf meat.

The Alpha took a step forward and lifted his hand to comb his finger through my tangled auburn strands.

Inhale, one, two, three.

Exhale, one, two, three.

The problem with my internal coaching was that his woodsy scent overwhelmed me with each inhale. Such a feral, masculine flavor, and very unlike all the boys at home.

He was clean, too. Another abnormal trait for this time of year, as it was hard to bathe outside when all the streams were frozen. Of course, that wasn't a problem for Andorra Sector.

"You seem to be the only intelligent one of your crew," he murmured, drawing his finger across my jaw. "Tell me what you were doing and maybe I'll let you live."

As he already knew our goal—it was too obvious for him not to—I had no problem giving him the truth. Even though

I doubted very much that he would actually let me live. But playing along was my only option.

Better to try than to give up.

I cleared my throat. "Maxim told us he found a food source. What he failed to mention was the owners of that food source, something the rest of us learned too late." The words came out raspier than I wanted, mostly due to the unexpected sprint through the woods in the dead of winter.

"And who is Maxim?"

Very slowly, I gestured toward the bloody pile to my right where the wolves were still feasting. "Him."

"I see." His touch drifted down to pinch my chin. He jerked my face upward, his dark eyes searching, studying, caressing each of my features all the way to my knees. "My, but you're a pretty one."

My heart skipped a beat, not just because of his words but because of the dark flare of interest blossoming in his gaze. Male wolves didn't ask for permission. They took what they desired, when they desired it. And while they usually preferred to mount their own kind, it wasn't unheard of for a shifter to take a human pet.

He tilted my head to one side and then the other. "What's your name, human?"

It took me a moment to reply, my tongue too thick for my mouth. "Kat."

"Kat," he repeated, his lips curling. "How apt. You *do* remind me of a curious kitten." He glanced over my head. "I do enjoy purring felines."

Chuckles met his remark, causing goose bumps to skate down my arms.

"Stand up, pussycat," he demanded, releasing my chin. "I want to get a better look at you."

He held out his hand.

I didn't use it, choosing to rely on my own strength to rise instead.

The smirk gracing his full lips told me he approved and found my hint of defiance amusing. Maybe I should have taken his hand after all.

"Turn," he instructed, using his finger to gesture a circular motion in case I didn't understand his command.

Prick.

With a thick swallow, I did what he demanded and tried my hardest not to notice the carnage around me.

But it was hard to unsee all the blood.

They're all dead.

Even Molly.

When they told her to shut up, I thought she'd listened. But no. They'd silenced her. Indefinitely.

I was completely alone and surrounded by at least twenty shifters. Likely more.

There was no question regarding my fate. If I survived, it wouldn't be because they allowed me to leave.

New plan, I decided as I faced the Alpha again. *Play along. Escape when able.*

I knew the walls of the dome well, knew where all the entrances and exits existed. Because I'd spent my life avoiding them. For the first time, I'd be seeking them—to run.

"Hmm…" His midnight gaze flickered with curiosity and something darker. Something that made my stomach churn.

He could kill me with a swipe of a paw, and the intensity radiating from his expression confirmed he was considering it.

"You claim Maxim was the organizer of this asinine attack," he said thoughtfully. "Unfortunately for him, he can't verify the truth." He took a step closer, forcing me to tilt my head back to continue looking at him. "Riddle me this, sweetheart. What food source were you expecting to steal from if not one from Andorra Sector? We're the only colony in over a two-hundred-mile radius."

"We didn't realize it was a food shipment." I cleared my throat, hoping to dispel the rasp from my voice. Maintaining his gaze took serious effort. My instincts roared to kneel and drop my eyes to his boots. But I needed him to see the truth in my features. It was the only way he might allow me to live— if he believed my innocence.

And I was, in fact, innocent.

"I thought we were going hunting," I continued hoarsely. "I didn't know our target was a truck until we reached the road."

The Alpha considered me in silence. It physically hurt to continue staring at him, my insides begging me to yield.

Too big.

Too strong.

Too domineering.

I blinked, my lower lip beginning to tremble.

He said nothing, his pack as lethally quiet as him.

My limbs shook.

My heart rate accelerated.

Until I couldn't take it a second longer, a gasp parting my lips as my legs gave out in a wave of unerring submission that took me to the ground.

It *hurt*, my knees slamming into the earth. My jeans did little to protect my skin, the scent of blood an iron flavor in the air. Maybe it was mine. Maybe it belonged to the massacre around me. I didn't know, my mind otherwise consumed by the heady intoxication of male Alpha.

I wasn't a wolf, but I *felt* his dominance down to my very soul. While I wasn't unfamiliar with his kind, I'd never been this close to a shifter, let alone a clan of them.

I'd much rather face an army of Infected. At least I knew how to kill them—with a bullet between the eyes.

Shifters were an entirely different animal.

Literally.

"You submit beautifully," the Alpha praised, petting my hair. His fingers trailed to my neck, his touch deceptively gentle. "I admit, I'm curious to explore the color inking your skin."

I shivered.

He meant my tattoos. They decorated my left side, adding splashes of pigment to my alabaster skin. Each piece held a unique meaning, and he stroked the most important one of all against my throat. It was a flower blossoming into claws—the design one my mother had drawn shortly before her death.

"Beautiful, but deadly, that's my Katriana," she'd said. *"It suits you."*

"Shall we keep her?" The Alpha asked the masses, his palm sliding to the back of my neck in a purely dominant hold. "I think she'd make a nice little pet for the border unit. She might even purr."

Rumbles of agreement met his proposal, each one reverberating down my spine and shooting pangs through my stomach.

Play along, I whispered to myself. *One-on-one, I'll stand a better chance.*

I'd fought my fair share of walking-dead creatures over the last two decades of my life, and while the Infected might not be as intelligent or strong as the wolves, defensive mechanisms were universal in a fight.

I can do this, I vowed. *It's just going to take—*

Something hard slammed into the side of my head, knocking me sideways.

My vision blurred, pain ricocheting through my limbs.

As everything went black.

CHAPTER TWO

ANDER

ELIAS KNOCKED ONCE before entering my office. I knew it was him because no one else would dare to make such a bold move, but my second-in-command didn't fear me. Which was exactly why he served as my right-hand man.

"Any complications?" I asked without looking up from my telecom screen.

My best friend collapsed onto the leather couch, kicking his feet up onto the coffee table—a habit he knew irked me to no end. "A minor one involving the Outsiders."

I cocked a brow at the unexpected comment, raising my gaze to his. "Really?"

He lifted a shoulder. "It's the dead of winter and they're starving. Fucks with mental faculties."

Their desperation wasn't the part that surprised me. "How did they know about the shipment?"

"I don't know yet, but I've put some men on it," he confirmed, proving his value as my Second. "The leak has to be from inside, considering the proximity."

Yes, because the Outsiders were without technology or means to communicate with our suppliers.

The lowly humans only survived because we allowed them to play in the mountain caves. They provided the occasional hunting sport for our wolves and served as the first line of defense against the Infected. We'd hear their screams long before the brain-eating fuckers fell upon us, providing ample time to enact our defenses.

The zombies were more of a nuisance than anything since wolves weren't susceptible to the virus that had turned nearly ninety percent of the human race into the walking dead. I just preferred to keep my streets clean and untouched. It was hard enough maintaining order without the addition of mindless creatures.

I returned my focus to the telecom, reviewing the technical specs from Drake—my research-team lead. "I assume you dealt with the humans appropriately." Not a question, just a statement. Because Elias knew how I felt about the Outsiders. Their use was just that—to remain *outside*.

"Killed five, kept one," he said, causing me to blink at my monitor.

"Kept one?" I repeated, drawing my focus back to him. "Why the fuck would you keep one?"

"Two words: submissive redhead."

I rolled my eyes. "For fuck's sake, man." The last thing we needed was another mouth to feed around here.

"Doc is looking her over now to determine if she's viable for the change." He checked his watch. "In fact, he's probably already injected her. Then I plan to give her to the border patrol as a plaything to break. Consider it a gift to the troops."

"One you intend to sample first," I muttered.

"Of course." He grinned. "Want to properly initiate her with me?"

I snorted. Elias loved sharing his female toys—it served as a way to expel some of his Alpha aggression. If only it worked for me. "She'd shatter between us."

"Probably," he agreed, linking his fingers behind his head, the dark brown curls a stark contrast to his pale skin. "But that's half the fun."

"The last time we fucked an Outsider, she died before we finished." Which had thoroughly ruined the moment.

"Yeah, a decade ago," he scoffed. "And she was still human."

"Which is why I don't fuck Outsiders anymore," I reminded him. Mortals were too fragile to satisfy my needs.

"And also why I asked Doc to inject her," he pointed out. "Shifters—even brand-new Betas—are harder to break."

I leaned back in my chair. "You really are bored," I drawled.

"Speaking of boredom…" He cocked a brow. "Finish that agreement with the Ash Wolves yet?"

My mood instantly soured. The Shadowlands Sector Alpha was driving a hard bargain. "He wants ten vehicles— land and sky—per Omega."

Elias whistled low. "Shit."

"Yeah." I palmed the back of my neck and glanced at my screen again. "Drake drew up specs for me. It's going to be an expensive investment." But it would certainly cure my second-in-command of his boredom. It'd cure mine, too. Assuming one of them was a potential mate match.

I scrubbed a hand over my face, shaking my head. "He knows we don't have a choice," I added, unable to hide my irritation.

Andorra Sector hadn't experienced the birth of an Omega in over fifty years, despite our researchers' endless tests and fertility treatments. The few we had left were mostly kept in protective captivity by their Alpha mates. And, unfortunately, all their pairings had yielded only Alpha and Beta progeny.

"He's agreed to send over the biological samples next week," I continued. "But he wants a down payment in the form of ten vehicles to show good faith first."

"And if the Ash Wolves prove to be incompatible with X-Clan genetics?" Elias countered.

"Then we're going to have one hell of a problem," I growled. Because none of the X-Clan Wolf sectors would send us any of their prized Omegas for mating. Not even my father had any to spare from Norse Sector. Which left me no choice but to try dealing with Dušan's pack. Their hierarchal structure differed from ours; however, the general principles applied. They had Alphas, Betas, and Omegas, just like us.

"Counter him," Elias said. "Tell him to send an Omega over for the first shipment of vehicles. We can take our own samples."

My lips twitched. "That's the message I sent him thirty minutes ago. I'm still waiting on a response."

Elias chuckled. "I bet he loved—"

A blaring alarm cut him off, sending us both to our feet.

"It's coming from the lab," Elias said, already heading toward my office door.

"Go."

He didn't need my command because he was already gone.

I checked my monitors, searching for the source of the issue, and found a petite redhead sprinting across my feed in nothing but a hospital gown.

My eyebrows shot up as she took down two researchers with a scalpel, her skill admirable for a human. That she managed to subdue two shifters only impressed me more. Of course, they weren't trained fighters like my guard or the border patrol.

She pressed her back to the cement wall, glancing around the corner before darting into the view of the next camera.

I folded my arms, amused. Maybe Elias was right about wanting to break this one. She certainly required some discipline.

She ducked into an examination room as two sentinels appeared, causing me to snort. "Bad move, little one." She'd effectively trapped herself.

I sighed. *So much for that entertainment.*

I started to sit, when her red hair flashed across the screen again, blood splattering as she took down both of my officers just as they crossed the threshold.

"Well, shit," I breathed, clutching my desk.

She was already running again.

I tracked her trajectory, calculating where she would end

up, when she paused to brace herself against a wall, her palm to her abdomen. Zooming in, I searched for any sign of injury. All the blood on her gown made it hard to tell, but she certainly appeared to be in pain. Given she'd just taken on two Beta male guards, I could understand why.

Determination lined her features as she forced her bare feet onward.

"All right, sweetheart. You have my attention," I told her, pushing away from my desk and leaving my office. There was only one place she could go on her current path. And I'd happily meet her at the end.

Speaking into the device on my wrist, I ordered everyone to stand down, including Elias.

This little deviant belonged to me.

And she'd rue the day she intrigued the Alpha of Andorra Sector.

You're mine now, pet.

CHAPTER THREE

KAT

Five Minutes Earlier

UGH... I had no idea what that asshole Alpha had hit me with, but my skull ached.

Slamming me into a world of unconsciousness hadn't even been necessary either. I'd have played along. Temporarily, anyway.

Now I didn't have a clue where I was within the dome. Some kind of clinic room being poked and prodded. They'd bathed me. I could tell because I smelled a thousand times better. Sweet, like fruit. Or maybe that was the dude—I assumed he was a male by the size of his hands—jabbing shit into my arms.

My medical torturer shifted positions, the clink on his tray suggesting he'd dropped the latest needle. It took considerable effort to remain calm and keep my eyes closed, but I knew the only way out of this was through the element of surprise.

The heat around me changed as the male stood, his steps echoing in the clinical space.

Snick.

That sounded like a door.

The click confirmed it.

I waited, trying to sense anyone else lingering in the room. Nothing.

Not even a breath beyond my own.

It can't be this easy. There had to be cameras on me, or a guard at the door, *something* to ensure I stayed put. Of course, I was just a lowly human in their minds. How could I possibly be a threat?

Well, they were about to find out.

I peeked at my surroundings, finding a slate of medical equipment and not much else. *Wow.* I'd never seen such a pristine space in person, only in photos. Medicine in the new world mostly consisted of surviving the Infected. Which really just meant one thing: don't get bitten.

Because all it took was one bite and the virus spread, turning humans into literal zombies.

There were rumors of humans sequestered away in labs searching for a cure, but I learned long ago that those were merely fairy tales told to children to help provide hope.

There was no cure.

Only death.

Not today, I thought, rolling off the table. My limbs protested, suggesting I'd been out for a while. The needle in my arm pulled, drawing my attention to some contraption with a bag that I'd been connected to. *Intravenous pump,* my mind supplied. *Huh. I guess those research books Mom made me read as a kid were finally coming in handy.*

I eyed the injection point and gently pulled the sharp stick out of my arm. With a glance around, I found some tape to put over the wound—the last thing I needed was the scent of my blood drawing attention to me.

Now to find clothes.

Clearly, they weren't in here.

Picking up two sharp instruments from the table, I pressed my back to the wall beside the door and stole a deep breath. *Now or never, Kat.*

Now.

I opened the door and flinched as alarms spilled into the hallway.

Fan-fucking-tastic. Apparently, there'd been some sort of code needed to exit without alerting the entire damn building.

At least there weren't any guards. *Yet.*

I took off down the hallway just as two males in white coats turned the corner. I didn't think. I acted.

The scalpel sliced across their throats, and they reacted appropriately with their hands coming up to press against the wounds. It wouldn't kill them—as I assumed they were wolves—but it would slow them down immensely.

I sprinted around them, down another corridor, and pressed my back to the wall. This place was like a white maze. Once I found an exit and could see the sky, I'd be better off. The mountains would guide me. Because the dome had all glass walls. Well, not real glass. Some enhanced technology that kept the wolves happy and safe from outside influences while still allowing them to see the scenery beyond.

Rich fucks.

Stealing a glance around the corner, I found the space empty and took a step. The echo of boots hitting the concrete floor reached my ears, forcing me to dive into the nearest room.

Their wolf-enhanced hearing and sense of smell would give my position away.

I had maybe twenty seconds.

Scanning the room, I found only more medical devices. Grabbing another scalpel and what appeared to be a saw of sorts, I crouched by the exam table and waited.

The two shifters burst into the room, their growls fueling my resolve. *Not today, fuckers.* My one strength revolved around misconceptions regarding my size—everyone underestimated me.

Just as these two did now, spotting me a few feet away and sharing a bemused look that said, *Really?*

What they failed to realize was that being small made me fast and lithe. Which allowed me to slide across the ground between them. The saw in one hand caught the ligaments of one of their ankles while the scalpel in my opposite palm sliced across the back of the other's knee.

Down the big boys fell, where I rammed my sharp instruments into their chests and took off through the door.

Quick.

Fast.

Efficient.

Adrenaline pumped through my veins, fueling me forward until a cramp hit my abdomen so sharply I slammed into the wall.

A groan parted my lips, causing me to crumple in on myself. I checked my stomach, searching for signs of a puncture or a wound, and found nothing. "What the…?" I breathed, flinching as the pain intensified.

Some sort of defense mechanism in the air?

I need to move, I told myself, forcing myself forward on a stumble. *Ignore it. Breathe. Run.*

Because the alarm was still blaring overhead and I had no doubt more guards were coming.

This was my only shot.

I'd given up my game far too soon. In hindsight, I should have remained in that room and allowed myself to obtain a better grasp on my surroundings.

Too late to reconsider.

I had to keep going. *Now or never*, I told myself again, pushing myself onward.

The alarms died as suddenly as they had begun, giving me pause. My lips curled down. *Was I not the one to set them off?* I wondered, glancing up and down the vacant corridor. *No. Coincidences don't happen.*

Which meant someone had turned off the blaring noise.

Why?

I crept forward, my senses on high alert as another excruciating pang stabbed at my insides and nearly sent me to the floor.

What the hell is happening to me?

17

My knees threatened to give out beneath me as I doubled over on a gasp.

This can't... I need...

Black dots danced before my eyes, the world blurring.

"*Fuck*," I breathed, shaking as I forced myself to take a step forward, just to fall back into the wall again. "*What. The. Fuck?*"

"You're going through the change," a calm voice informed me, the deep tenor an icy blanket that prickled my insides. "You should have remained in your room. The IV would have made the process easier."

I shivered, my gaze inching upward to find the one who had spoken. He shifted in and out of focus, his large body relaxed as he leaned against the wall opposite me. I hadn't even heard him approach.

Definitely an Alpha.

And not just any Alpha, but a merciless one, if the cold quality of his golden eyes was any indication.

My stomach heaved, drawing my focus back to the floor as I fought to stay on my feet. Running was no longer an option. Not in my current condition. Not with the predator looming across from—

Fingers combed through my hair, the male having moved on silent feet once more. Warmth bled across my frigid skin as he crowded me, his breath hot against my neck.

My hand shot up—a scalpel still clasped tightly in my palm—but he caught my wrist with ease, tsking as he forced me to drop the weapon. "You'll regret that, little one."

I already did.

Because now he had me effectively trapped against the wall. Painful spasms consumed me, eliciting a curse from my lips and a harsh "*Why?*" He said I was going through the change. What the fuck did that even mean?

They wouldn't have—

An agonized scream ripped from my throat as I collapsed to the ground, my insides rioting.

Growls erupted down the hall, a threat the male above me replied to with a snarl of his own. And all hell broke loose.

Blood.

Shouts.

Howls.

Chaos.

I whimpered, curling into a ball, terrified and alone. It *hurt.* Like fire and ice mating in my blood, stirring a maelstrom of sensation in my lower belly.

Weak.

Broken.

Can't breathe.

It felt like I was dying.

I'd experienced pain countless times, but nothing like this. My soul was literally detaching from my body, giving birth to a new form. Only, I remained human the whole time, my limbs quaking violently.

Warmth engulfed me, doing little to calm my chattering teeth.

Vibrations met my back.

Air floating beneath me.

Vaguely, I understood that I was being carried, but everything was so dark.

Words floated over my head.

Demands.

A general aura of disbelief.

I tried to concentrate, to *hear*, but my mind couldn't focus beyond the buzzing wrongness engulfing me. *What was in those needles?* I wondered, delirious.

Going through the change…

Into a wolf?

Or had they infected me?

My head lolled against a hard slab of hot male.

The Alpha?

Why?

I attempted to blink, longing to *see.* But I remained in a sea of black, my surroundings quieting with each passing second.

Until all I heard was my heartbeat.

Thump, thump.

Thump, thump.

Thummm…

CHAPTER FOUR

ANDER

MMM. I pressed my nose to the delicate female's neck, inhaling deeply. *Addictive perfection.*

She didn't stir in my arms, her body fraught with exhaustion. Surviving the chemical shift in her blood required strength and constant nutrition. While she possessed the former, she'd cut off the latter when she removed the IV from her arm.

Honestly, she was lucky to be alive.

I'd expected to watch her die in the hallway.

Until her scent began to evolve.

It was like a punch to the gut, her natural aroma shifting from standard to beautifully unique in a flash of a second. The results were instantaneous, her blood singing to every available male in the underground lab and sending them all running in her direction.

Had I not been there, the results would have been catastrophic.

The males would have ripped themselves limb from limb to claim her.

A rare, *unmated* Omega.

I marveled at the gift in my arms, her presence a miracle I never thought possible. All chemically induced shifters were Betas. It was part of the reason we rarely changed humans. What was the point? We had plenty of Betas already.

But this one somehow defied the science, morphing into a gorgeous, petite little treasure.

I nuzzled her neck once more, reveling in the beauty of her existence. My instincts had rioted at her earlier pain, forcing my inner wolf to act. She required comfort, and so I gave it to her, the soothing rumble radiating from my chest the only reason she slept soundly in my arms.

She still needed to change, to accept her wolf, but the worst of it was done.

When she woke, she'd be a new version of her former self. A shifter.

My future mate.

The air stirred at my back, an approaching presence causing all the hairs along my arms to rise. "Have you come to challenge me?" I wondered aloud as I settled the Omega into my bed, purposely bathing her in my scent.

Silence met my question, Elias standing at the threshold to my room.

It didn't take a mind reader to know what he was thinking.

"I know you found her," I said, tucking my sheets up to her chin before turning. "But I'm claiming her."

A muscle ticked in his jaw, an internal debate reflected in the dark depths of his eyes.

He was my oldest friend. My *best* friend. My Second. But he was also an Alpha in his prime, just like me. And the Omega in my bed lay unclaimed, ripe for the taking.

I cracked my neck, prepared to do what I needed to do.

This female belonged to me. My wolf had decided her fate the moment her changing scent reached my senses.

Elias's gaze narrowed, but he held up his hands, taking two

steps back. Then two more. Until he stood squarely in the hallway leading to my living area.

"Good choice," I told him, stalking forward to stand in the threshold, unable to move any farther. "What's her name?" In my haste to whisk her to safety, I hadn't been able to grab any of her records.

"Kat," Elias spit out, palming the back of his neck and beginning to pace. "Fuck. I *knew* there was something about her. I thought it was just her feisty energy that intrigued me. Now I get it." He halted and looked at me with a ferocity that was all Alpha male. "What if there are more, Ander? What if we can turn others?"

"You know as well as I do how rare this is," I replied, folding my arms. "How many humans have we experimented on over the years? All Betas. Most dead now because of the rations." We couldn't feed them all, not with our extended life spans and the problems the Infected inflicted upon the world. "Besides, there are barely any humans left."

"You wouldn't be saying that if I'd claimed her first," he countered, a snarl in his tone. "You'd be scouring the coast, searching for more, just to see if one met the criteria."

He was right, so I didn't bother to argue.

"Ceres is already demanding samples," Elias continued. "The entire council will want her genetically devoured to see how we can make more. Especially Artur and Enzo."

A growl vibrated my chest in response to the very real threat lying in the air. "Those two old fucks can kiss my ass. They will not touch what is mine." And if they wanted to threaten me with a revolution again, so be it. I'd annihilate them just like I did during their last challenge for my position.

Elias scoffed, his palm scrubbing over his face. "Fuck, Ander. *Fuck.*" He shook his head then and resumed pacing. "Artur and Enzo are going to advocate for testing humans over a deal with the Ash Wolves. And I think several others are going to agree."

This was why I kept him on as my Second. He provided the harsh truths I needed. But on this, I refused to budge. "I'll deal with them."

"Yeah?" He huffed a laugh. "When? Because I think

you're about to have your hands full with that one." He gestured over my shoulder with his chin. "She took down two researchers and two guards."

As I'd watched her do it via the security monitors, I didn't comment.

"Shit." Elias punched the wall, cursing again. Then repeated the motion with more intensity.

"Take a walk," I told him.

He flipped me off but did exactly as I suggested, his feet carrying him out of my suite quickly and the front door slamming behind him with a bang that vibrated the walls.

His words rattled around in my thoughts, each of his statements holding a variance of truth.

No one liked the deal I'd proposed with the Ash Wolves, despite our dire need for more Omegas. There was a very good chance the females wouldn't be compatible. They also weren't the same shifter breed.

An Omega's entire purpose in life was to procreate with Alphas. We couldn't mate with Betas. They weren't built to handle our knot. If the Ash Wolves were too genetically different, there'd be a moot point in the trade.

And now we had another potential path.

I glanced over my shoulder at the sleeping female in my bed, her luscious auburn hair fanned across the pillows.

"Are there more of you?" I mused out loud, stalking toward her. "More humans with a predisposition for submission and mating?"

My wrist began to buzz, Ceres's name scripting itself through the air in a wave of electricity.

I ignored him, my focus on my intended. Little frown lines marred her brow—lines that disappeared as I began to hum for her again. It sounded more like a low growl and was essentially a wolf's equivalent of a purr. As expected, it quieted her distress immediately.

I smiled. *Mmm, her body recognizes her fate already.*

Training her mind, however, would be another task entirely.

"You'll fight me," I acknowledged on a soft murmur, brushing a stray lock of hair out of her face. "But I'll win in

23

the end." I leaned down to press my lips to her temple before drifting toward her ear. "I'm going to enjoy breaking you, little one."

I nuzzled her pulse, my incisors elongating from the desire to meet her flesh. It would be so easy to take her, to claim her right now. But I wanted to make her beg.

And she would, too.

They always did.

"You'll submit in the end," I promised her. "Because you're already mine."

* * *

ALLOWING ANOTHER MALE to touch *my* Omega provided the biggest challenge I'd ever faced for self-control. Ceres being a Beta male was probably the only reason I allowed him to continue breathing.

Elias stood just over the threshold in the hallway, arms crossed, awaiting the verdict.

He wouldn't dare come any closer, not with the agitation lining my shoulders. I'd only allowed this bullshit to pacify Enzo. That damn Alpha was going to earn his excommunication soon if he continued to test my leadership boundaries. He'd managed to maintain the majority vote, forcing me to subject my intended mate to these tests.

I growled—not for the first time—irritated by my council's display of disrespect. Another problem for me to fix after I handled the Omega issue.

Somehow, Ceres managed to maintain a professional calmness as he took another sample of blood from my future mate. I growled low in my throat, displeased with the idea of him running tests on her genetics. But that was my wolf's possessiveness coming out.

The leader in me understood that this was a breakthrough moment in our research. If this human could become an Omega X-Clan Wolf, how many others out there could be turned similarly?

We had to learn more about her.

Which was precisely why I intended to authorize Elias's

raid on her home. If she had sisters or brothers, I wanted them. The others in her cave, well, I'd allow Elias to use his judgment. I trusted him as my Second for a reason—he'd never failed me before, and I doubted he would now.

So I gave him a subtle nod, acknowledging the request he'd arrived with and providing permission to proceed. "But I'm still going through with the Ash Wolves deal. At least the preliminary one." Dušan hadn't been pleased by my counteroffer. However, reason and need had won out over pride, and he'd capitulated. "The girl arrives next week."

Approval radiated from Elias's dark eyes. "Covering all your bases, as always."

"The day that stops, you can challenge me for the top."

He snorted. "Like I'd ever desire your job."

My lips curled as I glanced at the beauty lying in my bed. "There are benefits to being in my position."

"Just as there are benefits to being in mine," he replied, giving me a knowing look.

The Ash Wolf coming next week would belong to him— assuming she met our requirements. My chin dipped down once in confirmation.

His lips curled. "I'll gather all the information I can on your new mate."

I gazed down at her, curious about the girl called *Kat,* who seemed rather clever with a scalpel. "Yes. Do." I fixed my gaze on the doctor. "And I want a full report on her blood by nightfall." She'd been unconscious for twelve hours. Removing her IV and cutting off the solution pumping into her veins had been the cause of her mis-shift. Had she been a mere Beta, we would have left her to face her chances.

But I couldn't do that with an Omega.

So we'd brought in all the available technology and serums to ensure she survived the change. Once she woke, I'd correct her misbehavior appropriately. Then we'd proceed from there.

Including indulging in the final shift from human to wolf.

And after that, I could induce her estrus.

Just thinking about it made me hard. Never had I indulged in an Omega, but I knew what they could endure, knew what *she* would endure.

The future had never looked so bright.

We're going to determine your limits, little one. And then I'll push you beyond each of them, one by one. I stroked my finger across her cheek, smiling. *Welcome to Andorra Sector.*

CHAPTER FIVE

KAT

I STRETCHED MY ARMS OVER MY HEAD, the shoulder joints popping with a crack that startled me to awareness.

White engulfed me, reminding me of a cloud. It was too warm to be snow. Yet the faint hint of pine taunted my nose.

I sniffed.

Pine and something starkly masculine.

Something *good*.

I rolled in search of the intriguing scent, desiring more, and found it all around me in the disorderly sheets. *Mmm.* I curled and uncurled, reveling in the glorious aroma. I wanted to paint my skin in the paradise of this bed, to engrave it into my very being.

With a contented sigh, I smiled up at the tall ceiling, noting the silver beams and glass roof. It led to another, which bled into the blue sky, and to the sides, the mountains, covered in a fresh wintry mix.

Beautiful.

I'd never felt more alive or content. It was such a stark contrast to—

I shot up in the bed on a gasp.

Wait…

I glanced around the too-modern room, the vestiges of my dream state leaving me in favor of the reality I'd failed to remember.

The truck.

Maxim.

Being surrounded by wolves.

Waking up in the lab.

Excruciating pain.

I checked my abdomen, searching for signs of injury, and found only creamy skin beneath my palms. My hospital gown was gone, leaving me clad in nothing but the white cottony sheets.

Where am I? I wondered, trying to recall anything that could answer my inquiry.

Cold gold eyes flashed in my mind, startling me. I scrambled backward on the bed, hitting the headboard.

No.

No, no, no.

Why would he bring me here?

I took in the view once more, noting how we were in the highest room of the tower, lording over the dome.

Ander Cain.

This had to belong to him. The entire fucking sector did, but this space specifically… "Oh…" I swallowed, drawing the sheets around me in a makeshift dress and attempting to stand.

Only to stumble into the nearby window.

My limbs protested, my body immediately bowing as I began to shake violently. *Going down,* I thought just as my knees hit the plush carpet with a dull thud.

I curled into a ball, my stomach protesting at the same time a groan left my lips.

A rumble of sound pierced my ears, followed by a rich,

masculine aroma that caused my insides to clench. *Want… Oh… Very much want.*

I fisted my hands into the carpet, growling at the foreign voice in my head and at the strange sensations racking my body. Fire licked through my veins, stirring a heat in my lower belly that bled down onto my thighs.

Wet…

"What's happening to me?" I growled, trembling beneath the confusion and something else… something *hot*.

"Your wolf wants to play," a deep voice replied, the sound stroking my senses in all the right ways.

I leaned toward it without thinking, my body already submitting to the dark power caressing the air. A moan slipped through my lips as I found the source. The silk of his dress pants taunted my fingers, hiding the strength beneath that I desperately craved.

The whimper climbing up my throat caught between my teeth as reason began to trickle into my thoughts.

What am I doing?

My nails dug into the fabric as I forced my head backward to meet a pair of amused golden eyes. "Begging me already?" he asked, arching a dark brow. "And here I thought you would pose a challenge."

Ice replaced the fire inside me, sending me back several feet until my back hit one of the windows. "Wh-what have you done to me?" The question came out raspy, so unlike the growl from before.

How many days was I knocked out for?
Why does everything look so bright?
Why does he smell so damn good?

Ander crouched before me, the sleeves of his dress shirt rolled to the elbows. "Are you hungry, Katriana?"

"I…" My stomach churned, stirring a spasm between my legs that left me shuddering against the glass. A moan slipped from my mouth, one that only heightened the intensity brewing inside my lower abdomen.

Yes. I was definitely hungry.

But not for food.

I closed my eyes, fighting the craving my body had

29

awakened without my permission. It was his *scent*.

No, his nearness.

His size.

Those piercing golden eyes.

Thick black hair.

Broad shoulders.

Tapered waist.

Oh, I wanted him naked. Writhing. Screaming my name.

My brow furrowed. *My name.* He knew my name. "How?" I asked, breathless. "How do you know my name?" No one called me Katriana except my mother. Everyone else knew I preferred Kat.

"I've had three days to learn all about you, Katriana Cardona," he murmured, his fingers drifting across my chin to tilt my face toward him. A predatory gleam dilated his pupils, sending a shiver down my spine. "Twenty-one years old. Born in a cave—as are all the humans in my region. But I hear you're quite skilled with a bow. I'd like to see that for myself at some point."

"H-how?" I demanded. Although, my voice seemed to lack the force I originally intended. The husky quality of my tone was foreign to me. As were the sensations twisting inside me.

"Elias required a distraction, as did several of my men. So I sent them to investigate your home."

I sat up straight, my chin jerking away from his touch. "No." I shook my head. "No. They had nothing to do with Maxim's insane plan to steal food. None of us knew what he intended. I swear." Fuck, if that moron wasn't already dead, I'd kill him myself.

Because of him, the wolves had targeted our families.

Mine was already dead, but the others... I winced, my shoulders falling. They wouldn't stand a chance against a pack of angry wolves.

I hadn't been there to defend them, to help them, because I'd been here. Doing what? *Sleeping.*

Ander palmed my cheek, tilting my head backward again to search my eyes. "Are you aware that as wolves we can scent a lie?"

"If that's true, then you know I'm telling the truth."

"Yes, as did Elias when he questioned you after the attack."

Ah, so that was the dark-eyed Alpha's name. Elias. He must serve as Ander's second-in-command, I guessed. It was an educated assessment based on the power I'd felt radiating off Elias in the forest. It almost rivaled Ander's presence now, but not quite. The two of them together, however, would be a force of nature.

Yeah, avoid that, I decided.

Ander canted his head, those golden eyes seeing too much and giving nothing away at the same time. "It's my understanding that you're an only child."

His switch in topics caused me to frown. "Yeah, my parents weren't too keen on bringing much life into the hell of our world." Not that I actually knew my father. My mother mentioned him sporadically, usually with a wistful look in her eye before returning the topic to something training related. She wanted me to have the necessary tools to cope with the cruelty surrounding us and often claimed it was her primary purpose as my mother.

"I created you. Only fair that I teach you how to survive," she'd often said.

Our world was literal purgatory for a human.

Bringing life into this hell served only to torture the young, most of whom stood little to no chance for long-term survival.

Most of my friends died in our teens. And our parents were lucky to live into their forties. My mother had survived longer than most, dying at the old age of forty-eight. She'd served as a matriarch of sorts.

My father, however, I never met.

Ander's palm slid to the back of my neck. "Come. You need to eat." He tugged me forward and upward, not giving me a chance to comply on my own.

I swayed on my feet, blinking as black dots danced before my eyes. *Too fast. Too much. Ohhh…* I shook my head, trying to clear it, and clutched his shirt for balance.

Heat poured off him, swathing me in a warmth that had

me curling into him on a sigh. *Strong, powerful male*, I thought, pressing my nose against his chest. His size dwarfed mine, making me feel petite and protected in his arms.

Until he lifted me into the air and started walking.

"Hey!" I protested, trying to roll out of his grip.

And, oh, holy crap, I'm naked.

I futilely threw my arms over his shoulders, like I could somehow reach the sheet I'd left on the ground. What the hell had gotten into me? His presence somehow overpowered my common sense, stirring all these strange cravings and sensations I'd never before experienced.

"What did you do to me?" I demanded, my voice finally finding its resolve. "And put me down!"

Amusement teased his full lips. "You're making me hard, sweetheart. I suggest you stop before I feed you my cum instead of the food in the other room."

I gasped. Who the hell said something like that to someone they didn't even know? And talk about crude. *Dear God.* "*I'll do no such thing.*" The growl in my tone surprised me. *Is that my voice?*

"Oh, you will," he replied with a rumble that had my thighs clenching. "And you'll enjoy it, too."

Unintelligible words left my mouth because I had no idea what the fuck to say to that other than "No" and a bunch of curses.

Because fuck *that.*

No, *fuck him.*

A riot of images burst behind my eyes of the very idea, causing me to gasp for an entirely different reason. This male would be potent, thorough, and, oh, so—

Gah!

I really needed my insides to stop tingling.

Whatever spell he'd woven over my body was playing tricks on my lady parts. In no way should I *ever* be attracted to Ander Cain. His ruthlessness and superiority were legendary, and not in an admirable way.

He dumped me into a chair at an elongated table in what must have been the dining area and said, "Eat."

A plate sat before me beside a steaming mug of something

brown.

I sniffed the contents, prepared to decline on principle, until my stomach growled eagerly in response.

The defiant part of me wanted to fight his command and demand at least a shirt. However, the smarter part of me acknowledged the benefit of eating a meal. I had no idea when I last indulged in food, but I was starving.

So much so that I ate—naked—in the chair while he observed me with those fathomless eyes. He gave nothing away, his full lips flat and his jawline practically etched from stone. He merely sat adjacent to me at the head of the table, fingers clasped on the mat before him, silent.

When I couldn't stand another bite, I pushed the dish away and folded my arms to cover my breasts. He wasn't the first male to see me naked. We often bathed in groups during the summer months—safety in numbers and all that.

But I'd never been *alone* with a male in this manner.

Nor had I ever received this much scrutiny from one. He seemed to be memorizing every inch of my skin on display, even through the table. And I didn't like how it left me feeling warm all over instead of cold.

"Why?" I finally asked. "Why am I here?"

He tilted his head. "Because I brought you here."

I fought the urge to roll my eyes. This man of short answers and stoic commentary was really starting to grate on my nerves. "*Why* did you bring me here?"

"Because you're mine."

My eyebrows shot up. "*What?*" I mean, I understood in principle that all the subjects beneath his dome belonged to him in some way, but the comment earlier about my drinking his, uh...

My cheeks heated.

Not finishing that thought.

Nope.

Not happening.

Nor was I okay with being *his* in the way that I suspected he meant.

"I'm starting to question your intelligence," he said slowly. "Or perhaps your hearing. I'll have Ceres look into it." He pushed away from the table and held out his massive palm. "Come along, pet. You require more rest before we begin our mating."

My mouth opened, then closed, and then opened again.

He arched a brow, impatience coloring his features. "*Now*, Katriana."

"You can't just say something like that and expect me to obey," I snapped, jumping off the chair—to the opposite side of where he stood.

His gaze narrowed. "Surely living so close to Andorra Sector taught you about wolf hierarchy?"

"Oh, I'm well aware of your position at the top, *Ander Cain*." I waited to see if he denied my suspicion as to his identity. When he didn't, I added, "But that doesn't mean I respect it." I could practically hear my mother cursing at my audacity, her accusations of teaching me better than this rioting in my mind. But fuck this shit. I was *not* about to... to... *mate* this jackass.

He took a step forward.

So I took one back.

Fortunately, I felt much better after eating. Actually, I felt more than better. I felt amazing.

"Careful, Omega," he warned, his voice holding a lethal edge that scattered goose bumps down my arms. "You're exciting my predatory drive."

I snorted. "You're a shifter. That's your constant drive." And an Alpha male to boot. From what I understood, he constantly wanted to fuck, maim, or kill.

The look in his eyes now confirmed that assessment, which should have terrified me. But, instead, all I felt was a thrill of potential escape.

Like all men, he would underestimate my size and abilities. The fact that I was naked only added to my advantage because I could use my body to distract him.

He tracked my movements as I rounded the table, his nostrils flaring. "This is how you thank your protector and intended mate? By challenging him?"

"Protector?" I repeated, not touching the *intended mate* part. "You mean kidnapper, right? I don't recall ever asking for your *protection,* or to be brought here."

"No, you were too busy *dying,*" he retorted.

"Dying?" I didn't recall that part, just a pain in my abdomen unlike any I'd ever experienced.

And Ander arriving to say I was in the middle of the...

My eyes widened. "You turned me," I realized out loud. Or did he? I glanced at my hands and arms, finding—

My back hit the wall on a whoosh of air that had me yelping. I clawed at the hand encircling my throat, my feet kicking below as my toes barely scraped the ground.

Golden irises captured my gaze, the smoldering quality leaving me breathless against the wall. "This is not how—"

He bit off on a curse, his grip weakening, as my knee connected perfectly with his groin. I wiggled out from between him and the wall and took off running toward the door.

Or what I *thought* was the door.

Unfortunately, it led me to another bedroom.

Shit!

I spun around, searching for the exit point, only to run headfirst into Ander's chest. He grabbed me by the hips and threw me onto the bed before slamming the door behind him with a booted heel.

"All right, Omega. I tried the gentle route. But I can see that won't work with you." He began unbuttoning his shirt. "So let's try this another way."

I scrambled backward into the headboard. "Wait—"

"Consider this an introduction to your place in our society—which is on the bottom." His dress shirt hit the floor, revealing a torso rippled in solid muscle. And his palm dropped to his belt. "Now spread your legs like a good little Omega and maybe I'll go easy on you."

CHAPTER SIX

ANDER

KATRIANA FROZE, her petite little hands gripping the comforter on either side of her hips. "Ander, please—"

"Oh, we're past the point of begging," I told her, sliding my belt through the loops. "Spread your legs, Omega."

She didn't, her instinct to rebel too strong.

Breaking her of that habit was going to take time.

Fortunately for us both, patience came naturally to me.

I dropped the leather to the ground and flicked open the button on my pants. "You'll find that I do not enjoy repeating myself, Katriana." Her eyes followed my movements as I slid the zipper down. "You're also about to learn what happens when an Omega misbehaves."

Wolves maintained a hierarchy for a reason. Alphas at the top, Betas in the middle, and Omegas at the bottom, though they were cherished treasures owned and protected by their

Alpha mates.

Katriana was mine.

To punish.

To fuck.

To impregnate.

To protect.

And I couldn't proceed with the latter if she was hell-bent on ignoring my commands.

I toed off my boots and socks, followed by my pants, leaving me clad in a pair of boxers that were far too tight for my growing arousal.

Katriana's eyes grew wide. "*No*," she breathed.

"It'll fit," I promised her. Despite their petite forms, Omegas were built to accommodate Alpha cock.

But she shook her head in the negative and pulled her knees up to her chest. "*No*," she repeated on a snarl.

My lips twitched.

She wasn't the only one who could make those sounds.

I returned her rumble with one of my own. However, mine held special properties. A call of sorts that an Omega couldn't deny.

She convulsed violently in response, the hairs along her arms dancing in appreciation. "*Oh God.*"

"Ander," I corrected her, placing a knee on the mattress. "And that's just the beginning, pet." I allowed another growl to follow, her answering arousal an alluring scent I wanted to bury myself in.

Her thighs clenched as a moan parted her lips. "Wh-what…? How?"

"You're an Omega," I murmured, prowling toward her on the bed. "*My* Omega. Your body will always answer my call." I grabbed her knees. "Now *spread*."

Her legs came apart without resistance, her pretty pink flesh drenched with slick. My cock throbbed, assuring me she was already primed and demanding I take her.

Not yet.

I prided myself on my control, and while I wanted to teach my little kitten a lesson, I knew she couldn't handle me in her current state. She needed to experience the full transition first, to truly become an X-Clan Wolf. Then, and only then, would she be ready.

"N-no," she whimpered, trying weakly to move away, her head swaying as if she were trying to clear it. "St-stop."

"You're mine, Katriana." I gripped her thighs to yank her down the bed, positioning my mouth above her hot core and inhaling her sweet scent. "Mmm, I've never tasted Omega pussy before. I may be down here for a while."

She tensed, her lower body locking in fight mode.

I growled once more, right against her clit.

Katriana screamed, her back bowing off the bed.

"Don't fight it, kitten," I told her softly, nuzzling the curls between her thighs. "Your body was made for mine. Let me show you."

As far as punishments went, there were far worse things I could—

Slender fingers wove through the strands of my hair and harshly tugged my head to the side. The movement caught me off guard, allowing Katriana to twist beneath my hands.

She didn't get far, my grip tightening and pulling her beneath me completely. I trapped her wrists over her head, bringing us nose to nose as I settled my hips between her soaked thighs.

"Continue to defy me, little one. I dare you."

She spit in my face.

I narrowed my gaze. "You're going to lick that off."

"Fuck you," she snarled, wiggling beneath me.

"No, darling. I'm going to *fuck* you." I gripped her throat with my free hand, keeping her arms above her head with my other. "I'm done trying to explain pack hierarchy to you. I'm going to show you instead."

Finally, a sliver of fear permeated the air, the scent intoxicating as it mingled with her growing arousal. Because try as she might, she was attracted to me. Simple genetics made us compatible. Her wolf yearned for mine, just as mine yearned for hers.

She opened her mouth—likely to argue—and I silenced her with a kiss.

Not a pleasant, gentle one, but a dominant, forceful one

that demanded her submission. Her sound of protest melted into a groan, pleasing my inner beast immensely.

That's it, kitten. Accept me.

Her tongue tentatively touched mine, the caress sweet in a feminine way. Exploring. Seeking. I allowed it, gave her this small piece of me to taste before taking over and setting the rhythm I preferred.

More slick dampened her center, soaking my boxers all the way through and taunting my dick into responding.

Heat consumed my being, the need to *claim* stoking my inner fire and inflaming me to heights I'd not yet experienced.

This female was *mine*.

I wanted to bite her.

To shred her apart.

To impale her.

To nest with her.

To destroy her and put her back together again.

I pressed my shaft into the softness between her thighs, cursing the fabric between us and nearly ripping it from my legs.

Her breasts were heaven against my chest, the stiff little nipples begging for my mouth, my tongue, my *teeth*. I gave in to the instinct, trailing my mouth down her neck, memorizing her creamy skin along the way.

So colorful, I mused, noting all the intricate designs lining her skin.

One of these days, I'd demand she tell me the story behind each tattoo.

But today, I just wanted to explore every inch of her with my tongue.

She shivered as I drew one hard peak into my mouth, my teeth grazing her tender flesh. I released her wrists and throat but watched her closely for signs of rebellion. Her lips parted on a moan, her head tossing back and forth with the inner battle between her mind and her body.

I knew which one would win.

We were animals for a reason.

Our wolves drove our instincts, not our human penchant for overthinking.

She gripped the pillows beneath her head, a strangled sound slipping from her throat. Oh, my Omega had spirit; I'd give her that. Even now, she tried to fight.

"You won't win," I warned her while slipping downward again to the real prize. "You became mine the moment you approached that truck, kitten. My territory, my rules. And I want you, so I will have you. Any. Way. I. Want."

I closed my mouth around her sensitive little bud. She bowed off the bed on a scream that went straight to my groin.

"Mmm, that's it," I encouraged her softly, my words a whisper against her damp flesh. "Listen to your body. Just *feel.*"

She mewled, thrashing beneath me and arching in time with each of my licks and nips. A flattering pink hue overtook her pale features, her pleasure mounting and blossoming before my eyes.

Exquisite.

In my near century of existence, I'd experienced many females in the throes of passion, but none quite as beautiful as this one. Katriana's possessed a raw quality, one underlined in surprise and a becoming innocence that lit my soul on fire for her all the more.

Omegas were made for sex.

And I saw the proof of it in the way she came apart below me now, her ecstasy an aphrodisiac that blanketed the room in pure lust.

She cried out, over and over, her limbs trembling and her chest heaving beneath the exertion. Electricity hummed over her skin, charging the air.

I jolted backward, my eyebrows flying upward in surprise.

She curled onto her side, her moans turning to pained sounds as the shift vibrated across her petite form. Terror filled the room, her limbs beginning to fracture beneath the change.

I went to my knees beside the bed, trying to bring us to eye level. "You're forcing it," I growled, irritated.

She'd called upon her wolf—something I suspected was done on purpose to dismantle the sexual chemistry brewing between us.

Stubborn female.

I could force her back into human form with a command, and her wolf would be compelled to heel. Ignoring an Alpha's demand—not just a verbal one but a *real* one underlined in power—went against our nature.

But it would hurt her a hell of a lot to stop the change now and coerce her into transforming back. Although, the agony would serve as a worthy punishment for her rebellion.

No. I'd allow her to punish herself instead.

"Have it your way, little one," I said on a sigh, pushing back from the bed. "But I'm not comforting you through it."

Leaving the door open behind me, I walked to the kitchen to pour myself a much-needed glass of brandy and downed it in two gulps.

Her whines from the guest bedroom had me shaking my head. "You brought it on yourself," I told her, fixing myself another glass.

Shifting for the first time as an adult was rumored to be quite agonizing. She would eventually grow used to it after several rounds of experiencing the change. And a rumbling purr from me now could help her as my intended mate, but she hadn't earned it.

So I stood in the kitchen and waited, listening to her breath hitching and her tiny cries. This was why I allowed her to progress—to turn her back would hurt far more, and while I was irritated by her defiance, I didn't wish to be the cause of her pain.

Her current suffering was on her, not me.

I set my glass to the side and flicked a button on my watch to bring up a glowing screen. Oh, how technology had improved over the last hundred years.

Andorra Sector housed some of the best researchers in the world long before the zombie virus plagued the human population. It was our claim to fame among the X-Clan Wolves, our ability to advance via technical means. The dome overhead was a glowing example. Our transportation another. And intelligence devices—like the one affixed to my wrist—was my favorite advancement of all.

Flicking through the images, I brought up my computer

screen from the office and started sifting through my messages.

Dušan had set a drop-off time. Good.

I skipped down the list to Katriana's blood report from Ceres, my eyebrows inching upward as I read.

Only to be interrupted by a fierce growl from my Omega.

I glanced over my screen at the beautiful red wolf snarling in the entryway to the kitchen.

"Yes?" I asked, knowing she could understand me perfectly well despite her furry form. "Would you like a mirror to admire your new figure?" Because she was rather exquisite with all that auburn fur, even if it was standing on end as she openly challenged me.

She took a step forward, her intention clear.

With a flick of my wrist, the screen disappeared.

She wanted my attention? She had it.

I squared off with her, baring my teeth in a similar manner. "You've made a lot of foolish mistakes today, Omega. I strongly encourage you to reconsider this one."

Her tail twitched, aggression filling the air.

"Try it," I dared.

She might be fierce, but she stood no chance, even in wolf form. Not only was she new, but she was also small. And one growl from me would have her whimpering in a corner.

But I'd let her try if it made her feel better.

I dodged her first lunge.

Then jumped up onto the kitchen island for her second, landing deftly on the marble top on the balls of my feet. I cocked a brow as she slammed into the cabinets below. "You're going to hurt yourself."

She ignored me, of course, trying again to jump after me and failing.

"You're a wolf, not a cat," I reminded her.

Her resulting snarl made my lips twitch.

She attempted once more and fell on her rump.

I crouched, capturing her gaze. "Are you done yet?" Because I couldn't allow her challenge to go unanswered. No one attacked an Alpha without answering for it. Especially not *me*. I owned this entire fucking dome for a reason.

She snapped her jaws at me, causing me to smile.

"Oh, Katriana. You have so much to learn."

Her response was another snarl before taking off into the living room to begin shredding my furniture. I jumped off the island and folded my arms, watching as she threw her equivalent of a tantrum.

The female clearly had a death wish.

She began to pace around my penthouse, searching the windows, doors, and rooms, clearly looking for an exit. As if I'd allow her to leave. She wouldn't get farther than ten feet from this building without a pack of Alphas trying to mount her, even in wolf form.

I hadn't claimed her yet.

That left her available and fertile—a lethal combination for an Omega.

My wrist buzzed with an incoming call. A translucent screen populated the space before me as I accepted it. "I'm a little busy at the moment, Elias."

Right on cue, the chair in my living room crashed to the floor with an angry red wolf flying along with it, half the cushion in her mouth.

I turned the screen to show him the carnage.

He whistled low. "Just force her to change back."

"It's crossed my mind," I admitted. But despite her bratty behavior, I didn't want to hurt her. Not in that manner, anyway. "Do you need something urgently, or can it wait?"

"Just calling with an update—of the three viable candidates, only one survived the change."

"And?"

"Beta."

I nodded. "Not surprised." Particularly after what I'd read in Katriana's blood report. My little wolf had some explaining to do.

"Neither am I," Elias replied. "But the others want to keep searching."

By "others," I knew he meant Enzo and his merry little band of followers.

"Stall them." I needed time to process what I'd learned from Ceres's tests before I addressed the Alpha council.

"Busy them with preparing for the Shadowlands Sector deal. I want the dome reinforced and ready for their arrival."

"Understood." He chuckled as Katriana moved into the dining area to tug all the plates and cups to the floor from the table. "You're going to whip her ass when she's through, aren't you?"

"I'm going to do a lot more than that," I vowed, narrowing my eyes at the menace destroying my penthouse.

"Good luck."

"Not needed." I'd let her have her little romp around my flat. Then I'd make sure it never happened again.

I hung up, knowing Elias had nothing else useful to say, and leaned against the island.

Her rampage continued for another twenty minutes, which I found impressive considering how exhausted her body had to feel from the change. She started to slow down, her movements not as sharp, her head beginning to sway as though dizzy.

Every minute or so, her bright blue eyes flicked to me, a hint of alarm dilating the pupils. Oh, she knew she was in trouble, could sense my Alpha wolf biding his time and waiting for her to fall.

Roughly ten minutes later, her legs gave out beneath her from the fatigue of her first shift. She let out a keening noise that echoed through the condo, her body folding into itself on the floor, just before her mind gave way to unconsciousness.

I pushed off the wall with a tsk under my breath, padding toward her as she began to morph in her sleep.

Long strands of auburn hair decorated my carpet, her colorful skin slowly appearing beneath the fur. The reverse back to her human state went faster because her mind was no longer functioning; only her body worked now. Fortunately, that also meant she wasn't suffering.

As soon as her change was complete, I scooped her into my arms and cradled her against my chest. She snuggled into my heat, causing me to smirk. "Yeah, you like me now while passed out and oblivious," I said, giving her the soothing rumble I knew she craved as I started toward my bedroom.

"But you're going to hate me in the morning."

Because that little show she just put on? I would not be allowing a repeat.

"Such a troublesome little mate," I whispered, laying her on my bed and retrieving a fresh set of blankets from the linen closet.

After wrapping her in them, I kissed her temple and nuzzled her throat. "Sleep well, Katriana. Because you're going to need your rest for what I have planned for you tomorrow."

Her little disobedient streak was about to come to an end.

Swiftly and efficiently.

"Good night, little mate." I turned off the lights. "See you in the morning."

CHAPTER SEVEN

KAT

SILENCE.

Such a bizarre concept, one I'd never experienced. Surviving required traveling and sleeping in groups. But I awoke alone to a too-quiet room.

My new sense of smell told me Ander hadn't gone far, his woodsy scent lingering in the air. But for whatever reason, he'd granted me a moment of solitude.

I didn't question the temporary gift and instead chose to use it to find a shirt or something to wear.

His room lacked storage space, the two nightstands housing objects, not clothing. All right, he had to have something somewhere.

I wandered into the bathroom in search of a closet.

And caught my reflection in the mirror.

"Holy crap," I breathed, noting my wild hair and the dried

blood on my arms. I winced at the memory of scratching myself up in wolf form while throwing a major fit in Ander's living room. My goal had been to turn off the hormones driving my responses to him, and it'd worked. Sort of. Parts of me still ached for him, and just his scent had a fresh surge of need pooling between my thighs, but my mind seemed to be in working order once more. I'd take that as a win over my treacherous body.

Giving in to his mouth yesterday, or whenever that was, had been the highest and lowest moment of my life.

No man had ever touched me *there,* and I'd enjoyed it more than I cared to admit.

Which was why I also hated everything about it.

He'd used his pheromones to seduce me. Rather, he'd *growled,* and it had provoked my animal side to come out and play.

I refused to let it happen again.

Mind over matter, I told myself, checking my reflection once more. *Yeah, okay. Bathe first. Clothes second.*

Except… I had no idea how to turn on the water.

My lips twisted. *How hard can it be?*

I'd seen photos of showers in magazines and recognized the marble monstrosity in the corner as the place to rinse off. The bottles beside it were probably soaps or fragrances to help clean.

I've totally got this.

I totally did not have it at all.

The water was blazing hot, then too cold, then splashing left and right, and by the time I finished, I was pretty sure I still had soap in my hair. It felt sticky and not at all clean, but a glance in the mirror told me it at least made me more presentable.

Dripping water all over the damn floor, I grabbed a small cloth hanging near the sink and began patting myself dry. The drawers all had foreign things in them, so I tried a cabinet door on the left. "Ohhhh…" I grabbed a much larger towel and wrapped myself up in the plush fabric.

It warmed my skin and left me sighing in content. A girl could get used to this. Except it would require me to stay here, which was so not happening.

Clothes, I reminded myself, pushing through a door that led to the jackpot of outfits.

Suits.

Jeans.

Dress shirts.

Coats.

Boots.

All masculine. All belonged to Ander based on the scent. My stomach twisted at the familiarity, my thighs clenching.

This reaction to him needed to end, and there was only one way to do that—escape. Which required me to wear something other than a towel. Hmm, wearing his clothes should allow me to smell like him and not me. That could be a benefit. And if I wore enough layers, I'd appear bigger, too.

I perused the selection, mentally cataloging the items that would work. The shoes were out of the question, but I could run in thick socks.

This will work. Just need to find a way out of here next.

I traded my towel for a button-down shirt that ended at my knees, then combed out my hair with a brush from one of the drawers. Not the best I'd ever looked. Not the worst either. As I didn't want to attract him to me more than I already had, I decided my appearance was for the best and wandered toward the living area. To my utter shock, it was not only clean but also stocked with all brand-new furniture.

For fuck's sake, how long was I asleep? Seriously, I'd slept longer in this condo than I had in the last month. At least I felt rested. No, I felt better than rested. I felt *alive*. Powerful, even.

Because Andorra Sector had turned me into an X-Clan Wolf.

A shifter.

An—

"Omega." Ander's deep voice rumbled across the room from his position in the corner of the living area. He resembled a king in his chair, his legs splayed and his massive forearms resting on his thighs. His expression was unreadable, but I sensed his underlying aggression. His anger. His profound disappointment.

It made my knees quiver and my heart jump in my chest.

I'd severely pissed him off. Which was my goal yesterday. Today, however, I somewhat regretted that decision.

But he kept pushing me. Growling. *Licking* me. My body kept taking away my own choices, forcing me to endure and enjoy his offerings while my mind protested every step of the way.

I'd never allowed a male to touch me, let alone *fuck* me. While he might think he could fit down there, I knew he wouldn't. Not after the reveal of his size in those too-tight boxers—an image that would be forever ingrained in my mind, because *wow*.

I shuddered, chastising my errant thoughts and the sequences that followed. I didn't want to be attracted to him. I didn't want to be his mate. I didn't want to be here.

Yet, no one gave me a choice and my body seemed hell-bent on forcing the issue. Even now, I wanted to kneel, to crawl to him, to beg forgiveness. It took physical effort to remain upright, to hold his powerful gaze.

"Challenging me is a mistake, little one."

"No. Capturing me was the mistake. I'm not the kind of girl who heels, not even to you." I folded my arms, striving for confidence while my insides turned to putty beneath the weight of his stare. The male was potent, dominance radiating from his pores and suffocating the room. But I couldn't let this continue. He needed to understand that I would not submit, even if his growl and tongue did wicked things to my nether regions.

He pushed off the chair, his height an intimidation to my five-foot-two frame. He had over a foot on me. Not to mention the width of his shoulders. There wasn't an ounce of fat on this man, all toned, hard, masculine muscle. Yet he moved gracefully toward me, his steps not making a single sound.

"There's a matter that requires my attention," he said, gripping my chin between his forefinger and thumb. "When I return, we're going to have a discussion about pack hierarchy. You will be naked for that conversation, and my palm is going to become very well acquainted with your ass. And by the time we finish, you will be aware of what I will and will not tolerate."

I glared up at him. If he thought I would let his palm anywhere near—

My lower body jolted as his hand connected with my ass and squeezed. "You will agree with a simple 'Yes, sir.'"

"Fuck you," I said instead.

His hold on my chin tightened. "You're lucky I have a meeting, or I'd put you over my knee right now and beat your ass red."

"I'm not a child," I snapped.

"Your behavior says otherwise," he countered, releasing me as quickly as he'd caught me, then spinning me toward the sofa and pushing me over the back of it to present my backside. He promptly lifted the shirt to expose my rump and pretty much everything else to his view in this position.

"You can't do this!" I squirmed, trying to move out of the inferior position, but his palm against my lower back held me in place as he used his thighs to pin my legs to the back of the couch. "Let me go!"

A sharp pinch bit into my fleshy bottom, causing me to freeze.

What the hell...?

It was too thin and quick to be his teeth.

A needle, I realized, likening it to the pricks from the other day. "What did you just do?" I demanded as he stepped back. Whatever he'd injected me with was already gone, both of his hands tucked into the pockets of his dress pants.

"Consider it an introduction to your fate," he replied cryptically, walking toward the door. "Riley is on her way over to supervise. Be kind to her, or I'll let Jonas deal with you."

With those parting words, he left.

I chased after him, just in time to see the door slam.

No lock.

No code.

Just a regular exit point.

No way could it be that easy.

After slowly counting to five hundred, I traced his steps

and twisted the handle softly to find a metal set of doors looming on the other side.

Better than Ander waiting for me—which was why I had lingered for a beat.

Slipping into the hallway, I eyed the exit point. No handle or hinge. It seemed to slide open. *An elevator*, I realized, awed. I'd read about these but had never seen one.

So how does it work?

Spying a panel to the side, I studied the arrow buttons. Surely selecting "down" was too obvious. Hmm. There had to be another way, stairs maybe, that allowed me to escape this tower in a more obscure way.

A blinking light appeared above the doors, followed by a ding as the metal began to slide open.

Shit! I sprinted back to the main door, but not fast enough.

"You must be Katriana," a feminine voice murmured, her sweet scent clouding the hallway and causing my lips to curl into a snarl before I even turned around. "I'm Riley," she added.

Short.

Vibrant blue hair.

Pale skin.

Curvy.

Smiling.

I didn't return the welcoming gesture, instead glaring at her. "I don't need a babysitter." Ander had called her a supervisor, technically, but I knew what he meant.

She laughed, the sound far too cheerful for the situation. "Good thing I don't feel like babysitting. How about we just talk instead? I think you'll find that we have a lot in common."

I eyed the dress flirting with her calves and the dainty little shoes on her feet. "Yeah, somehow I doubt that."

"Looks can be deceiving."

"No shit." I turned and stalked back into the penthouse. Ander was gone, which left me with an opportunity I might not get again. This chick would be easy to subdue. But maybe I could trick her into telling me about the exits first. She also probably knew the code that activated the elevator, since she'd used it to come up here.

A plan quickly formed in my head. It wasn't perfect, but I didn't have time to improve all the hard edges.

Ander wanted to teach me a lesson later, and I had no intention of being here. Nor did I want another injection in my ass.

What was that? I wondered again, rubbing my abused cheek. It hadn't made me feel any different. It just pinched a little.

I'd have to work it out later.

Escape first.

Questions after.

I turned to make small talk with the chick who had made herself at home in Ander's space. My inner wolf wanted to snarl at her for being so familiar with the Alpha, but I swallowed the instinct. Who cared if he fucked other women? I wasn't going to stay around to be *his*, so he could make whatever choices he wanted.

"Here," Riley said, handing me a cup. "Enjoy that. I'll prep something for the oven, then we can chat."

As much as I wanted to get this show on the road, food probably wouldn't be a bad idea. I could run fast and far on a full night's rest and a recent meal. And maybe I could get some details out of her while she played in the kitchen.

"Okay." I sat on one of the stools near the counter overlooking the dining area.

She rummaged through the refrigerator—another item I'd only seen in books until this week—and pulled out several savory cubes of meat.

My jaw about hit the floor.

"What are *those*?" I asked, my mouth watering already.

"Beefsteaks. Or, well, pre-cut ones, anyway. They're usually long and thick, not bite-size." She dropped them on the counter and went back to searching. "Ander sources some of the best products from the farming regions. We trade healthcare products and technology in exchange for sustenance." She added some vegetables to the pile, only hers appeared far more edible than the ones I grew up eating.

My eyes continued to grow rounder with each added item. While I'd indulged in the meal Ander provided yesterday, I hadn't truly registered the richness of it. Now that I felt better—at least physically—I could *smell* the quality.

"Wow," I said, awed.

Riley glanced up at me with bright blue eyes that matched her vibrant hair. "There are perks to being Ander's intended mate."

And just like that, my appetite was gone.

There might be perks, as she proclaimed, but I wouldn't be staying to enjoy them.

I picked up my cup and wandered into the living area, effectively ending our conversation. Oh, I'd eat whatever she gave me. Then, I'd be on my way. With, or without, her help.

CHAPTER EIGHT

ANDER

"HOW LONG WILL THIS TAKE TO WORK?" I asked, dropping the empty syringe on Ceres's desk.

He picked up the item and tossed it into a nearby red box. "Given her current hormonal levels, I'd give her five or six hours at most."

"Then this meeting better be done in less than three hours," I said to Elias, who stood waiting for me out in the hallway.

"Give the council what they want and that shouldn't be a problem."

I snorted and walked past him, leading the way to our meeting. "Enzo and his idiotic pups want to gather a bunch of human females, fuck them, and see what happens with the offspring later in life. Do you have any idea how many resources that is going to waste?"

It would take eighteen to twenty years for each experiment to be viable for the change, and the majority—if not all—would turn out to be Betas.

My Second grabbed my arm, halting me before I could reach the elevator that would lead to the conference area. "They're desperate, Ander." Soft words meant for my ears alone. Even with shifter hearing, no one else would have heard the confidential statement.

"I know. And I have a potential solution that is much faster than rounding up a bunch of humans for experimentation," I reminded him in the same tone.

Most of the Alphas were already in agreement. It was Enzo and Artur who whined about the Ash Wolves not being acceptable substitutes. Only X-Clan Omegas would ever qualify for mating in their eyes. They preferred the old world, pre-Infected, and refused to assimilate to change.

It would one day be the death of them.

Likely by my hand.

Elias nodded. "Pitch it in a similar manner and they'll be more agreeable. But be prepared to make a compromise."

I already was. I knew how this council operated forward and backward, and I was their leader for a reason. "I know what I need to do." It was all about proving the opposition wrong, and I had a suggestion lurking in the wings that none of them would be able to refute. Unless Enzo and Artur wanted to renege on their argument. In which case, they'd lose respect from their minions.

Checkmate, I thought with an internal grin.

Elias released me, his chin dipping in an indication of trust. "Then let's get started. You have a mate to fuck and claim in a few hours."

"Assuming the serum works," I muttered, hitting the code for the bottom floor. Katriana's human habits were overriding her wolf's common sense. Once she came to terms with her position in the pack, she'd be much more agreeable.

Omegas were treasured and revered. They were the protectors of our children and the only ones capable of a true mating with an Alpha. Fighting our chemistry was futile. And the shot I administered before I left would help her understand that.

Once I completed this meeting, I'd return, have a little discussion about the hierarchy, and then wait for her estrus to take over. Spanking her ass would just serve as a sexy prelude before our instincts assumed control. She'd enjoy every moment, once I broke through her insubordinate shell.

I was lenient with her last night because she came from a different way of life. However, the sooner she allowed her wolf's true nature to rule, the sooner we could facilitate our inevitable mating.

And I needed to claim her.

Particularly before someone from the council decided to challenge me for her. There were already rumblings of it, and her lab results only worsened matters.

Katriana wasn't just turned into a wolf through science. The markings for lycanthropy already existed in her blood. She'd been born with Omega genetics, which our serum had strengthened and unleashed during her transition. It made her even more worthy of being my mate. Because it meant one of her parents was a wolf.

Unfortunately, this revelation also increased her appeal to all the other Alphas as well.

While the Omega Ash Wolves also appealed to them, they weren't X-Clan Wolves.

Katriana was an X-Clan Omega.

That set her above the rest and made her the prize everyone desired.

Mine, I thought, exiting the elevator toward the conference room. *Katriana Cardona is mine.*

CHAPTER NINE

KAT

"I USED TO LIVE WITH HUMANS," Riley said after we finished eating. "Back before the Infection, I mean." Her lips curled down. "So I can understand how all of this might be difficult for you to accept. I wasn't all that accepting myself, and I grew up as an Omega."

"You're an Omega?"

"Can't you smell it?" she countered, arching a brow. "Jonas says I remind him of a Georgia peach, which I think is a play on how we met."

"What's a Georgia peach?"

"A delicious fruit," she replied, her lips twitching. "Jonas is Icelandic, so it's not he like ever had a Georgia peach. By the time we met, there weren't any left, and I was too busy trying to find a cure to introduce him to one." Her amusement seemed to fade. "That was a troubling time, but it brought us here. Eventually, anyway."

"Jonas is an Alpha?" I guessed.

She nodded, her cheeks reddening. "Yes. He's my mate."

"By choice?" I wondered out loud, then shook my head. "Sorry, I mean—"

"No, no, it's fine. I get it. As I said, I used to live with humans. And there was a reason for that—I didn't want to be an Alpha's mate." She let that settle for a second, likely making sure she had my undivided attention.

"Is that normal?" I prompted.

She laughed. "No. Well, not in my former clan, anyway. We lived in a time where the females were permitted a college education, but only because the Alphas felt it helped with the education of the young. Long story short, I pursued a pre-med path, then applied to medical school. Everyone expected me to return afterward. I didn't. And when they found out I was using my medical knowledge to suppress my estrous cycles, the pack disowned me."

"Estrous?" I repeated, searching my mental dictionary for the definition. "Like fertility?"

She nodded. "Omegas go through it regularly. And we, uh, require an Alpha during that period."

My eyebrows shot up. "*What?*"

"It's not as bad as it sounds. Actually, it can be quite pleasing with the right Alpha." Her face flushed again. "But my point is, I once rejected that part of me. I went to work for the Centers for Disease Control and Prevention, specializing in infectious disease, which was how I became involved in the zombie crisis. My team was looking for a cure." Her lips twisted. "We never found one."

Clearly.

"Jonas worked with the Iceland Crisis Response Unit, which became affiliated with the global armed forces. He was assigned to my post in Atlanta at the time. My suppressants gave me the scent of a Beta, so he didn't realize what I was until we found ourselves in a compromising situation. And, uh, yeah, I went into estrus and he claimed me."

I gasped. "Against your will?"

"Not exactly." She squirmed a little. "I mean, the

attraction was always there—it's only natural between Alphas and Omegas. But yeah, I wasn't thrilled with him at first."

"Did he apologize?"

She snorted. "Jonas apologize for giving in to his instincts? Ha. No. He told me to deal with it."

"Sounds like Ander," I muttered. He hadn't said that to me exactly, but he seemed pretty hell-bent on me just accepting this fate and his ownership.

"That's just the Alpha way, honey," she replied, smirking. "They pick a path and expect everyone to fall in line."

"And did you?" I wondered out loud. "I mean, obviously you did. But…?" *Did you fight him?* was what I wanted to ask. I just didn't know how to phrase it without giving my motives away.

"Yes and no." She winced. "I gave chase a bit at first, but he caught me in the end. They always do." Those ominous words were accompanied by a look, suggesting she already saw right through me.

I said nothing.

I didn't even blink.

But her expression told me she knew, which didn't bode well for my plan.

"What happened when he caught you?" I asked, swallowing.

"He dragged me to Europe—to Ander—and we joined Andorra Sector. It's always been a higher-tech sector of X-Clan Wolves, and my background with the CDC made me a viable candidate to work in their labs."

"And that's it?" *You just accepted your fate?* I wanted to demand.

She shrugged. "I continued trying to find a cure for a while, but it became less and less relevant. With over ninety percent of the human race turned or dead, my focus shifted to the survival of those who are left. I still help today, much to Jonas's chagrin."

My brow furrowed. "He doesn't want you to work?"

"It's more, he doesn't like me around the other males." She rolled her eyes. "He's always worried about my safety, even within the dome."

"And that doesn't bother you?" I pressed. Because it sounded suffocating to me.

"Most Omegas are kept in the nest, breeding, caring for the young, and so on. Jonas and I have an understanding—I require my independence, and he craves my submission. It's a constant negotiation, but it works for us." Her eyes brightened while she spoke, her affection for her mate obvious.

I had to wonder how much of it was *her* versus her hormones. If yesterday taught me anything, it was that my body could not be trusted to make decisions regarding Ander. Or I'd end up on my back with my legs spread every time he walked through the damn door.

"Well, I've intruded on your space long enough for today." She leaned closer. "I know how territorial Omegas can be with their Alpha's quarters." She winked and picked up our plates from the table to carry to the sink.

Frowning after her, I called out, "Oh, I'm not territorial."

"You snarled at me when I arrived," she returned. "So while your human mind might not be territorial, your inner wolf definitely wanted to shred me alive. But don't worry. I'm not offended. And Ander will be thrilled when I tell him."

The water flickered on, hiding my groan.

She could tell the Alpha whatever she wanted because I had no intention of being here when he returned.

Except, I'd just wasted a hell of a lot of time hearing her history and learning about estrus.

That… that's going to be a problem, I thought, shivering.

From what little she said, it sounded like I would lose control of myself completely to the heat cycle.

Hopefully, that wouldn't happen anytime soon. I needed to get the hell out of here first.

"Well, if you want to visit again, let Ander know. I'm sure he won't mind us being friends. And I think you'll find I understand you better than you think I do."

That remains to be seen, I thought back at her. Outwardly, I smiled. "I'd like that. Can I walk you out?" I was totally thinking on my feet here. I needed to see the hallway again, to search for any signs of the stairs or another door or exit.

Maybe she'd give something away.

"Sure," she replied, her lips curling. "I suspect Ander has his hands full with you."

"I have no idea what you mean," I replied, brushing my palms against the dress shirt.

Her glance told me she knew exactly what I meant. And her words proved it. "He will catch you."

"You assume I plan to run."

"Don't you?" she asked, opening the front door. "It's what I would do." She punched the arrow pointing down and turned to face me. "I wouldn't suggest it, Katriana. You're unmated and on the verge of your cycle. If you leave this building, the wolves will go into a frenzy over your scent. You might not feel safe up here, but you've never been safer than in Ander's quarters."

"I appreciate your concern," I said, forcing a smile. "I'll be fine."

She sighed. "You're very much twenty-one-year-old me."

The door opened.

"Good luck, Katriana," she said, her smile sad as she did something on the internal panel. "Do us both a favor and stay here."

"Nice to meet you, Riley," I replied, giving her a little wave.

She shook her head as the doors closed, but not before I caught the glimmer of respect in her features. Hopefully, that meant she wouldn't go straight to Ander with my plans. But I doubted it.

Which meant I needed to move.

I ran to his closet, pulling the items I noted earlier and dragging them on.

His shorts fit me like pants.

Two pairs of socks were almost as good as boots.

And his coat came equipped with a hood that hid my hair.

Not the most covert outfit of my history, but it should work to at least block my scent. What I should have done was demanded she get me one of the suppressants. However, there was no time.

I sprinted across his flat to the door, found it still

unlocked, and tried hitting the button for the elevator just like Riley had done.

Please don't open with anyone in it. Please. Please. Please.

Ding.

Empty.

With a relieved sigh, I stumbled inside and stared at the panel on the side. "Uh…" It was a standard keypad of numbers, but it stopped at nine. As the penthouse was well above nine stories high—given my view out the windows, anyway—the numbers probably didn't tie to the floor level.

Which meant I needed a code.

Nibbling my lip, I tried the bottom three numbers first, hoping it would take me to a basement or the ground level.

It took me to a sky lobby—something I determined upon sticking my head out and seeing an array of bright windows.

Right.

I selected two buttons this time.

Nothing.

Okay… I tried four next, and it opened to a cement hallway that reminded me of my first night here. *Next!*

The elevator whooshed back up—in the wrong direction—and then down again as I punched more codes. It felt like I was even moving sideways at certain points, almost as if the elevator could shift horizontally.

Oh, yep, that's exactly what's happening, I thought as I moved clearly to the right.

Huh. This is some high-tech shit. All the documents I read back in the caves defined elevators as up-and-down modes of transport only.

When the doors opened to reveal two men in suits standing outside waiting to enter, I darted out, deciding this was my exit point because sharing a small space with two wolves would not end well.

I really should have at least grabbed some knives before leaving. Not that I knew where they were kept. I suspected Ander had hidden them since my meat was *pre-cut* and Riley had only allowed me to use a fork.

Regardless, I should have planned something other than to trap myself in a damn metal box.

With a growl to myself, I headed right down a corridor lined with doors, which ended in yet another threshold. I twisted the handle to find it locked and took off in the other direction, trying a few knobs along the way.

The last one gave way to a stairwell.

Yes! I started downward, skipping steps as I went, searching for the bottom.

Endless floors passed by, the sounds of idle chatter drifting in and out as I approached various exit points.

The chill sweeping up my spine grew as I descended. I couldn't tell if it was real or imaginary, but as I hit the final level, a frosty blast caused my teeth to start chattering.

And I finally found a door that led outside.

I shoved it open and took a deep breath, reveling in the fresh air for all of a split-second before an alarm sounded.

Shit!

I took off around the building, searching for the mountains I knew and loved. Once I spotted the familiar landscape, I'd be able to establish a trajectory and—

A male stepped out in front of me, blocking my path, his head cocking to the side in a wolfish manner that had my blood running cold. *This is why I should have grabbed at least a knife.*

I stumbled back, then darted around him in a sprint.

He shouted after me, but I didn't listen, my need to run taking over. So much for a stealthy escape. Not that I really expected one.

My feet flew beneath me, carrying me aimlessly down the street, past buildings and the few people wandering around outside. Growls snapped at my heels, sending me faster, my heart racing inside me as a pang hit my middle abdomen. I ignored it, pushing on, refusing to slow.

I couldn't let them catch me.

Couldn't allow Ander to find me.

Couldn't—

My insides tensed violently, the sensation causing me to stumble into something hard, much like the last time I tried to run. *The change?* I wondered. *No. This... It's...* I shook my head, trying to clear it, to force myself onward, but a palm caught my shoulder and yanked me backward.

I yelped, then punched the male who dared paw at me.

He snapped out a reply, his opposite hand coming down on my hip.

Wait, no. That one didn't belong to him. There was a guy at my back. I threw my elbow at his face and squirmed out from between them, running again, only to be caught by a third male, this one much larger than the other two. He lifted me and threw me back at something hard. Darkness blinked before my eyes, his angry face looming over me. Somehow I'd ended up on the ground, the snow seeping in through my clothes, freezing my limbs and joints.

"Well, well. What do we have here?" a deep voice drawled.

"I don't know, but she smells fantastic."

"Aroused."

"Omega?"

The words began to blur together, my abdomen tightening to a painful degree. Something was very wrong, and it had nothing to do with the hit I'd taken against the brick siding behind me.

Yet, I now had an even bigger problem in front of me because the males had attracted attention from others. There were five, no *six*, hungry sets of eyes fixated on me.

And none of them belonged to Ander Cain.

CHAPTER TEN

ANDER

"I'M GOING TO FUCKING KILL HER," I growled.

Riley's report, coupled with the blaring alarms, told me exactly what my intended mate was up to. I left the conference room on a wave of aggression, the need to get to Katriana first heating my blood to a boiling point.

If another Alpha caught her in this state, I'd lose my claim.

Artur and Enzo were already sniffing around my property enough as it was. If they realized she'd escaped while on the verge of her heat cycle, we'd have a war on our hands.

I'd win. No question. But I'd end up losing a good male in the process. Because there'd be no choice but to fight to the death. An Omega in estrus caused even the strongest Alphas to lose their common sense, especially when provoked by violence.

I should have locked her in her damn room. I just never expected her to try something so foolish.

Riley seemed to think otherwise, reminding me that Katriana wasn't a typical Omega.

Didn't I know it.

"Distract them," I demanded, referring to the room of council members eyeing me with unveiled intrigue.

"On it," Elias said, moving to address the crowd.

I trusted him to at least give me a head start.

The rest fell on my shoulders.

Pulling up the screens on my watch, I searched for the source of the alarm and took off toward the stairwell. My Omega's scent mingled with mine all the way down to the door she'd shoved open only moments earlier.

I traced the path her little feet made in the snow, my nose scenting her the entire way, until I spotted a group of Beta males pacing restlessly.

An Omega in heat served as a beacon that called to all unmated wolves, begging them to help procreate.

My growl caused the crowd to part, my dominance clear with each step.

Several ran off, not wanting to test the claim of an Alpha.

Others lingered, likely hoping for a show.

Most Alphas lacked control when around an Omega in Katriana's position. Fortunately for her, I knew how to temper my urges.

Her eyes widened as I crouched before her.

It seemed that shot had worked even faster than Ceres anticipated because she was already on the edge of estrus. Her pupils flared, little whimpers escaping her mouth as she curled on her side, and her slick began to permeate the air.

I needed to get her the hell out of here, and fast.

But I needed her to understand her situation first, and there was only one way to do that.

"You're going into heat, Omega," I informed her. "In about an hour, likely less, you'll be inconsolable in your need to fuck."

She flinched. "Ander—"

"These Betas will try," I continued, gesturing to the salivating crowd. "And you'll welcome their efforts, but it won't be enough because you need an Alpha to knot you. Only, you're unmated, so it's going to send the available Alphas nearby into a frenzy. As you're a wolf, you should physically survive their rampage. Omegas are, after all, built to receive our brand of aggression. But it won't be pleasant."

I kept my hands loose at my sides, the growing aggression singeing the air behind me. It wasn't unmanageable yet, but it would be soon.

"You have a choice to make, Katriana. You can either choose to come with me—and let me take care of you and your current state—or I can leave you here to your fate, to be claimed and fucked by whoever manages to mount you fast enough."

Her eyes narrowed. "Fate..." Knowledge registered in those blue depths, her lips parting. "That's what was in the needle. Y-you d-did something to me."

I wouldn't apologize for igniting a process her body was only days from experiencing anyway. Nor would I acknowledge the accusation in her gaze.

This was not a time for debate or discussion.

She had a decision to make, and she needed to choose while I could still help her.

A growl sounded in the distance—an Alpha scenting an Omega in need. She moaned right on cue, her arms wrapping around her stomach as she curled tighter into herself.

"I know how to make you feel better," I promised. "But I'm not going to help you until you ask."

She created this situation with her foolish escape attempt. If she wanted me to fix it, she'd damn well admit it.

I folded my arms and waited, the approaching snarls growing louder. If they reached us, I'd be forced to fight. Katriana might not want to accept me as her mate, but I'd chosen her. Leaving her defenseless wasn't an option, even if it was what she deserved.

"Ander," she whimpered, the scent of her slick growing stronger with every inhale.

"Hmm, I was wrong. It seems you have minutes before you begin begging. I recommend you make a decision quickly, Omega. Before one is made for you." If she forced me to fight on her behalf, I would fuck her in the aftermath up against that wall, just to make my dominance clear to everyone under this dome.

No one questioned me, and certainly not my intended mate.

"Stop thinking like a human and let your wolf guide you," I suggested. "The Omega in you knows how to survive. It's your human inclinations that will be your downfall."

She writhed, the scent of approaching Alphas tainting the air.

Her Omega instincts would drive her to select the strongest potential mate—me—and she'd beg me to take her. It was only a matter of time.

"Choose, Katriana," I growled, not wishing to provoke bloodshed. "*Now.*"

"You!" she cried out, her body convulsing beneath the layers of clothes she'd donned for this senseless outing.

"Good choice," I said, my voice low and filled with warning for those around us. Scooping her into my arms, I took off at a clipped pace, growling and snarling at anyone who dared step into my path along the way.

Two of my council members were among them, their nostrils flaring, hostility a cloak around their necks. Challenge lined their shoulders, indecision weighing in their eyes.

"Move," I demanded when they threatened to block me.

Darren and Tonic.

Two of my younger Alphas—both of whom supported Enzo on every decision.

Their self-control was nowhere near as strong as mine, and it showed in the way they took a step forward, not backward.

The hairs along the back of my neck danced, and Katriana moaned wantonly in my arms, the Alpha presence drawing her Omega out in full force. If I allowed her, she'd strip naked and accept all three of us at once, her instinct to procreate overriding all thought and reason. Having a trio of viable candidates surrounding her only intensified her needs and desires, her mind fully quieting to the beast within.

"Ander," she breathed, nuzzling into my throat, her lips trailing a path up my neck. Seeking. Searching. Begging for more.

"*Move*," I said with more force, the growl in my voice only exciting the Omega more.

Growls met my command, the Alphas losing themselves to their instincts.

Elias came plowing out of the building, his pupils dilated, his lips curled back into a furious expression, though it wasn't me he set his sights on, but the two weaker males. "*Stand. Down.*" He shoved them both aside, allowing me to pass. "Get her the fuck inside, Cain!"

Any other time and I'd have taken issue with his tone, but I gave him a much-deserved pass. Swallowing his urges had to hurt, his need to knot her likely as powerful as mine.

Violent sounds trembled in my wake, Darren and Tonic squaring off with Elias—who, fortunately, possessed as much control and experience as I did. It would likely be the only reason Darren and Tonic might survive, assuming my second-in-command decided they were worthy of keeping their lives.

"Thank fuck," I muttered, noting the empty lobby.

Elias had cleared the floor, providing me with a straight path to the elevator. I nearly jumped inside, punching the code to my floor. The entire system would lock down when we arrived at the top, preventing anyone else from reaching us.

I leaned against the metal wall, my arms tightening around the disobedient little brat in my arms. "Oh, little one. You have no idea what you've done." And I couldn't lecture her in this state.

Her teeth nibbled my jaw, her mewling going straight to my groin.

"Ander," she whispered, licking the stubble along my chin and trying to move in my arms.

"No." I held her tighter.

She whimpered, the scent of her arousal suffocating me in the small space. I practically charged out of the elevator as soon as it announced our arrival, then carried her swiftly through the threshold of my penthouse. The door slammed behind me, a switch near the wall throwing up the locks that would keep everyone out—including raging Alphas.

I dumped her unceremoniously onto the couch in the living area.

"Undress," I demanded.

Katriana would be begging me to fuck her before I gave in. We'd call it a lesson in hierarchy—Omegas needed their Alphas just as much as Alphas needed their Omegas.

She'd disrespected me to the extreme.

And it was past time she learned what happened to disobedient little wolves.

CHAPTER ELEVEN

KAT

TOO MANY CLOTHES.

Too hot.

Need air.

Ander…

Oh, I could feel his anger like a lash against my skin as I stripped out of his coat, shirt, and shorts. It both terrified me and excited me. I wanted to hide from him as much as I wanted to jump him, leaving me conflicted, confused, and very naked.

Every part of me ached.

My heart raced.

Dampness unlike any I'd ever experienced coated my core and thighs.

I *needed* him. His warmth. His touch. His tongue. His *cock*.

A shiver traversed my spine at the thought. Never had I

desired a man like this, nor had I ever felt so helpless to one.

Some voice in the back of my head tried to shout reason, the inclination to fight surfacing and fleeing in between every breath.

This isn't me. Fight this!

Oh, but his scent, how I longed to roll around in his scent.

Ander approached with a glass filled to the brim with a brown liquid, his golden eyes caressing every inch of my body. "Mmm, I think I may keep you naked for days, Omega."

A sound I hardly recognized fell from my mouth as I started toward him.

He stopped me with a shake of his head. "Kneel."

My knees wobbled and then buckled, sending me to the floor on a wince. Part of me wanted to rant, while the stronger part of me yearned to obey.

"Why?" I whispered. "How?"

The Alphas outside had been primed and ready. I'd sensed their eagerness like claws digging into my skin. But Ander remained poised. Confident.

Sexy as fuck.

"Take me," I breathed, arching my back in a manner I'd never tried before. That nagging voice in my head whispered something about how wrong this was, how I shouldn't be giving in, but I was so wet and ready. "Touch me. Please." I reached for him and he stepped back.

"You don't deserve my touch."

My gaze narrowed on the profound erection threatening his zipper. "You want to touch me." Just like all the others outside. Only, he wasn't.

"No, I want to fuck you," he corrected. "And I will. Soon." He took a healthy swallow of his drink, then set it aside. "But you need to understand and accept a few things first."

This male possessed a control that only made me burn hotter, the urge to force him to fall overwhelming me with wanton ideas and thoughts.

Why had I run from him?

Why had I run from *this*?

Because he took away your choice! that voice reminded me.

72

Well, he technically gave me a choice outside, and I chose the stronger Alpha. I chose *him*.

Is it a choice when he forced this on you?

I frowned. Did he force it on me? Or was I a victim of circumstance?

The sound of leather sliding through the loops of his pants put me on high alert, drawing me out of my internal debate and compelling me to focus on the masculine perfection before me.

"You're fighting your cycle," he murmured, dropping his belt to the floor. "I'm equally impressed and infuriated with you, Omega."

While I heard him, my attention was on the button he'd just popped open, my mouth salivating for the prize that lurked inside.

My thighs clenched.

My mind raced.

This was so very wrong, but just as right.

I groaned, lost somewhere between reason and the illicit cravings stirring inside. *More…*

"An Omega in heat requires a mate," he continued, unzipping his pants. "Without one, she suffers. I think you require a demonstration to understand exactly what I'm saying." He kicked off his shoes right beside me, his warmth causing me to lean. "Stay on your knees."

A shiver of longing coursed through me, my wolf submitting to Ander's dominant tone.

This is so bizarre, I thought, goose bumps dancing along my limbs. I'd never felt this wild and free before, as if I lived on my urges alone and nothing more.

Ander's impressive erection slid free, eliciting a deep moan from my throat, the precum on the head calling to my tongue. I'd never tasted a man before, but I desperately wanted to now. Especially him.

The foreign desire hit me square in the gut, my sex pulsing with *need*.

His size had seemed so daunting yesterday, but now I couldn't wait for him to fill me. To fuck me. To take me to new heights.

Virgin…

Wait, that's important. That—

"Suck my cock, Omega."

"Oh, yes." I leaned forward, licking the bulbous head and salivating over the addictive flavor of him. This was what I needed, what I craved, what I was dying to have inside me. Ander. His seed. His manhood. His everything.

I sucked him deeper, eager for his primal scent and masculine taste. I no longer recognized myself. No longer cared to try. All that mattered was the throbbing shaft inside my mouth and the essence only he could provide.

He didn't touch me.

But his gaze captured mine, encouraging me to accept more of him. I pushed myself to the limit, allowing him into my throat and swallowing more of his delicious arousal. Each suck and pull left me whimpering, the experience not nearly enough.

I wanted his hands on me. His cock buried deep within me. To feel his mouth. His tongue. Everything. Yet he held me hostage, his stare demanding I continue, the taste of him a growing addiction I couldn't ignore.

Maybe making him come would be enough to satisfy these strange yearnings. Or to quiet them, anyway.

"You're still fighting," he whispered, a glimmer of respect brightening his gaze. "One growl from me and you'll be putty in my hands. But I want you to cross that line yourself. To truly give in."

He threaded his fingers through my hair, forcing me to take even more of him into my mouth. Tears welled in my eyes, my airway cut off by his member as he held me to him.

"Completely at my mercy," he mused, his pupils dilating. "Do you feel my knot throbbing beneath your lips, little one?" He pushed impossibly farther, something hard and pulsating reaching my mouth. "Mmm, yes, you do. That's the part of me you crave. You just don't know it yet."

My vision began to color with black dots, my lungs yearning for air.

His grasp loosened, allowing me just enough room to breathe before setting a rhythm that forced me to inhale at very specific points. It should have bothered me, debased me, and infuriated me, but all it did was excite my competitive drive.

I wanted to force him over the edge, to steal his control, to drink more of that intoxicating fluid. I moaned, "*Yes.*" Yes, that was what I desired most of all.

The frenzy overcame me in a wave, driving my instincts, hollowing my cheeks, and forcing my mouth to work as I all but begged him to come down my throat.

He remained steadfastly in control, his grip in my hair a leash more than a caress. His gaze still boasted a flicker of anger, one I knew was directed at me, but I couldn't remember why. My only thought was about pleasuring him. Mounting him. Fucking him. Moaning beneath him.

More.

I sucked harder.

More.

I drew my nails up his thighs, clasping his hips.

More.

I swallowed around his head, groaning at the precum teasing my tongue.

More.

His pace became my own, my movements driven by impulse alone. He grew impossibly longer as a result, that harsh bulb vibrating beneath his skin and compelling me onward. I wanted him. Wanted this. Wanted him to unleash his power and *come.*

I whimpered.

Cried.

Begged.

All with my tongue and my eyes. His jaw clenched, a vein pulsating along his thick neck. And then he exploded on a roar that provoked a fresh surge of dampness to blossom between my legs.

I writhed, the seed spilling into my mouth not nearly enough. Ropes of his hot substance coated my throat as I gulped him down, my moans turning animalistic in nature. They turned to whines when he finished, my body unsatisfied. Pained. Requiring something different.

Pleasure.

"Touch yourself," he demanded. "Rub that little nub and let me see you come."

I didn't think.

I obeyed.

But no matter how close I came, I couldn't bring myself over the edge. It was all wrong. Cold. Not enough.

Tears poured from my eyes, my body convulsing on the edge of an orgasm that refused to peak.

My nipples ached.

My pussy clenched.

I tried sliding a finger inside, then two, then three, but nothing worked. A sob racked my spine, the pain overwhelming me from the inside out. "*Please*," I whispered, falling to the ground at his feet. I had no idea what I wanted, but I knew he could help me. "Please, Ander."

He stood over me, his size and presence so overwhelmingly right.

His pants remained unbuttoned and unzipped.

His shirt on.

"Why?" I asked, curling into myself. I couldn't finish the question, but I conveyed it with my eyes. *Why are you rejecting me?*

Because that was what this was—a rejection. My Alpha refused to take me, to bring me the pleasure we *both* craved. Instead using my mouth as a poor substitute, pouring his seed down my throat rather than into my womb.

Oh, I had become a puddle of incessant *need*. And if he didn't fuck me, I would die.

Agony ripped through my torso, my hand still lodged between my thighs. No amount of touch or friction was enough. "*Ander*," I cried, rolling around, begging him to fix this, to *fix* me.

"This is why you need an Alpha," he finally said, still unmoving. He'd even put his hands in his pockets. "Now beg me to fuck you, Omega."

I was already begging! What more did he need? Anguish almost split me in two. I reached for his ankle, pulling myself to him, rubbing my face against his calves. "Please, Ander.

Fuck me. Please. Take this pain away."

"Better," he murmured. "Say it again."

"*Fuck me.*" It came out on a strangled growl.

Flames licked my insides, scorching me and bringing me to that crest of pleasure all over again without the release.

"Please, Ander," I added, shaking violently. "It *hurts.*"

"It would be even worse had you allowed those Betas to fuck you," he said from above. "They'd be spilling their seed inside you right now, bringing you to this point over and over again with no true satisfaction. And those young Alphas out there—the ones without control—would have ripped you apart just to be inside you." He bent and scooped me into his arms.

I pressed my damp face into his neck, inhaling deeply.

Oh... Just his scent...

My legs tensed, my arousal heightening to new levels.

"I'm still going to hurt you, but you'll enjoy it." He brushed the hair away from my face. "And do you know why that is, little one?"

I didn't.

And even if I did, I was too busy rubbing myself against him to reply coherently.

"Because I'm not some young pup consumed by a single need to fuck. Nor am I just an ordinary Alpha. I'm the Alpha of this fucking X-Clan Sector." He dropped me onto the mattress. "And you, my darling Omega, are about to learn exactly what that means."

CHAPTER TWELVE

ANDER

FUCK, SHE SMELLED AMAZING.

It took considerable restraint not to rip off my clothes and mount her. While coming down her throat had temporarily taken the edge off, the violent need to knot her was quickly overriding my control.

Katriana fighting her estrus had actually helped because it diluted the scent of her arousal just enough for me to focus. However, now that she'd fallen headfirst into the oblivion of her heat cycle, I was losing that focus.

Unbuttoning my shirt, I watched as she writhed wantonly on the bed, her hands roaming her body in an attempt to evoke the gratification she craved. But it only heightened her yearning. That was the lesson I needed her to learn——Omegas were miserable without their Alphas.

She'd chosen to run and had put herself and the entire

sector in danger. That wasn't something I could just ignore.

Which was why I had the ultimate punishment in mind for her.

A lesson she would never forget. One that would bring her to her knees.

What she wouldn't know was how much it would hurt me to see this through, but her little stunt today proved how badly she needed this.

So I would provide the tutorial she required because my intended mate needed to respect our ways. Everything she did reflected back on me, and I needed a mate who acted responsibly around my wolves.

She'd done the exact opposite today.

And for that, she would pay severely.

My shirt hit the floor, followed by my pants and socks, leaving me as naked as her. But rather than go to the woman on the bed, I stroked my shaft while observing her.

"Ander," she whispered, agony in her tone as she reached for me. "*Please.*"

"You want my cock, kitten?" I purred at her.

"Yes," she hissed, arching her back.

"Show me how badly you want it. Spread your legs. I want to see just how wet you are."

Her thighs parted on a groan, a fresh wave of slick permeating the air. My sheets would be soaked with her arousal by the time we were through, which was exactly what I wanted. It would provoke her nesting instincts, force her to accept my bed as her own.

And then I'd remove her from it.

A wordless whimper left her, the anguish underlining her need calling to my instincts. As her Alpha, it was my duty to take her. To fill her with my seed. To fuck her through her cycle. The longer I withheld, the more she suffered. That made me cruel, yes. But she needed to understand our roles.

Fate could be ruthless, but it was how we survived that defined who we were, and so far, I wasn't all that impressed with her choices. Strong she might be, but her decisions the last two days proved to be childish at best. I needed a mate worthy of my status. Not an Omega who defied me at every turn.

Even if that defiance also turned me on.

I knelt on the bed, growling deep in my throat.

She mewled in response, my animalistic nature calling to hers and driving her wild.

"I'm going to fuck you, Omega," I warned, grabbing her legs and parting them as I crawled over her. "And it's going to hurt in the best way." She fisted the comforter on either side of her hips, her body primed and ready for my claim.

Her virginity in a human state would be problematic. However, in her enhanced condition with immortality flowing through her veins, she wouldn't feel a thing other than an urgency to experience my knot.

A sliver of fear permeated the air as I settled between her slick folds.

Somewhere inside her, the Omega's human sensibilities were peeking through.

I had just the remedy for that.

With another low growl, I invited her wolf to the surface, unleashing the sex drive I knew existed deep down. *Come play with me, little wolf.*

Katriana responded by wrapping her legs around me and pressing her hot cunt against my shaft in invitation.

I wasn't the kind of man who took things slow. When I wanted something, I went after it with everything I owned. This would be no different.

"Grab my shoulders," I demanded.

She did, her little nails biting into my skin. "Take me," she breathed, her thighs squeezing my legs in emphasis.

"Ah, Omega. As angry as I am with you, I can't hold back any longer." I lifted my hips, the head of my cock lining up with her slick entrance. It would be a tight fit, but Omegas were made for this. I'd just have to work myself into her. "Now scream for me."

CHAPTER THIRTEEN

KAT

TOO BIG.

Too fast.

Too hard.

Too right.

I arched into the beast rutting into me, my body on fire from his touch. This was what I needed, what I craved, what I loathed, all wrapped up in an emotional inferno burning inside.

Ander wasn't gentle.

But I didn't want gentle.

I wanted *this*—the Alpha losing his steadfast control. He growled, the sound a rumble that made me even wetter. He wasn't all the way in yet, his cock splitting me in two, something that both pained and excited me.

I'd completely lost my mind to this insatiable lust.

Words that were foreign to my ears fell from my mouth. They left in screams, pleas, moans, and growls. I clutched his shoulders, crying out as he drove into me again, hitting me deeper with each thrust.

Fuck, this should be breaking me in half. His power. His strength. His size. Oh, but it stoked the flames licking through my veins. My pleasure mounted higher than ever before, dancing along the edge of oblivion.

Something was missing.

Some sort of climax to push me over the cliff.

It stirred a whimper from my very soul, mingled with a cry of agony as he finally filled me to completion. I shivered, my nails scraping along his skin. He didn't stop, his lips falling to my neck, his pants branding my skin. He had a tight hold on my hips, holding me at an angle to better receive him. My core ached and throbbed for him at the same time, the delicious mix of pleasure and pain calling to a wanton side of me I never knew existed.

I wanted more.

And I told him that.

My lips chanting the word over and over, his name mingled in between the command.

He growled something in reply, but it was lost to my scream as he picked up his pace. I couldn't think, couldn't breathe, couldn't do anything other than *feel*.

"Fuck," he breathed, his teeth skimming my pulse. His grip tightened to a harsher grasp, no doubt bruising me down to the bone. But it paled in comparison to the quake building within me. I was on the verge of an explosion that would render me unconscious.

Dangerous.

Violent.

Enthralling.

I bowed off the bed as he grew impossibly longer, his engorged shaft stretching me all the more. "Ander!" I cried out, my arms wrapping around his neck, my limbs quivering.

"Shh," he hushed, his mouth at my ear. "I'm going to knot you, Omega. I'm going to knot you for fucking days."

Oh, I liked the sound of that. Even though I had no idea

what—

He erupted into me on a roar that vibrated my spine. I flew over the edge into oblivion with him, his seed hot and searing my insides. It branded me, shooting me into an orgasm that brutally shook me from head to toe, eliciting a sharp gasp from within.

A scorching pain liquefied my insides as his cock anchored itself so deep within me that I couldn't breathe.

No.

Not his cock.

The *knot*.

Fuck, it'd shot out of him with his cum, clamping down on my intimate flesh and locking us together in an unending vibration of pleasure.

Tears fell from my eyes. It hurt in the best way, providing me with the relief I needed while destroying me at the same time.

I had no idea this was how X-Clan Wolves fucked. I both loved and hated it, my mind melting into a puddle of blissful confusion.

Ander's tongue met my cheek as he licked up the tears that had fallen. His nose nuzzled mine. And he rolled us so I straddled his waist, our bodies still engaged below in a dance of savage rapture.

I quivered, a blanket of ecstasy wrapping around me and holding me captive in a sea of passion I couldn't escape from. Not that I wanted to, not with the oblivion blossoming between my legs.

He continued to spill into me, his knot vibrating as I milked everything from his shaft with greedy pulsations.

It wouldn't stop.

I couldn't stop.

Yet something was missing. Beneath the incredible pleasure was a hollowness I didn't understand. Ander wrapped his arms around me, holding me tight to his chest, his lips brushing the top of my head. And still, I felt empty. A whimper mingled with a moan as he moved below, his cock still pulsing deep within, but I didn't feel right.

I required more.

I tried to move my hips against his, to demonstrate my need, but his palm drifted down to my ass to hold me still. "Not yet."

"Please." I pressed into him again.

"Not. Yet."

Another tear fell, my rapture morphing into devastation. My pussy throbbed, my legs tensing around his hips. "Ander…"

He gave my rump a slap that jolted me inside, stirring a fresh wave of euphoria. I moaned, craving another. But he went back to holding me, his fingers drifting through my hair. "Relax, Omega. I'll take care of you."

A shiver of anticipation skated down my spine.

Ripples of pleasure continued to engulf us both, his knot doing things to me I never knew were possible. Yet, I craved a deep connection. Something to glue us together. I wanted him to give me everything.

He tilted my chin up, his golden eyes swirling with power. "That was only the beginning, sweetness. I'm going to consume every fucking inch of you and own you in every way but one."

I had no idea what he meant by that, but found my lips whispering, "Yes," in response. Because yes, I wanted him to devour me. To take me over and over and over again.

His erection finally began to calm, the connection between us loosening and the knot disappearing from my core. Liquid heat pooled between my thighs, soaking us both in the combination of our fluids.

"I want you to crawl down and lick me clean, Omega. Every damn drop. And then, I want you to suck until I'm hard enough to fuck you again." He pulled out of me, leaving me even emptier than before. "Now."

I swallowed a whine and descended to the place he demanded, only to be immediately distracted by the mingled scents of our arousals.

Oh God…

My thighs shook, mounting need growing within me as I took him into my mouth.

Utter ambrosia.

I'd never tasted or experienced anything like this, my instincts demanding I run my tongue over every inch of him. There wasn't enough. I needed more. My mouth sealed around him, my throat working harshly, my desires increasing by the second.

His fingers wove through my hair, tugging, guiding, clenching.

He hardened again, his groan going straight to my gut. My back hit the mattress in the next move, his cock thrusting into my sensitive pussy as his mouth claimed mine.

Feral energy settled over us, an animalistic urge taking over to drive our movements. I moaned, screamed, and begged him never to stop. He growled in return, giving me everything I asked for.

On and on.

For hours.

Days.

Everywhere.

Everything.

He varied harsher sex with fleeting tender moments before flipping me onto my stomach and taking my ass. I howled for him, demanded he give me his all. And he did. Over and over again. Swathing us in a cocoon of semen and slick, his sheets soaked through and bundled around us.

My hands worked while my mind hummed in contentment.

Ander provided piles of silk woven with cotton, the scents all too clean for my preference. So I fucked him on the fresh sheets, soiling them to my satisfaction, and added them to our nest afterward.

He seemed pleased, his naked form lounging beside me as he watched.

All muscular, strong Alpha male.

I wanted to lick him all over again, but his palm against my neck guided me to his mouth instead. He kissed me thoroughly, his cock sliding into me once more. I welcomed him with widening legs, reveling in his slower movements. He took his time, grinding my hips into the bedding and forcing me to feel every throbbing inch of his shaft as he took me deep.

My thighs cradled his, my heart thudding wildly in my chest.

Time had completely escaped us, lost to our desire to mate.

"You're fucking beautiful like this," he whispered against my neck, his lips tracing a path up to my ear. "I love being inside you." His knot thrummed along his shaft, warning me of his intending orgasm right before it hit.

I panted beneath him, his explosion setting off one of my own.

Stars blasted through my vision, cascading me into an ocean of black. He did this to me. Ander. My beast. My Alpha. He wrung every ounce of pleasure from me, driving me to the brink of death so many times only to bring me back with his kiss.

I moaned into his mouth, my tongue twining with his in a sinful dance. My fingers threaded through his thick hair, my legs wrapping around his waist. He tugged me over him, keeping us joined below while he continued to come inside me.

His kiss turned soft with little nips and licks that caused me to melt against him.

"You're beginning to fall out of your mating high," he murmured, nuzzling me gently. "I can sense the change coming over you. Just as I can sense the life we've created together." His palm drifted from the back of my neck down my spine. "My seed grows inside you now, Omega."

I sat up to palm my belly, his knot still latched on to keep us connected while his orgasm coaxed pleasure from me in kind. But something about his words left me uneasy.

A baby? I glanced down, frowning.

It wasn't something I ever desired. Bringing a child into this chaotic world had always felt wrong. But that was when I lived on the outside, fearing the Infected, X-Clan Wolves, and all the other supernatural creatures of the world.

Andorra Sector played by different rules.

Children grew up here protected by the wolves. They didn't starve. They didn't worry about being bitten by an

Infected. They survived.

Ander reached out to lift my chin, his golden eyes holding a warning in them. "Run from me again and I'll lock you in a fucking cage until you give birth."

I gasped at the vehemence in his statement. His dick remained erect, his knot affixed to me in an intimate trap I couldn't remove myself from, and yet he spoke to me as if we weren't naked and joined.

"I mean it, Omega," he said. "I will not tolerate another escape attempt. And you will be guarded at all times when I'm not here to do it myself."

Why was he saying this now? After everything we'd shared?

Because even after all the fucking, he's still pissed, I realized. It was why he hadn't used my name once out loud. Always "Omega."

He gripped my hip as I made to move off him, not caring what it did below. "Don't. You'll regret it."

"I'm regretting a lot right now," I retorted, my voice hoarse from days of screaming. Or was it hours? I really didn't know. It felt like at least a week, perhaps longer. Yet not nearly long enough.

We were surrounded in silk and cotton, a nest I'd created for us to fuck in. All the warmth it'd given me had deflated with his words and the stark realization that we were no better off now than when we started.

No. We were *worse* off.

Because *he* put me in this position.

He shot me full of something that triggered my hormones, convinced me to fuck him within an inch of my life, impregnated me, and then had the gall to threaten me?

My blood boiled for an entirely new reason, my hands balling into fists, ready to inflict damage. But he caught my wrist and flipped us, dragging both my arms over my head with ease and trapping them beneath one of his palms.

He shifted his hips sharply, drawing a sharp sound from my throat. "I can still fuck you like this, Omega."

I gritted my teeth against the pleasure his movement awoke. *Again.* God, how long was I going to be like this? My thighs dampened with a fresh wave of slick, my body accepting his punishing thrust with ease. It hurt, his knot not yet subsided, but I felt his anatomy shifting to ready himself for another round.

Endless intimacy.

Covered in semen and sweat and sex.

And while I longed to stir free, to lash out violently against him, the little movements of his pelvis against mine drew me right back into the intoxicating cloud of sexual energy.

I kissed him with a ferocity, longing to punish him and adore him at the same time. And the way his tongue battled mine said the feeling was absolutely mutual.

This time wasn't kind or gentle.

It was hard and brutal, the kind of fucking that made us both bleed.

And I loved it.

Hated it.

Wanted to do it all over again.

And cried when it was done.

He cradled me against him a long while later, my back to his chest, one massive thigh between both of mine. "It didn't have to be this way, Omega," he whispered against my ear. "I would have claimed you as mine. Yet you had to push. And that left me with no choice but to do this the hard way."

Ominous words.

The kind that left my stomach rolling with unease.

What did he mean by *claiming*? What had the last few days together represented? He put a *baby* in me. There was no deeper way to create a bond with someone than that.

"I'm going to miss our nest," he continued softly. "But you'll make a new one on your own."

My lips curled down. Why did it sound like he was saying goodbye to me? He couldn't do that. Not after impregnating me.

Unless… I frowned. Was that how it worked in X-Clan society? Did Alphas use an Omega for procreation, then leave them to raise the children?

"Ander—"

He released me, sitting up. "I'll let you sleep here tonight.

88

But you're moving to your own room in the morning."

I rolled to my back to gape up at him. "What?" Wasn't his entire goal to get me into his bed? Now he wanted to kick me out of it?

"You're not my mate, Omega," he said, staring down at me with an emotionless expression.

I blinked at him, my mouth working over words I didn't know how to say. Not his mate? How? Why? What the hell had our time together been about, then?

And why did that proclamation hurt?

I didn't even like him, wanted nothing to do with his world or this place. His doctors turned me into a wolf against my will. I'd just wanted to go home. To escape.

Then Ander used some sort of shot to trigger my estrus, changing everything. He took all my innocence, placed a baby in my womb, all to what?

"Why did you do this to me?" I asked, my voice barely a whisper.

"You were an Omega in heat and I did my job. I provided the seed your body craved, and now you'll give me a child." Harsh words. Cold golden eyes. Stoic expression. "That said, as the mother of my future offspring, I'm duty-bound to protect you. And so I shall until you give birth."

"How kind of you," I seethed, livid.

How dare he put me through all this bullshit just to… just to… put me in my own room!

I wanted to smack him.

To rant.

To rage.

To destroy his fucking penthouse all over again.

Yet the energy zapped right out of me beneath a wave of despair unlike anything I'd ever felt.

He doesn't want me.

Why that thought rose above the others, I didn't know. But it hurt more than all the others.

After everything he'd put me through these last few days, he hadn't chosen me to be his. He hadn't truly claimed me. *That* was the feeling I'd been missing, the reason I hadn't been able to achieve true satisfaction in my hormonal state.

I'd been good enough to fuck, to spread his seed, but at the end of the day, I wasn't a worthy enough mate.

My shoulders crumpled, my body curling into itself, the fight leaving me on a breath.

Ander Cain had rejected me. In his own bed. Covered in his seed.

It was exactly what I should have desired—a chance at freedom. A way to disentangle myself from the Alpha.

Yet all I felt was utter desolation and loneliness and a subtle little heat blossoming inside my belly, thriving with new life.

Maybe that last part was my imagination, but I clung to it. Because of all the thoughts rioting through my mind, it was the only detail that gave me solace.

A baby, I thought, closing my eyes. *My baby.*

It was perhaps the only moment of happiness I'd ever be granted in this life. And for the moment, I allowed it.

A little glimmer of hope, surrounded by an eternity of darkness.

My fate.

CHAPTER FOURTEEN

ANDER

"I CAN'T BELIEVE YOU DIDN'T MATE HER," Elias muttered, rubbing a hand down his face. "And then you just left her in another room?"

My jaw clenched. "I don't want to talk about this." We had more important tasks on deck today—like receiving the first shipment from the Ash Wolves. They were scheduled to arrive in ten minutes, my own jet having gone to retrieve the package. If we were satisfied, I'd allow the Ash Wolf Alpha to take the jet back with him—to keep.

That was our deal.

"How are you going to handle her being around other Alphas?" Elias pressed. "She's unclaimed, Ander."

"With my child growing inside her," I growled back at him, "another Alpha would have to be insane to touch her."

"It's not unheard of to claim another's pregnant mate," he

tossed back at me. "Especially under our circumstances."

Meaning with her being one of the few Omegas under the dome, another Alpha might be just suicidal enough to take her—repercussions be damned.

"Then I'll kill the asshole who thought to challenge me," I replied. "Problem solved."

"You're just asking for a fight."

"No, I'm asking for some goddamn silence on the issue," I threw back.

He whistled. "A week of fucking your Omega and you're even crankier than you were before she arrived. I'd blame her skills, but I suspect it's your *lack of a claim* that's the result."

"Shut the fuck up."

"Make me." He squared off with me, aggression rolling off him in waves.

I grabbed him by the dress shirt, yanking him forward. "Are you trying to provoke me into kicking your ass?"

"I'm proving a point," he snapped back, his hand settling over my wrist as he dropped his voice to a level only meant for my ears. "We're outside awaiting a transport, and a handful of words from me have you ready to kick my ass in front of an audience. This isn't you, Ander."

I released him just as quickly as I'd grabbed him, irritated as fuck that he'd pushed my buttons on purpose. It hadn't been easy to leave Katriana unclaimed, but it was the best way for her to understand our dynamic.

After her little stunt last week, I knew forcing the bond would only worsen our situation and make her fight me that much harder. Once she understood our society a little better, she'd have a bit more respect for what I had to offer her.

"Pull yourself together," Elias continued softly. "You're making the other males nervous."

He was right.

Fuck, I hated that he was right.

I paced in a circle, hands on my hips, and fought to rein in my emotions.

Not biting Katriana had taken a great deal of physical restraint. Couple that with all the fucking this last week, and I was exhausted.

"She's going to be the death of me," I grumbled, palming the back of my neck.

Elias gave me a look. "Still not understanding why you didn't just claim her, Cain."

"Punishment."

"Seems like you're punishing yourself more than her," Elias pointed out.

I snorted. He had no idea. Except the devastation radiating from her last night said my punishment had not only worked, but it'd nearly destroyed her. I hadn't expected her to react so sullenly. She hadn't stopped fighting since she arrived, and I expected more of the same. To my surprise, however, she'd sunken into her nest without a word beyond her snappy retort about my kindness.

When I checked on her this morning, she hadn't moved.

I'd planned to tell her to get her ass out of my room, but the words had refused me. Instead, I'd showered and changed and come straight down here to assist with the trade.

The whole purpose was to get my mind off of Katriana. Elias, however, thwarted my plans the second he saw me, riding my ass for the last half hour about not claiming my intended.

As if I needed his shit.

"It'll sort itself out," I promised.

"See that it does," he replied, arching a brow in challenge. He was my Second for several reasons, including the fact that he knew how to hold my ass accountable when needed. "Maybe try heading to the gym after our meet and greet. Blow off some steam."

Oh, I had every intention of taking care of this aggression back upstairs with Katriana. Assuming she left my damn bed.

I blew out a breath and checked my watch. The transport would be here any minute. *Thank fuck.*

Right on cue, the glass at the top of the dome began to open.

Elias inhaled, testing the air with the rest of our team out on the runway. Our wolf senses could pick up on scents for miles upon miles. But nothing seemed off other than the approaching fumes. Jet fuel always left a certain stench in the air, the kind that made my nostrils flare in irritation.

Wolves were meant to run, not fly.

But I couldn't deny the usefulness of certain modes of transportation.

Such as today's little trip to Shadowlands Sector and back. We'd delivered half of what they desired up front, in expectation for the Omega to be returned to us. Then they could have the rest of the technology sitting on the tarmac, along with the jet.

Elias's posture shifted, his spine erecting as the sounds of running engines approached.

"We have the package," the pilot said through the comm connected to my ear. Yazek was one of ours, and we had a code in place should he be coerced into speaking.

As he didn't use it, I gave a nod and replied, "Good. Proceed to the landing site."

"Roger that." The Beta signed off, leaving us to wait for him to land.

Which happened several minutes later.

I folded my arms, eyeing the transport with a bored expression. Mad, Dušan's second-in-command, was notoriously quiet during all of our previous negotiations. He struck me as a pensive sort with a calculative mind, someone I didn't want to underestimate.

So I stood my ground, waiting as the stairs unfolded from the side of the jet.

An Ash Wolf Beta appeared first, followed by Jonas, my chosen lieutenant for this mission. As a mated Alpha, I knew I could trust him to escort the Omega unharmed. He gave me a subtle nod, confirming everything had gone smoothly.

Mad appeared next, his expression void of emotion. His size rivaled that of a typical X-Clan Alpha, but his pensive nature struck me as undeniably lethal. A hint of violence lingered in his ice-blue eyes as he approached me, his casual attire of jeans and a sweater belying the danger lurking beneath. "Cain," he said by way of greeting.

"Mad," I returned, holding his gaze.

He might be a powerful Alpha in Shadowlands Sector, but on my turf, I was the one in charge. Mad smartly accepted my leadership with a respectful cant of his head. "May I introduce Daciana?"

Elias stiffened beside me as a petite ash-blonde female appeared in the entry, her shoulders curved in a frightened manner as Yazek gave her a gentle nudge from behind.

"They won't bite," the Beta told her softly, his words carrying on the wind.

She shivered visibly, her heeled boots hitting the stairs with a light clack as she took a wobbling step. Anxiety radiated from her, causing all the hairs along my arms to dance. She was practically crying out for an Alpha protector, her submissiveness evident in her stature and meek movements.

So very different from my Katriana. She would descend those stairs with an air of defiance underlined in confidence. And she'd stare me down while she did it, not focus on the ground.

Daciana's lower lip trembled as she reached Mad's side, her legs bending in an awkward curtsy. "Hello," she whispered.

"Hello, Daciana," I greeted, using my hand to lift her pale blue eyes to mine. "Welcome to Andorra Sector."

A tear caught on her light-colored lashes, her throat working over a swallow. "Thank you for having me," she managed to say, her voice hoarse. Her terror warmed the air, a sort of aphrodisiac for the Alphas present.

We all enjoyed chasing, and this one was clearly ready to run.

Mmm, definitely nothing like Katriana. While my Omega desired to flee, she didn't exude the stench of fear while she did it. No, her actions were underlined in determination, not terror.

"The rest of your shipment is over there," I told Mad, my gaze still on the Ash Wolf Omega before me. "I assume your Beta is here because he knows how to fly?"

"He does," Mad confirmed.

"Good. Then our initial exchange is complete." I finally met his icy gaze. "I'll be in touch with the lab results."

"Dušan will be pleased."

"I know." I refocused on the Omega. "Come along,

Daciana. We'll introduce you to the medical team." I wrapped my arm around her, giving her a soft little rumble from my chest to help calm her nerves. Assuming that even worked on an Ash Wolf.

She trembled against me, but her shoulders relaxed a fraction. That was a good sign.

Elias led the way to our nearby car and opened the door for her to enter the backseat. Jonas was already behind the wheel in the front seat. Seeing him had the girl calming even more, suggesting either he told her about his mate or she sensed it. Given Jonas was a man of few words, I suspected it to be the latter.

Which meant she knew Elias and I were unmated.

I turned to him after she slid into the car. "Ride in the back with her."

He arched a brow, his hand already on the front passenger door. "Right." That was all he said, taking the seat beside her in the rear of the SUV. I slid into the front and caught his gaze in the mirror.

Yeah, I'd deviated from the plan. Just slightly. But the idea of sitting near her, allowing her to think of me as available when I wasn't, left me feeling off. Like I was somehow being unfaithful to Katriana. A ridiculous notion considering we weren't even mated yet, but it tugged at my gut uncomfortably.

Besides, he was the one who had first dibs on the girl. Might as well give him a chance to start acquainting himself with her now.

I'd just make sure to escort her into the labs. That would ensure everyone understood she was under my protection. We needed to know if she was a viable candidate for procreation and mating. If she was, my deal with the Ash Wolves could move forward. But if something happened to her before we had a chance to confirm her viability, we were utterly fucked because Dušan would not be sending another female for testing.

That was why I'd tasked Elias personally with her security. It would have been me if I didn't have a flight risk on my hands, because I didn't trust Katriana to heed my warning.

Trying to calm a nervous Ash Wolf Omega while also attempting to tame an X-Clan Omega would be a fucking nightmare.

Fortunately, Elias was more than happy to accept the task.

No one said a word the whole way back to headquarters. Daciana's fear permeated the interior, her scent an allure I knew had to be driving Elias mad. Jonas would be able to ignore it, his bond to Riley resolute.

And for whatever reason, I didn't find it all that enticing.

I preferred the fragrance of my feisty female.

I glanced up at the top of the building from the outside, wondering what she was up to right now. Had she left her nest yet? Was she already plotting another escape? Mmm, part of me hoped she would give me a reason to chase her down. Pregnant with my child, she didn't pose as much of a risk.

At least until her second trimester.

But we'd handle that when the time came.

Jonas parked, and the four of us exited.

Elias hovered at Daciana's side as she walked between us.

"Jonas," I said once we were inside. "Can you have Riley meet us in the lab?" I'd tasked her with watching over Katriana upstairs. That she hadn't reached out told me nothing of importance had occurred and my Omega was probably still asleep in our nest. I'd bring her something to eat when I returned, then. Soon. Once I finished assisting with Daciana's transfer to Andorra Sector.

In typical fashion, Jonas responded with a nod and nothing else.

Daciana watched him go with panicked eyes.

"Riley is his mate," I told her softly. "She'll be the one administering your lab work."

The Ash Wolf blinked, her shock palpable.

"I'm starting to think she's heard the rumors about our knots," Elias said conversationally. "She seems quite timid and terrified of us."

Her jaw clenched subtly, the only indication his words irked her. But she remained outwardly submissive, her Omega instincts in full control.

I gave my Second a look, telling him to knock it off, and

he smirked in reply.

Making jokes was his way of easing tension.

Something told me that wasn't going to help the fragile female between us.

I wrapped my arm around her again, rumbling just enough to ease her shoulders, and led her toward the elevator bank. Once she met Riley, the situation would improve.

Of course, I'd thought the same about Katriana, and she'd tried to run minutes after Riley left.

Once downstairs and in the lab, I released Daciana and nodded to Elias for him to take over. There were no cameras in here, no way for any of the other Alphas to see me providing him favor with the girl.

While I trusted most of my brethren to handle themselves, I couldn't rely on them all.

As was evident last week when Darren and Tonic tried to take my intended mate. Not to mention Enzo and his shenanigans.

This was a delicate situation requiring the strongest of our kind to handle. And the way Elias looked at Daciana now, I knew I'd chosen correctly.

Despite his crude remark about knots, I knew he wouldn't hurt or touch her inappropriately.

Riley and Jonas stepped into the room moments later, their fingers locked in their usual way. I met the gaze of the Omega and arched a brow, expecting an immediate report.

"She's in the shower," she said. "She needs food, Ander."

The latter statement had Jonas giving me an apologetic look and Elias arching a brow.

But Riley wasn't done.

"I don't know what you did to her, but she's a mess. So get up there and fix it. Right now. I'll handle our new addition. You go fix the one you broke."

My jaw clenched, unused to taking orders from someone so small and beneath my station. "Watch your tone, Omega."

She didn't even flinch, her glittering gaze reminding me of a blue flame. "She's not used to our ways, Ander. Should she have run? No. But can you blame her? She didn't grow up a wolf. She grew up human. She won't just assimilate to our ways overnight."

"Enough, Riley," Jonas said, tugging her protectively into his side.

Smart move because I was ready to throttle her for daring to come at me with this accusative attitude. I'd done nothing wrong. The woman didn't even want me. She should be thanking me for not forcing a mating bond on her.

Of course, I still intended to.

I just wanted to make sure she understood our society first.

"I'm going about this my own way," I informed Riley. "Not that I owe you or anyone else an explanation for my methods."

Riley hmphed loudly, her irritation more than clear.

I arched a brow at Jonas. "Your Omega requires a stern lesson on how to properly address an Alpha, particularly the highest-ranking Alpha in her sector."

His lips twitched. "I suspect a lesson is exactly what she's seeking."

Riley elbowed him in the side, her expression furious.

He wrapped a palm around the back of her neck, tugging her toward him in a move that would have caused a less agile wolf to stumble.

"I take that back. It's a fight she's in the mood for," he corrected, his bright blue eyes engaging hers. "But I think she's forgetting our guest in the room."

The misbehaving Omega studied her mate for a long moment, then pursed her lips. "Fine," she said, replying to whatever secret conversation they appeared to be having with their eyes.

He nodded. "Good." He pressed his mouth to hers before releasing her. She caught the collar of his shirt to yank him back to her and tugged his lip into her own mouth, biting down. Hard.

He growled.

She smiled.

Elias just shook his head, and I took a step back.

That was my cue to leave because just watching them interact had me craving a battle of my own.

"Let me know what you find," I said, leaving them without

another word.

My Omega needed food, so I'd feed her.

And afterward, I'd fuck her.

CHAPTER FIFTEEN

KAT

THE WHOLE SHOWER EXPERIENCE was not working for me, but there hadn't been a choice after seeing my reflection in the mirror. I'd been covered in fluids, creating a complex knot in my hair.

Fortunately, between the shampoo and the brush I found in Ander's bathroom, I'd been able to comb it free. But my skin held a sharp red tint, thanks to the scalding water.

At least all of Ander's semen was gone.

I shuddered, recalling how it felt spilling between my thighs. Then I remembered his final words, the way he informed me of the place in his life—as a glorified breeder.

No, not even that.

He fucked me because I was in heat, something *he* had induced, and then told me I would be living separately until I gave birth.

What happened after that? Did he take my child away, too, then pass me to the next Alpha to breed again?

My teeth clenched as a snarl worked its way out of my chest. *Not. Happening.*

He had another think coming if he thought I would willingly go along with that insanity. Although, if the last week was anything to go by, he didn't require my mental consent to gain approval from my body.

A part of me loathed him for everything that had happened, crying out that I never had a choice. But I learned a long time ago that nothing in this world was ever fair. It was how we survived that mattered.

I could accept that my body desired him.

I could even accept that *I* wanted him.

But to use me as a breeder crossed the line.

He'd called me his intended more than once yet took it all back with a few cruelly worded statements. Because I didn't please him enough? Because I'd tried to run? Could he fucking blame me?

No one asked for my permission to turn me into an X-Clan Wolf, let alone an Omega.

They *stole* me from the woods, unconscious, and pumped me full of a bunch of chemicals to force my change. Then Ander took me and placed me in his penthouse, stating I now belonged to him.

No one with a conscience could blame me for running.

Yet, clearly, Ander did.

Okay, yeah, it hadn't been the brightest idea, because I went into heat around a bunch of hungry wolves. But *he* was the reason my cycle hit me early. He was just as much to blame for the incident as I was, if not more.

And he denied me.

Left me pregnant with his child, told me to move out of his room, and coldly stated I wasn't his mate.

"Asshole," I grumbled, dropping my towel on his floor and marching into his closet for a shirt. I refused to let him break me. Nor would I allow him to take my child away from me, just because he was an Alpha.

There had to be a way around all of this—a way out.

I grabbed a shirt from a hanger and threw it over my head, then pressed a palm to my flat stomach, pausing.

It would be so easy to run away again, this time with better planning. But I had to consider another life now. While pregnancy might not have been on my dream list of future choices, it wasn't something I necessarily hated either. It was just an experience I never allowed myself to consider, the cruel world around us not a place I ever thought to raise a child.

Andorra Sector was different.

A world of wolves unaffected by the Infected.

But this new world contained rules I didn't understand, a hierarchy that placed me at the bottom without any semblance of choice.

Ander Cain could take my child from me, and likely would.

How do I stop him? I wondered, padding across his bedroom to the door. Our nest of sheets and blankets taunted me along the way, a reminder of our time together—a time he'd claimed to be his duty and nothing more.

My gaze dropped to the carpet.

I hated how his words made me feel, hated even more that he'd spoken them. How could I feel so attached to someone I hardly knew? A male I should logically hate?

Because he'd awoken a passion in me I'd never known existed.

Maybe another Alpha would stir a similar reaction? Did I even want that?

With a shake of my head, I ventured into the living area and toward the kitchen, my stomach growling out a demand for sustenance. I couldn't even remember my last meal.

Ander stood just beside the stove, his back to me as he focused on whatever he was doing. I took a moment to admire him from behind, noting the way his jeans fit his perfectly sculpted ass and how the gray T-shirt he wore stretched across his broad shoulders.

Why does he have to be so ridiculously good—

My nose twitched, scattering my thoughts. He didn't smell right. Too sweet. Not masculine. "Where have you been?" I asked, my voice underlined in a demand I hadn't meant to deliver. But I didn't like this new scent. It unsettled something deep inside.

My wolf, I realized.

I could feel her pacing beneath my skin, itching to escape, to lash out at the Alpha. But I didn't understand why.

He ignored me and instead released a demand of his own. "Sit at the table. You need to eat."

My eyes narrowed. "Not until you tell me why you smell so weird." The statement sounded ridiculous out loud, but my wolf nodded in approval. So I folded my arms and waited.

And waited.

He said nothing as he put together two bowls of savory food. I couldn't identify the ingredients, despite my heightened senses. They were foreign, rich, and meaty.

Mmm… I wanted to taste it.

Until he stepped by me and that sweet scent assaulted me once more.

My brow furrowed. "I don't like the way you smell."

He snorted and set the bowls on the table. "You weren't complaining in our nest yesterday."

The reminder of our *nest* had my hackles rising, a sour note creeping up my throat to my tongue. Not wanting to think about that or how it ended, I chose to sit and lose myself in the meal he'd provided.

While I enjoyed the flavor, I couldn't get rid of the agitation creeping along my spine. It all came down to that damn intrusion—the sweetness I didn't like.

When I finished my bowl, I shoved it aside and glowered at him across the table. "Tell me why you smell wrong."

He took another bite before meeting my gaze. "Is that your version of gratitude for feeding you? To issue more commands at me?" He arched a brow. "Do you require another lesson of your place in the hierarchy, Omega? Because I'll gladly supply you with one."

I wanted to take my bowl and break it over his head.

Then pick up the sharp pieces and stab him over and over again.

"You made yourself clear yesterday when you informed me I'm nothing but a breeder to you," I replied, my heart racing with each word. "I was an Omega in heat and you did your job. So no, I will not thank you for feeding me. You only provided food because of the child growing inside me." My voice rose with each word, my fury bubbling over. "You'll take care of me until the birth, right? Isn't that what you said?"

I pushed away from the table, everything spinning through my head.

Being turned into a wolf against my will.

The shot he administered to my ass, also against my will.

Trying to escape, only to have my heat cycle stop me.

Fucking him for days in every way imaginable.

Learning what he considered my place to be in his life and his world.

Him coming home smelling like another—

My eyes widened, understanding sending an ice cube down my spine. "Another Omega," I breathed, stumbling backward. "*That's* why you smell wrong."

He said nothing, studying me as one would an experiment. Like my reaction somehow intrigued him, but not enough to comment.

"*Say something,*" I hissed, my fingers curling into fists at my sides.

"Topping from the bottom will never work with me, Omega."

Omega.

Omega.

Omega.

I growled. "My name is Kat." And if he called me "Omega" one more time, I would slap him.

"Your name is insignificant. Your commands are as well. I will tell you what I want to tell you when I want to tell it to you. Until then, you do as I say. Now sit down while I refill your bowl."

"Fuck you," I snarled. "I'm done eating. I'm done with this. I'm done with *you.*"

He stood, blocking my path as I charged toward the hallway without a real destination.

I reared backward not because of his nearness but because of the sickly scent coming off his shirt. My nails itched to shred the offending fabric from his body. An Omega had touched him there. It wasn't Riley, but another one.

An unmated one, some foreign part of me thought.

My lips parted. How did I know that? No, better question. "Why were you with an unmated Omega?"

His jaw clenched. "My business does not concern you, *Katriana*."

Well, it was better than "Omega." I also liked the way my name sounded from his mouth. Decadent. Like a treat he was tasting and enjoyed.

He took a step toward me, that stench slapping me across the face once more. I screamed and grabbed at his shirt, ripping it off him in a fit of rage I didn't realize was happening until I finished.

Ander's eyebrows shot up.

As did mine.

Because wow, I hadn't meant to do that.

And it still wasn't any better!

"Wash it off," I snapped. "Get rid of it!" I was borderline hysterical, my thoughts raging between wanting to kill him and needing to calm down.

Pull it together.

How dare he come home smelling like unmated wolf!

What the hell is wrong with you?

I'm going to kill him!

Ander's palm circled my throat, my back slamming into the wall of the dining room. I clawed at his grip, my feet kicking wildly as he lifted me a hair off the ground.

"Calm down, Omega."

I screamed my name, but it came out as a harsh cry due to his grip. I shifted to knee him, but he blocked me with his leg, then slid it upward between my own.

A shiver ran through me at the rightness of having his muscular thigh pressed to my core. I arched on instinct, a new desire running through me. If he wouldn't wash off the scent, I'd override it with my own.

Releasing his wrists, I went for his nape, yanking him down to take his mouth in a harsh kiss. I dragged my teeth along his lower lip sharp enough to draw blood and arched into him at the same time.

He froze in response, his grasp turning to stone around my neck. I didn't let it stop me from plunging my tongue into his mouth, branding him with my flavor.

Ever since arriving here, he'd been in charge. Never me. He chose how we kissed, how we fucked, how we touched, and when. So I took this for myself, asserting my own version of control as *I* kissed *him*.

It was empowering.

Liberating.

Glorious.

Addicting.

I wrapped my arms around his neck, hugging him with all my strength and kissing him to within an inch of my life—literally, since he still had ahold of my throat.

His grip would leave a bruise.

So I scratched my nails down his back to leave my own wound and bit him again.

He growled in response, the sound eliciting a surge of wetness between my thighs. All I wore was one of his shirts, leaving me utterly exposed below. His jeans abraded my hot center, stirring a burn in my lungs as I tried to gasp and failed.

I felt delirious and drunk on power, my vision dancing with black dots.

Worth it, I thought, no longer sensing the other female on him. My arousal had soaked right through, branding him in a place she hadn't touched, marking him as mine.

Darkness loomed.

An oblivion of unknown.

I would have sighed, except I couldn't. My arms began to shake, my hold failing.

"Ander," I mouthed.

He hushed me against my lips.

And sealed his mouth over mine, his return kiss breathing air into my lungs as he released my aching throat.

His tongue soothed mine, his hands catching my hips and hoisting me into the air. My legs wound around his waist, my pussy finding his cock through his pants. It hurt in the best way, my clit throbbing against the rough fabric.

Slick poured from me, readying me for his entry despite the barrier.

It was irrational. I should hate him. But I chose this moment. I wanted to mark him, to claim him, to erase that Omega bitch from his very existence.

And he let me, his palms skimming up my sides as he removed my shirt.

I dropped my hands to his pants, unfastening and unzipping to release the part of him I craved.

He wanted to use me as a breeder? Then I'd use him for pleasure.

Fucked up.

Wrong.

But I stopped caring the moment his bulbous head touched my entrance.

I didn't give him a chance to reject me or taunt me. I squeezed my thighs and shifted to impale myself on his engorged shaft. He hissed a breath in response, his forehead finding mine.

His grip tightened, but not enough to stop me from rising and falling over him, the wall at my back a brace I used to set my momentum while I clutched his waist.

This was no longer about him, but about me.

I needed to come, to scream, to saturate his skin with my juices.

A moan parted my lips, my head falling back as rapture built inside me.

But I needed more.

I needed him to fucking move.

Dragging my nails along his skin to his lower back, I dug into his ass and attempted to yank him forward.

Damn male didn't budge.

"Fuck me," I whispered, still riding him in my own way. "Knot me."

Heat radiated from him, his palm sliding up to my throat once more. "You want me to fuck you, little one?" He squeezed, but not as harshly as before. His gaze burned into mine, the emotion one I didn't understand.

Annoyance?

Fury?

Sexual need?

Perhaps a combination of all of the above.

"Please," I added, hiking my hips to take him even deeper into me.

His nostrils flared.

A whimper left my lips, the sound of anguish both belittling and frustrating at the same time. I needed this—the control—and he wasn't giving it to me. He was holding back, and I hated him for it.

He wanted a submissive. An Omega. And he refused to accept the woman inside me, the person who survived twenty-one years of hell.

Tears prickled the back of my eyes, yearning ripping through my lower belly and leaving me breathless against him.

I knew what he was doing, the trick up his sleeve. He wanted me to remember my place, to submit completely. But I refused, and I showed him that with my hips, determined to bring myself pleasure even if he didn't want to give it.

His grip slipped to the back of my neck, his fingers threading through my hair. I expected him to pull me off him, to throw me to the ground as a reminder of my position at his feet. Yet he surprised me by kissing me fiercely and finally adding his power to the game.

I moaned into his mouth, my ecstasy mounting with every thrust.

This. This was what I needed. What I craved.

Tears dampened my cheeks, my pleasure grounded in pain, his pace turning savage. I clung to him, crying out at each deep hit inside and openly weeping as his knot began to pulsate.

More.

More.

More.

I needed his cum, my slick, our sex, to permeate the air with our coupling. To announce to the world that I owned him. At least in the moment. No one else compared. No other Omega, that dreadful scent long gone and washed away by the power of my own.

109

I'm in charge.
This is my Alpha.
I will not share.

Oh, but he wasn't mine at all. He told me that—we weren't mated. My wolf rioted in my mind, threatening to shred him apart for the cruel words. I let her free, growling my anger between moans of bliss.

Yes, yes. Right there.

His knot was mine, growing, moving, exploding into me and drawing me over the rapturous edge with him. I roared his name, raking my nails down his back once more while clinging on for dear life as violent spasm after violent spasm rocked me to my very soul.

Harsh.

Savage.

Amazing.

Euphoria.

Fuck.

He was bleeding, his coppery taste on my tongue.

I bled, too. Between my legs.

But I also wept in elation, my stomach convulsing over and over as orgasms rippled through us both.

I barely registered him taking me to the room he originally tasted me in, but the wrongness of the scent caused me to surface from my enchanted sea. My nose twitched, the sheets too new.

Not my nest.
Not Ander's room.
Not right.

He lay on the mattress, draping me over him as he continued to spill inside me.

No words exchanged.

None needed.

This was just another rejection, his way of reminding me of my new quarters.

My insides deflated, my heart aching. I might have owned him in the moment, but I didn't have any claim on him. Even if my marks were drawn up and down his back.

Vehemence struck me hard. He'd taken my beautiful

experience and dismantled it with his cruelty. Reminding me that while I might have chosen to fuck him, he chose not to claim me. He was still free to mate another.

Including that bitch who left her scent all over his shirt and torso.

My jaw clenched. *Not happening.*

His fingers ran through my hair, his touch a poor attempt at soothing. I started to squirm, no longer wishing to be connected, but a rumble from his chest gave me pause.

Not a growl. Something other. Like a purr?

I blinked, stilling as he repeated the sound, louder now.

He continued to pet my hair while that hypnotic rhythm hummed beneath me. I snuggled into him, wanting more of the comfort that purr evoked. It caressed me in a manner that left me boneless on top of him, lulling me into a state so very different from moments ago.

I sighed, content, my lips parting on a yawn.

Mmm, yes, this I liked very much. I nuzzled his chest, finding the right place for my head.

His touch drifted from my hair to my back, gently tracing my spine and back up again.

So tender and warm.

Protected.

Every part of me relaxed, the world finally feeling right.

At least for this second.

I accepted it with a smile, my eyes falling closed.

And when they opened again several minutes or hours later, it was to find myself alone in a bed that lacked Ander's warmth and his scent.

My new room.

Without a mate.

CHAPTER SIXTEEN

KAT

WE HAD DEVELOPED A PATTERN.

Ander left. I roamed his penthouse alone. He returned smelling of an unmated Omega. I initiated sex. He fucked me. Purred. And I awoke alone.

Every. Single. Day.

For weeks.

Every time, I vowed it wouldn't happen again. Every time, I broke that vow. But I couldn't bring myself to regret it, not when he gave me those few precious moments of control each day. I always started it, and he didn't punish me for slashing out at him and ripping his clothes off. He even went as far as to allow me to dictate the pace for as long as I desired, waiting until I begged before he took over.

It had become our dynamic, our way of coexisting.

However, today something was different.

The sweet scent lingered in the air as he arrived, but lacked the offensive note that usually set me off. It felt less threatening.

I sniffed him as I always did, his stance stiff while I ignited our routine.

Some days we ate first.

Most days, I raged and tore the offending fabric from his body before dropping to my knees to confirm he still wore my scent where it mattered most.

He continuously smelled like foreign Omega, but only on his torso. Never between his legs.

I cocked my head at him, my eyes narrowing. "What's different?"

His usual silence reigned.

He never answered me. Never commented on who the Omega was or why he continued to smell like her. Just showed up, fed me, fucked me, purred, and left again.

I hated our pattern almost as much as I relied on it.

But I didn't like this difference. It left me confused and uncertain about how to proceed. The instincts to wash him in my scent didn't come, just a casual curiosity over who—

My eyes widened. "Wait…" I sniffed him again. "She reminds me of…" I pressed my nose to his shirt, inhaling deeply. "That one Omega." *Riley.* I hadn't seen her since the day of my poor escape attempt. "The mated Omega." My lips parted. "Ohhh…" Someone had mated the female. *That* was why I no longer sensed a threat.

Because he hadn't been the one to claim her.

I dropped to my knees to rub my cheek against his thick thighs. Overwhelming relief settled over me. *He didn't mate her. He didn't choose her. He came home to me.*

Logical thought fled, my instincts taking over as I unzipped his jeans and took his hardening cock into my mouth.

I wanted to thank him.

To show my pleasure at him returning to me and not her.

Mine, I thought, sucking deep, pulling his essence into my mouth.

His pupils dilated as he watched me, one of those foreign

emotions flaring in the depths of his golden eyes. He didn't grab me or control my pace but allowed me my moment, gave me the opportunity to take him as far as I desired without his interference.

It emboldened me more. Pleased me. Gave me all the power. This was meant to be a submissive position, but I held his orgasm in the palm of my hands—literally, as I cupped his heavy sack.

He would come when I wanted him to come.

His pleasure would be mine because *I* would drive him over the edge.

He bit his lip, a low growl stirring in his chest, one that dampened the apex between my thighs. I wore another of his shirts and nothing else. It'd become my thing—I raided his closet, found something to wear, then added it to the nest.

Along with his pants.

Like these jeans.

I would take them back to my room when we finished. A trophy of sorts meant to scent my bedding.

Who am I? I often wondered, especially when I sat in the living area, staring out the window at the mountains beyond.

Escape seemed so fleeting, so trivial. But I yearned to taste the fresh air once more. To explore. To be one of the many wolves I saw wandering the street below. Yet I didn't ask. I didn't know how.

All my actions were orchestrated by the wolf beneath my skin, our bond growing stronger every day. She taught me how to exist in this new world, how to consider impulse over reason.

I'm becoming an animal.

I already am an animal, a part of me corrected.

Ander groaned, drawing me back to the shaft elongating in my mouth.

He was close, and still he allowed me to lead, his hands curling into fists at his sides. Somehow he knew this was more for me than for him. I thanked him with a twirl of my tongue, which set him off.

His palm slammed into the wall as he came, his restraint defined by the tightening of his muscles. He wanted to take charge—I could taste it in the way he pumped his hips against my mouth. But he didn't touch me. Instead, he threw his head back and howled, the sound turning my insides to mush.

"Fuck, Katriana," he breathed, his knuckles brushing my cheek before he threaded his fingers through my hair. He didn't take over, just held me as I drank every drop from him. I pushed down his jeans, and he kicked off his shoes to step out of the fabric, knowing what I wanted.

His knot throbbed at the base, signifying he desired more, but he always did. Neither of us was truly satisfied unless he came between my legs. But this wasn't so much about mutual pleasure as it was about me thanking him.

Part of me recognized how fucked up it was that I felt the need to thank him for not taking another mate. I still hated him. Hated that he made me sleep alone every night. Hated that he hadn't claimed me. Hated that he kept me here as his personal fuck doll.

Tears prickled my eyes at the thoughts, forcing me to swallow a final time and release him with a pop.

It's how we survive that defines us, I thought, standing. *I do what I need to do to live.*

But was I truly living?

That part remained to be seen.

Without looking at him, I walked to my room to add his jeans to the nest. It took me a few minutes to find the right place. The whole instinct to burrow into a pile of sheets and clothes was new, but I felt safe inside my little haven. I almost crawled inside now, but warmth from behind me had me glancing over my shoulder.

Ander stood naked in the doorway, his manhood heavy against his thigh. He held out a palm, and I knew without words what he needed.

This was how we communicated.

Not with our voices, but with our bodies.

I nibbled the inside of my cheek and considered the intricate design on my bed, searching for a piece I could give back to him. There were so many pairs of pants that he had to be running low, although his closet said otherwise.

Still, maybe these were his preferred pairs.

I shuffled around some of the fabric, grabbing one of the older pieces that smelled more like me now after nights of sleeping with it. His expression remained stoic as I brought him the jeans. He disappeared with them in his fist, leaving me alone once more.

Always alone.

My lower lip wobbled, but I refused to cry. I placed my palm over my abdomen instead, focusing on what little happiness I had in my world.

"Tell me about your tattoos," Ander said, startling me.

I hadn't felt his return, my gaze on the floor and not the doorway. Blinking up at him, I frowned. "My tattoos?"

He stepped into the room, still as naked as before, but without the pants I'd given him. "Yes. I want to know what they mean." He stopped before me and drew his knuckles down my shirt-clad arm. "Will you tell me about them?" Not a demand, but a question. Very unlike him.

Wariness mingled with intrigue.

We'd spent the last month—perhaps longer—letting our bodies talk for us. Hatred, blended with lust and need, defined our relationship.

But this... this was different.

He wanted to talk.

And I found myself wanting to answer him.

"They represent memories," I whispered. "My way of honoring the dead."

He cocked his head to the side and reached out to unbutton the dress shirt hanging on me like a dress. Usually, he ripped it off or drew it over my head, but he seemed to be in a gentle mood, like he wanted to cherish me in his own way.

The fabric parted to reveal my pale torso. My markings were mostly on my arm, with the exception of the name written across my collarbone and the flower above it. He traced the script with his finger. "And this one? What memory does it represent?"

"My mother." I swallowed. "It's her family name beneath the namesake she once drew for me."

"Namesake?"

I nodded, my throat going dry. "A flower blossoming into

116

claws. She used to say I was beautiful but deadly." Of course, I didn't feel all that deadly now. More subservient. Like a shell of myself. "At least the claws were appropriate," I added, thinking of my wolf.

His touch drifted upward to trace the purple talons. "On the contrary, I think it represents you adequately. Gorgeous, delicate, yet sharp." His finger slid along my jaw. "You just need to bloom, Katriana." He cupped my cheek, drawing me closer. "Tell me about the others. The colors."

I knew what he meant, the splashes of paint down my arm, leading to the bird on the back of my hand. "Loss," I replied, my voice hoarse. "Each one represents someone from my past that I've lost to the cruelty of this world."

"And the cardinal?"

"The father I never knew." I cleared my throat, emotion tightening my voice. "My mother used to say our relatives visit us in cardinal form, some old superstition her parents passed to her. I've never actually seen one other than in books and old photographs. So I had one painted into my skin as a reminder that while he may never visit, he's still part of me."

A child's dream, I supposed.

Ander pushed the fabric from my shoulders, leaving me as naked as him. His gaze roamed the colorful markings, leaving me warm all over. "Aside from the flower and name, you've only tattooed your arm and hand," he murmured. "Why nowhere else?"

I licked my lips and shrugged. "It seems wrong to allow anyone to share the space with my mother. Everything else is a memorial, a way to honor the memories while keeping them at an arm's length." It sounded ridiculous out loud, but it was how I processed loss. "To allow them closer would require me to feel."

He angled his head, his golden eyes capturing mine. "How does one in the mountains tattoo another?"

"Ink, needles, fire," I explained. "It's amazing what nature provides in terms of color."

His knuckles swept over my arm once more. "Sounds painful."

"It is," I admitted. "But it drowns out the sorrow of

death."

"There must have been a family in the caves with knowledge of tattooing," he added.

"Yes. The Dunkins." Jim Dunkin started tattooing me when I turned twelve. He'd claimed it would harden my emotions.

He was right.

Ander's palm settled on my hip while his other wrapped around the back of my neck. "Take me to your nest, Katriana. I want to hold you."

"Wh-why?"

"An Alpha doesn't require a reason." He walked me backward until my calves hit the bed frame. "Tell me where to lie so I don't disturb your work."

He usually chose his own place, regardless of what I had constructed, his focus on keeping us joined, not on my comfort.

Whatever had gotten into him today, I liked it. But I wasn't a fool to believe it would become our norm.

No. We had our pattern.

Except the other Omega had mated.

Did that mean he wanted—

"Katriana," he breathed, gently pressing his lips to mine. "Stop thinking and invite me into your nest."

I nodded and disentangled myself from him to find the right place on the bed, then slid over in silent invitation. He joined me, his heat and scent instantly welcome in my cocoon. I curled into his side, his arm circling my shoulders, and allowed him to just hold me.

No lust.

No fury.

No violence.

Just warmth.

"I like your markings," he admitted softly. "They give me insight into who you are."

"Who I used to be," I corrected. "I'm not that woman anymore." And I never would be again. He'd ensured that when he placed another life in my hands.

Our baby.

"Perhaps not, but we all evolve and change. Your former suffering and resulting strength are the foundation of who you are today, whether you feel it or not." He drew his palm up and down my arm. "This is a new stage in your existence, and while it may not be what you once hoped for, it's your fate."

"I know."

He shifted to pull me beneath him, his much larger body hovering over mine. "Do you accept it?"

"Is there an alternative?" I countered.

"No."

"Then I have no choice but to accept it."

He nuzzled my nose, the heat of his mouth taunting my senses.

Pine. Masculine. Spice. I sighed, content with how those scents made me feel. Wrapping myself up in Ander always left me satisfied, as long as I didn't think.

"Do you desire a choice?" he asked against my lips. "Is that what you need?"

"There is no choice," I whispered.

"That's not what I asked. Is it a choice you require to accept your fate?"

My brow furrowed as I sought out his golden irises. As always, he gave nothing away with his expression. "I don't know how to answer that."

"Don't think; just reply. Do you wish I would have given you a choice?"

"Of course I wanted a choice," I retorted, a fire lighting within me. "What person wouldn't?" But it was too late now, so why dwell on it?

He observed me for a long moment. "I've never been human, Katriana. Always Alpha. We make the decisions we feel are best for those under our care."

"Which, to you, meant turning me into a wolf, then forcing me to go into heat, and impregnating me," I summarized. "Not exactly what I would have considered for myself, but it doesn't matter now, does it?"

I couldn't help the note of irritation in my tone. Why bring this up now, weeks after everything he'd done? I was over a month along in my pregnancy, if my day count was right.

Likely longer, honestly, because I slept a lot.

Regardless, I couldn't change a damn thing.

And neither could he.

"I'm the Alpha of Andorra Sector, the highest-ranking official under this dome. To be mine means more than you seem to appreciate."

"Ah, but I'm not yours," I retorted, wanting to shove him off me and out of my nest.

How dare he take such a quiet and calm moment and turn it into this? I didn't want to think about these things, choosing to rely on my wolf more than my mind.

"What's the point of all of this?" I demanded. "Why are you making me feel?" It changed nothing. Did *nothing*. So why bother considering alternatives? Why discuss what happened? *Why? Why? Why?*

"You do not appreciate what I've offered you, have chosen to hide instead, and I am trying to understand why."

There was that word again. *Why*. I hated it. Loathed it. Despised *him*.

"Why," I repeated, the word bitter in my mouth. "You want to understand why I don't appreciate being taken from the woods, turned into a wolf, forced into heat, then impregnated against my will?" I gave a humorless laugh. "If you can't figure that out, Ander, I can't help you."

"My wolves saved you from a troubled life in the woods—where you slept in a cold cave, shivering all night, only to wake with a single hope of surviving the next day unscathed. You were then gifted immortality and a way to protect yourself far better than in your human state. And when you showed signs of your Omega genetics, I took you under my protection to save you from the experience of being taken by several Alphas lost to their rutting instincts."

He glowered down at me while I glared back up at him.

"Your version of events is missing the small detail of my consent—which I never gave."

"So you would rather I had left you to your cold, miserable fate than to provide you with the life I have thus far?" he countered.

I bristled. "All I wanted was a choice." Where, yeah, I

probably would have accepted his offer to become a wolf because who wouldn't in my position? "Some consideration for *my* wants would have gone a long way."

He considered me for a long, too-silent moment. "In my world, Omegas trust their Alphas to make decisions for them. And they respect them for it."

"In my world, humans make their own choices."

"In your world, humans die," he pointed out. "Often."

"I'd prefer death over not having a right to choose," I whispered.

"Then you're a foolish female." He rolled off me, leaving the nest. "Choose wisely, Omega. And remember, you were the one who desired this choice."

CHAPTER SEVENTEEN

KAT

A WEEK.

Seven. Fucking. Days.

I paced Ander's condo, agitated. He hadn't come home at all since the incident in my nest, his scent disappearing with every passing minute.

Oh, food arrived.

Always appearing overnight while I slept restlessly in the haven that no longer felt like a haven.

Everything was wrong.

I ran my fingers through my hair and went into his bedroom again. His perfectly made bed caused me to growl, my thoughts raging. How could he just leave me here? Like some glorified prisoner.

At least I had windows.

I went back to the living area to plop before them, staring

wistfully outside.

What I wouldn't give to inhale the fresh air, to roam in the trees, to feel the ground beneath my paws.

I hadn't shifted since that first time.

Maybe I should try again, but outside. I made to stand but faltered as Ander's warning hit me in the gut.

"Run from me again and I'll lock you in a fucking cage until you give birth."

"I'm already in a cage," I muttered back out loud. But my rump hit the ground once more, my head falling into my hands.

I sat there all day, watching the sun hit a high point and then dip low into the sky.

Continued to sit there long into the evening, gazing up at the stars shining brightly above the glass dome.

And eventually drifted off to sleep, only to wake with the dawning light all over again.

Countless hours passed.

Followed by days of nothing.

I ate and showered only because I needed to.

Then returned to my spot, my nest no longer appealing to me. Ander's scent was long gone, his presence a ghost of my past, and I hated how that made me miss him. I felt empty inside and more alone than ever. At least he visited with me before.

After finding a glass of water in the kitchen, I padded back to my spot, only to have all the hairs along the back of my neck rise.

My nose twitched at the approaching scent of sweetness.

Riley, I recognized, turning just as she entered the foyer. She froze when she found me sitting in another of Ander's shirts, my hair a messy bun on top of my head. "Oh" was her version of a greeting.

I replied by refocusing on the window and the outside world.

The mated Omega wasn't the one I wanted to see.

My heart dropped to my stomach because I didn't really want to see Ander either. Except I did. I wanted to scream at him. Fuck him. Mark him. Demand he tell me what the hell this was and why he left.

What the hell did abandonment have to do with making a choice?

"Kat?" Riley murmured, crouching beside me. "I'm here to do a ten-week checkup on you and the baby."

Ten-week? My lips parted. *I've been pregnant for ten weeks?*

That meant Ander had been gone for... for... well, I didn't know. My entire sense of time and space had been warped since my imprisonment here.

Because that was what this was.

Imprisonment.

Sure, I had windows and space to roam around, but there was literally nothing to do other than stare longingly outside, eat food, shower, and occasionally fuck Ander—when he showed up.

I pressed my palm to my still-flat stomach and frowned. While I could sense the life growing inside me, I didn't really *feel* the presence, too lost to my thoughts to notice. "Is the baby okay?" I asked, my voice a rasp of sound after days— weeks—of disuse.

Riley flinched, the back of her hand going to my forehead, then my cheeks. "Can we do this down in the lab? It would be easier with all my equipment."

"Are you worried about the baby?" I asked again, ignoring her request.

"No, I'm worried about you," she replied, her tone a low growl.

I blinked at her. "Am I doing something wrong?" I hadn't tried to escape. I wasn't being very active. I still ate and showered. Maybe there was more I should be doing for the baby growing inside me?

"You?" She let out a humorless laugh. "No. It's your mate that's the issue."

"I don't have a mate," I replied on autopilot. "I'm alone. Me and the baby." The words came out broken, my gaze dropping to my hands. "But we'll be okay."

"I'm going to kill Ander," she snapped, standing. "Come on. I need to check you out in the lab. Then I'm going to murder your damn stubborn Alpha." She held out her hand.

"Let's go."

"I'm not allowed to leave," I said, returning my focus to the windows.

"You're not supposed to run away," she corrected. "But a visit downstairs to my office is perfectly allowed. In fact, I'll teach you how to find me so you can wander around more often."

My brow creased. "Wander around?" Ander had been pretty clear about not leaving, right? Or had I misunderstood?

If he would fucking visit, I could ask for clarification, I thought bitterly.

Maybe I should leave. He'd already locked me in this pristine penthouse prison to wallow in my loneliness. What worse could he do?

Wandering, as Riley put it, might also bring him out of hiding. Or perhaps I'd find him in the labs.

What would I do if I saw him again? A vision of my fist meeting his face had my lips barely twitching at the sides. It'd be the least he deserved after—

"Kat," Riley said, her hand still wavering beside my head. "I really need to get you checked out. If you can't do it for you, do it for the baby."

My mouth curled down. She made it sound like I wanted to put my child in jeopardy, which irked me. "I would never do anything to harm my baby." It came out on a growl, a sound I preferred to my raspy tone before.

"I know," she whispered. "It's not you doing harm." She crouched again. "Come on. I just want to help. We'll figure this out. Then we can kick Ander's ass together."

"Where is he?" I asked, unable to help myself. "Where's Ander?"

"He and Jonas are overseeing the Omega transport from Shadowlands Sector."

"Omega transport?" I repeated. "Where's Shadowlands Sector?" I had never heard of it. Not really surprising considering how big the world was and how little of it I had seen.

"Have you heard of Romania?"

I nodded. "My mother had me study the geography of the

old world as a kid. It's former Eastern Europe."

"It's also where Shadowlands Sector is located. It's a clan of Ash Wolves."

"Ash Wolves?" I finally looked at her. "Are those different from X-Clan Wolves?"

She muttered something under her breath followed by, "I can't believe Ander hasn't explained all this to you."

"He doesn't speak much," I said, glancing down again. "He usually just..." I trailed off with a shrug.

Riley sighed. "Typical Alpha. Jonas is the same way—man of little words, but, boy, can he growl." She visibly shook herself. "But, yeah, not the point. Let's chat while I conduct your exam. I'll tell you everything I can about what's happening and why. Hopefully, it'll help."

That sounded promising.

It also gave me a chance to leave this condo.

My only other option was to sit here and stare out the window all day again. As entertaining as that sounded, I preferred answers. "Okay." I pushed myself off the ground, leaving my water beside the window.

Riley smiled, then took in my outfit. "Do you not have clothes?"

My lips pursed as I took in the button-down shirt hitting my thighs. "I, uh, wear Ander's shirts." They fit me like a dress, so it worked.

Her grin melted into fury once more. "I'm seriously going to kill him. Fucking Alpha." She stomped off toward the exit. "Follow me and I'll find you something to wear."

"I'd much rather you tell me what's going on with the Omegas," I said, trailing after her. "His shirts are fine."

She hmphed and pressed the button for the elevator just outside the door. I was actually surprised to see the vacant hallway, as I had assumed Ander stationed guards outside. Hadn't he claimed I would be guarded at all times to prevent any escape attempts? Well, apparently, he'd lied. Or maybe they were somewhere I couldn't see them.

With a dejected sigh, I joined Riley in the metal car, where she proceeded to explain which buttons to push to come find her in the future. I half listened, knowing I wouldn't leave the penthouse unless Ander gave me permission. Not because I wanted to obey him, but because I just didn't have the energy to fight him anymore.

"Has he at least explained that Omegas are rare? That Alphas outnumber us typically ten to one, in a balanced pack, and more like thirty to one in Andorra Sector?" Riley studied me for a reaction. Whatever she saw on my face had her releasing a string of curses that had my eyebrows hitting my hairline.

I'd already told her Ander rarely spoke. What did she expect? "We're rare?"

"Jesus fucking Christ on a stick," she said just as the elevator opened. A male on the other side cocked a brow. "Oh, don't look at me like that, Lionel. You've heard me say a lot worse."

The much bigger man smirked. "That I have, lass."

She waved him away with a tiny hand and gestured for me to follow her with her head. "Right, so we'll start at the beginning, then," she said, walking quickly while she spoke. "Omegas and Alphas typically mate because of the way our bodies sort of fit together. You see, Alphas can't knot a Beta." She glanced at me again, then frowned. "Something else I assume you didn't know. Yeah, I'll just assume you don't know anything."

"That'd be wise," I mumbled. I knew only what I'd observed of the wolves, which wasn't much.

"There are Alphas, Betas, and Omegas." She pushed through a door that led into an office. "Alphas are at the top of the hierarchy, Betas are in the middle, and Omegas, well, we're at the bottom. It's a matter of size and power, and most of us are rather petite." She shrugged. "Just how biology works."

This part I sort of understood—at least about the Alphas being the strongest and in charge. My mother once explained it to me, saying wolves valued order above all and an Alpha's words were law.

Ander certainly lived up to that expectation.

"While Omegas might be the weakest of our species, we're also the most revered," she continued, patting an exam bed for me to hop up on. "We're the only ones who can accept the knot."

Right, she'd mentioned that already.

"Which means we're the only ones who can bear them children," she added, looking pointedly at my stomach.

"Betas can't procreate?"

"Oh, they can with each other, and even with an Omega. But an Alpha needs to be able to knot and—"

"He can only do that with an Omega," I finished for her, having followed that part already.

"Yep. So they're desperate for our kind. Meanwhile, the Betas have a lot of options, with them outnumbering us and all. Lie down." She turned to start fumbling through her instruments while I did as she requested.

"So Alphas mate Omegas," I said, prompting her to say more. "But there are more Alphas than Omegas."

"Exactly." She turned with a metal instrument and set it on a tray. "And in Andorra Sector, there are significantly more Alphas. Which is why Ander has been busy making a trade with Shadowlands Sector to acquire more Omegas."

A sour taste hit my mouth. "Because Andorra Sector needs more Omegas." *And Ander needs a mate.*

She nodded solemnly. "We're in dire need of Omegas. There are only a handful of us here, and all of them are mated, except, well, you." She paused to stare at me. "You're the only available X-Clan Omega Wolf in our sector, Kat. It's why Ander has kept you locked up. As barbaric as it is, he's trying to protect you. Being pregnant protects you to an extent, but should anyone decide to question his rule, they would start by taking you—and that would likely lead to them destroying the child."

My jaw hit the floor. "*What?*"

"Alphas are territorial," she whispered, placing her palm on my shoulder to push me back down on the exam bed. "They don't take kindly to their Omega having another Alpha's child."

I frowned. "Are you telling me my baby is in danger?" I curled my hands over my abdomen. "That someone might try to... try to...?" I couldn't finish the question, my heart racing.

"No, no, no," she said, cupping my cheek to force me to look at her. "I'm just trying to explain what's happening here and why. You're not in danger. Ander would kill anyone who tried to touch you."

"But what about in seven months?" I asked, doing quick math. "When the baby comes… what does he plan to do with me?"

Her shoulders fell. "I can't answer that."

"Can't or won't?"

"Can't. Because I don't know," she admitted softly. "But he would be insane to let you go. The Alphas will be in a riot over mating you. Even with the new Omegas, you're still the one they'll all want—because you're X-Clan. The Ash Wolf Omegas will never compare, even if they are compatible."

"I don't… I don't understand." But I kind of did. Maybe. *I'm the only X-Clan Omega.* Which made me more valuable than the new ones coming from Shadowlands Sector. "Why wouldn't they find other X-Clan Omegas? Are there no others in existence?"

"Oh, they exist. The other sectors refuse to trade them. As I said, we're valuable." She gave me a small smile. "And here, you're the most valuable of all."

"Then why hasn't Ander claimed me?" I blurted out.

"Because he's a foolish idiot Alpha," she muttered, returning to her tray. "He's been consumed with this shipment from Shadowlands Sector, practically living in his office for weeks. Elias successfully mating Daciana was the final stage. Her being pregnant with his child proves we are indeed compatible."

Daciana, I thought, recalling the scent from Ander's shirts. "She was the unmated Omega."

Riley nodded. "Yes, she was unmated until a few weeks ago when she went into estrus. Elias claimed her."

Which was why the sickly-sweet stench had changed to a less threatening fragrance. "There are more Omegas coming?"

"Nine," Riley confirmed. "Ander exchanged technology—a lot of it—for ten total Omegas, including Daciana. They're arriving today."

Nine Omegas for Ander to choose from.

Nine competitors.

Nine females I would never compare to because I wasn't born a wolf.

"Hey, I saw that." Riley snapped her fingers in front of my eyes. "Don't you dare even think about it. Ander is yours. He's just putting the pack before his own needs. He does it often as our leader. But he'll come around. And when he does, I need you to do me a favor."

"Do you a favor?" I repeated, incredulous. "Like what?"

"Kick his ass," she said, speaking as if the conclusion was obvious. "Make him work for it. After everything he's done? He deserves a little hard to get."

"But he doesn't want me."

"Oh, he wants you." She sounded so sure of herself. "Why else would he keep you?"

"Because of the baby."

"That's part of it, sure. But he gave you his seed." She smiled. "Because he wants you."

"He only did that out of duty—I was in heat and he did his job."

She froze over her instruments, looking at me as if I'd slapped her. "Why the hell would you say something like that?"

I blinked at her. "Because that's what he told me." Just recalling that experience in his bed numbed me all over again.

Riley appeared positively mortified.

So I stared at my hands, his words repeating in my mind.

"You were an Omega in heat and I did my job. I provided the seed your body craved, and now you'll give me a child."

The coldness of his tone still sent a shiver down my spine, his statements forever branded into my soul. "He doesn't want me," I added softly, brokenly, my eyes falling closed. "Can we finish the exam? I want to make sure his child is healthy."

Riley said nothing for so long that I thought she'd left. But she eventually cleared her throat. "Yeah. Yeah, let's do an ultrasound. I'd like you to hear the heartbeat."

"Sure." I didn't open my eyes.

And when the thudding of the baby's heart filled the room

several minutes later, I remained utterly still.

This was my purpose.

To breed.

At least I'd done something right.

CHAPTER EIGHTEEN

ANDER

"WHAT DO YOU MEAN, THERE ARE ONLY EIGHT?" Dušan's deep tones came through the comm unit, his pale blue eyes fixated on mine through the screen. "We sent nine."

"Well, only eight arrived on the transport," I replied, doing my best to maintain a steady tone. "Your Second is here to confirm." I pinched the digital screen with my fingers and twirled it on my desk toward Mad. His white-blond hair practically glowed beneath the fluorescent lighting of my office.

The Ash Wolf Alpha didn't express any emotion as he confirmed my report. "Meira wasn't part of the transport."

"How is that possible?" Dušan demanded.

"You'll need to check with Mihai. He was the last one seen with the cargo before we took off."

"I thought I charged *you* with that task, Stefan?" Dušan

phrased it as a question, but as a fellow leader, I heard the lethal note of disappointment in the way he spoke Mad's given name.

How did one called Stefan take on the nickname of Mad? I wondered.

"I was working with Caspian in the cockpit, trying to help him with some of the more advanced controls. That was the primary reason you tasked me with this mission, correct? My previous flight experience?"

Elias arched a brow at me from across the room, my Second clearly catching the challenge in Mad's voice. He would never use that tone with me in front of another sector leader. Maybe in private, sure, but not in this manner.

"I also expected you to manage the shipment," Dušan replied after a beat. "Which clearly did not happen. Put Cain back on."

I didn't wait for Mad to touch my screen, reaching out to move it myself. The Shadowlands Sector Alpha ran his fingers through his long black hair, the tips brushing his shoulders. A scar ran up the side of his neck, starting at his collarbone. I wondered at the cause, as it didn't resemble the usual wolf claw mark, but something more jagged. Sharper.

"You can hold back one of the cargos while I locate our missing Omega," Dušan said, his jaw ticking with the words. "It won't be hard. I should have her to you within the week."

I considered him silently, debating whether or not to trust his word. The strain around his pale eyes told me accepting less of what he anticipated was going to create a problem on his side. It was already an issue on our part, as we'd sent the technology via transport two hours ago upon receiving word of the incoming shipment from Shadowlands Sector.

It'd been an execution of faith on behalf of both parties to exchange at the same time. "That's going to require you to send back part of our shipment," I noted out loud.

"A burden we will bear," the other Alpha muttered as he leaned against a nearby tree. Just seeing his surroundings compared to mine said so much about our different situations.

Andorra Sector boasted power, technology, and advanced medicine whereas his wolves lived in the wilderness. Yet he had an abundance of Omega wolves, while we had barely any.

Amazing how fate worked.

"It's a waste of resources for you to return the shipment," I added, running a hand over my face. "And you'll need time to charge the transport."

Because it required ample sunlight to activate the solar power necessary for flight.

"Returning the shipment will take days at a minimum," I continued, shaking my head. By the time he sent it all back, he'd probably have his wolf in custody already.

"I have a suggestion," Mad put in, his voice flat and emotionless, just like his expression.

Dušan remained stoic as he replied, "And that suggestion is?"

"Caspian and I will stay here as collateral while you find the girl. Once found, Cain can send his own pilot to retrieve her, and then we'll make our way back to you afterward."

Elias gave me a look from the corner, one I understood down to my core.

An outsider had just invited himself to stay in our sector for an undetermined length of time.

I didn't care for that solution, but it also afforded us an opportunity to do this a little differently. It would be a sign of good faith that Dušan planned to deliver on his promise and also grant us time to get to know the two Ash Wolves, which could lead to future trade deals.

Drawing my thumb over my bottom lip, I weighed all our options. Dušan appeared to be doing the same, his light eyes glowing like that of a wolf in the moonlight.

While Mad exuded a lethal air in person, Dušan maintained one even through the screen. I could practically see his wolf pacing behind his fathomless gaze, the animal just as dangerous as the human who contained him.

"I accept those terms, if you're agreeable," Dušan said after a long, drawn-out moment. He'd been waiting for me to speak, but I wanted his thoughts before I provided mine.

"You have a week," I told the Shadowlands Sector Alpha. "We'll renegotiate at that point, should the girl not be in your custody by that time."

"Oh, I'll catch her by then," he promised, his grin positively feral. "I'll be in touch soon."

The communication ended without a formal goodbye, Dušan clearly on a mission. I didn't take offense to it, because I'd be the same way in his position. The Omega had threatened our agreement. I expected he would punish her severely for it—before he sent her our way.

Mad pushed off the wall, his spine straight. "I need to inform Caspian of our change in plans."

Elias stepped in front of him. "Not so fast." He looked over the Alpha's shoulder to meet my gaze. "Where do you want them?"

I knew what he was asking. *Dungeon or a guest suite?* As I intended on making future deals with the Shadowlands Sector, I had no other option but to say, "Guest quarters."

If Elias disapproved, he didn't show it. Instead, he radioed Cedrick for our assistance. Our lead security officer appeared in seconds, confirming he'd been outside my office awaiting further instruction. "Caspian and Mad are going to be staying with us for a week. Can you arrange for their rooms and escort them as appropriate?" While phrased as a question, everyone knew it was an order.

My Second didn't make requests. He issued demands.

"Yes, sir," Cedrick replied. He gave me a polite nod before escorting a still-emotionless Mad from my office.

Elias caught my eye, and I hit the noise silencer on my desk to hide our conversation from anyone who might be listening too close to the door. "I don't trust him," I said, not wasting any time. "I want them both watched. They are not to go anywhere near the labs or my personal quarters."

"Understood," Elias replied. "Do you really think the ninth female escaped?"

"No." The shipment was far too important to Dušan for the Omega to have just vanished. "Someone sabotaged the deal."

"And you don't think it was Dušan."

"I'm positive it wasn't. He had too much riding on the trade to do something so stupid. He wants to enable trade between our sectors just as badly as we do, even if he doesn't

135

outwardly show it. There's too—"

My door slammed open with a force that had me jumping from my chair and Elias going immediately on the defensive.

Until we both saw who had entered.

Riley stormed over to my desk and placed her palms on the wood, her expression livid. "Did you really tell your mate that you only fucked her because it was your duty as an Alpha?"

I blinked at her, shocked by not only her intrusion but the lethality in her tone. "Riley—"

"Do you have any idea what you've done to that poor girl?" she continued, her voice a shrill tone bordering on a scream. "She's broken, Ander! She's fucking shattered!"

I opened my mouth to reply, when Riley sent all the items on my desk scattering to the floor in a rage.

"Have you lost your damn mind?" I demanded, shocked.

"No! *You* have lost *your* damn mind!" she shrieked. "Telling your intended— Oh, wait, no, I'm sorry. Your *breeder*."

Riley grimaced, her train of thought clearly morphing into another. One that painted her cheeks in shades of fiery red that matched her real hair color.

"She thinks she's a breeder, Ander! She kept repeating it over and over to herself during the exam, not listening to a word I said. Because you fucking broke her!"

"Is the baby okay?" I asked, the mention of Katriana's exam causing my heart to race. My staff hadn't reported anything out of the ordinary. She was eating all the prepared meals left for her in the fridge, suggesting she was fine. I just assumed she was busy nesting, as Omegas were wont to do while pregnant.

"Oh, your child is fine," Riley replied, her tone so cold it nearly frosted the air. "But your *breeder* is not. Telling her you fucked her as a duty. Are you fucking kidding me right now? Why the hell haven't you claimed her? You know how dangerous an Omega's pregnancy can be."

"You're overstepping your place, Riley," I growled, irritated at not only this woman's audacity but also—

My head jolted as her palm connected squarely with my

cheek, startling me even more.

"You're a bastard!" she shouted. "How dare you treat your intended mate this cruelly! Are you trying to kill her?! Because that's what you're doing, Ander. She's a shell of the woman she was two months ago because of you."

"What I do with my mate is not your concern," I snapped, taking a step toward her.

"Not my concern?" she repeated, her auburn eyebrows shooting upward. "She's my patient, Ander Cain. And what you're doing is dangerous for her health."

"You just said the baby is fine," I retorted, throwing my hands up in the air. "She's fine."

"Is that all you care about?" Riley asked, taking a step back, her expression aghast. "That your child is fine? What about the woman bearing that child, Ander? Or does she not matter? *Since you fucked her out of duty.*" She charged toward me, and I caught her wrists in my hands.

"I need you to calm down, Omega," I snapped.

She kicked at me on a vicious snarl just as Jonas stormed into the room.

One look at him had me releasing the female and dodging to the side. "She came at me, and I just restrained her so she didn't hurt herself," I told him, lifting my arms in a nonthreatening manner.

He didn't even look at me, his focus on the shrieking female losing her shit in my office. She collapsed into his chest on an anguished cry that startled me to my very soul. I never wanted to hear her, or any other female, make that sound in my presence ever again.

"I don't know what you did, Cain, but you better fucking fix it," Jonas said, picking up his mate and cradling her against his chest with a low rumble meant to soothe her. "It's okay, baby. I've got you."

"He's a monster," Riley whispered brokenly. "He's a fucking monster."

My lips parted at the proclamation, that particular designation not one that had ever been assigned to me before. "Riley..."

"No!" she screamed at me. "You've destroyed that poor

girl. How could you?" She shuddered against Jonas, her lower lip wobbling. "How could you?" she repeated, softer now, then buried her head against Jonas once more.

His blue eyes met mine, a lethal warning lining his stare. "Fix it."

With that, he carried the sobbing Omega from my office.

I gaped after them, at a loss for words.

In all my decades of knowing Riley, I'd never seen her lose her shit. She'd yelled at me a few times, mostly when I intruded too much into her research.

"You tasked me with this for a reason, Ander Cain. Now fuck off and let me do my job," she'd said a few times over the years. But nothing like this.

I'd certainly never made her cry before.

Nor did I ever want to again.

"Shit," I breathed, running my fingers through my hair and looking at Elias. "What the hell just happened?"

"You fucked up," my Second replied, his arms folded over his chest. "Clearly."

"I fucked up?" Now I gaped at him. "How the hell did I fuck up? I was talking to you when she stormed in here. And all I did was grab her wrists to try to calm her down."

"Yes, because grabbing a woman typically calms them down," Elias drawled. "But I'm not talking about Riley, Cain. I'm talking about Kat."

"What about her?"

"Did you really tell her you fucked her because it was your job or duty to do so?"

I sighed, gripping the back of my neck and glaring up at the ceiling. "I was trying to teach her a lesson, E. She put the entire sector at risk by trying to run away while on the brink of estrus." Had I not caught her when I did, she would have started a fucking riot. "I didn't know how else to bring her to heel."

"Do you want her to heel?" he countered. "Because I thought some of her allure was the fire in her."

"Yeah, it is, or, I guess, was," I admitted, thinking back to our first week together. After that, everything had changed. "Her wolf sort of took over after her estrus. It's been driving all her reactions since, which I enjoyed at first. Until I didn't."

It was seeing the way Daciana looked at Elias that changed everything for me. She gazed at him with adoration and respect, while Katriana barely looked at me. And when she did, it was as if her soul had left her gaze.

She'd started relying on her animal instincts alone to survive, not her emotions. "I asked her what she wants," I continued, swallowing thickly. "She told me she wants a choice. So I left her alone, giving her space to sort out her decisions on her own."

"That explains why you've been living in this fucking office," Elias said, gesturing to the couch I'd slept on for far too long. "You know I love you like a brother, right?"

"Yeah," I muttered. "I know."

"Good. Then I hope you'll understand me when I say, you're a fucking idiot, Cain. You claimed her as yours in every way but the one that counts. Then you fucking told her she was just a duty—a way to procreate—and left her *alone* for weeks in her miserable state. That's a pretty harsh punishment for trying to escape, man." His arms fell to his sides as he shook his head. "To quote Jonas, 'fix it.'"

With that profound statement, he stalked out of my office without even looking back.

Apparently, we were done discussing my love life and the issue with Shadowlands Sector.

Good.

Great.

Fantastic.

My fist hit my desk, cracking the glass top.

I growled at it, and the mess on my floor. "Fuck this," I snapped, leaving it for another day. "Fuck all this." I marched out of my office toward the elevator.

My goal wasn't to break Katriana. Not completely. I just wanted her to understand our hierarchy and how her stupid stunt put not only her life in danger but also those of my wolves.

Everyone under this dome looked to me for leadership. They relied on me for survival. They expected me to make decisions that best suited all their interests. It was a lot of fucking pressure, but I accepted it with my position at the top.

My intended mate didn't understand how her behavior reflected on me or how she continued to put herself at risk when she fought my dominance.

Maybe my words were cruel. But they were effective. She hadn't tried to defy me since that first week. She'd actually pleased me greatly following that period, her instinct to claim me gratifying me to no end.

Until I saw the difference in Daciana with Elias.

And realized Riley looked at Jonas much the same way.

Katriana was hollow when she gazed at me, her body doing what the wolf instructed her to do while her mind and heart remained completely off-limits. I tried to get her to open up, but she'd demanded a choice.

There was no choice.

She was mine.

Who else could she possibly choose in this sector? Who did she feel could offer her more? Elias was officially taken. Jonas, too. Which left only the Alphas on the council, and none of those males could compare to me.

But just knowing she wanted that choice infuriated me. Left me feeling inferior in ways I didn't anticipate. And so I had spent the last few weeks figuring out how to give her one, even though it killed me to orchestrate.

I punched the elevator button for my suite, counting the seconds as they ticked by. With each passing moment, I grew more agitated.

What exactly had Katriana said to Riley? Would she say the same to me or just let her wolf take over again?

Maybe I'd fuck her and then force her to speak while my knot tied us together. It'd help me expel some of this aggression and also bond us together. I also wore the scent of all the Omegas from today's transport, which I knew would drive my intended mate crazy. She probably wouldn't even let me speak before ripping my clothes off again like she did last month when I returned smelling like Daciana.

Yes. This plan would work.

We'd fuck, then talk.

I stalked out of the elevator as soon as it arrived on my

floor, then stormed through the door to my penthouse and slammed it behind me.

My nose jerked at the wrongness of the scents.

Devastation.

Despair.

Dread.

"Katriana?" I called, announcing my presence.

It only took me a few steps to find her. She sat beside the windows in one of my shirts, her shoulders hunched around her drawn-up knees.

No reaction.

I frowned at her back. "Katriana?" I tried again.

Nothing.

Not even a flinch.

My brow furrowed as I stalked toward her and around to her side to see her expression. Vacant, lifeless eyes gazed out at the window to the setting sun. I squatted beside her. "Katriana?" I said, softer this time.

She didn't even blink.

Shit. No wonder Riley was pissed at me.

"Katriana," I whispered, wrapping my palm around the back of her neck. She felt cold beneath my touch. I drew my thumb up and down the column of her neck, noting her slow pulse.

It was like she'd fallen into a catatonic state.

Fuck. How had this happened? I'd only meant to give her some time and space while I worked out how to offer her the choice she desired.

That had clearly backfired.

I gathered her into my arms, lifting her off the ground to hold her in a similar manner to how Jonas had held Riley.

A rumble started in my chest, one meant to soothe, but it did nothing for her lifeless form. She merely lay against me, her head on my shoulder, her arms limp across her abdomen.

"Let's go to your nest," I suggested, walking toward her room and freezing on the entryway. My lips parted at the destruction in the room. "You..." I swallowed, my voice failing me.

She destroyed it, I marveled, shocked.

141

Omegas needed a nest to feel safe. Pregnant Omegas even more so. To demolish her safe haven…

"Oh, Katriana…" My chest constricted even as my rumble intensified, needing to give her everything I could to help pull her out of this state. I didn't even understand how this happened. How had my feisty female fallen to this point?

"Smelled wrong," she muttered, her voice breaking my heart.

I pressed my lips to her temple, holding her tighter. "I'm so sorry," I whispered. "I had no idea." But I should have known, or at least anticipated it. Pregnant Omegas needed their Alpha to feel secure. And I'd abandoned her. No intention on my part could forgive my absence. Just as no amount of apologizing would improve this situation.

No, she needed something else from me.

Comfort and strength.

I walked away from her room, taking her to mine instead. "It's okay, sweetheart," I said softly, rumbling steadily in my chest. "We'll build a new nest. A proper one."

Then she would feel better.

I hoped.

CHAPTER NINETEEN

KAT

THE SCENTS SURROUNDING Ander had my wolf pacing and growling sharply inside.

Fertile Omegas.

Unmated Omegas.

Competition.

I wanted to rant and rave and demand he remove the perfumed fabric immediately. But I couldn't. Because that required too much effort.

Lying in his arms was easier.

Less work.

A way to exist without existing.

My lip wobbled as he placed me in the center of his bed, releasing me. This wasn't any better than the window. Just softer. With a view of the ceiling above instead of the mountains outside.

His rumbling purr strengthened, that sound a hypnotic caress to my senses that I refused to indulge. He would just take it away. Leave me all over again to wallow in my misery while his child grew inside me.

How had this become my existence?

So empty.

Unfulfilling.

Maybe this was how the Infected felt. Brainless with only one goal: survival.

Except I wasn't sure I longed to survive anymore. No, that wasn't true. I wanted to live. For the baby. But what then? Riley suggested the child might be in danger, that another Alpha might want to take the baby from Ander.

I shuddered at the thought, curling deeper into a ball, only to find myself being scooped into Ander's arms once more.

His bare chest rumbled beneath my nose, the fresh scent of pine tickling my senses.

Oh, the clothes are gone, my wolf practically purred, stretching out against him. *No more Omega stench. Only Alpha.*

My legs stretched out, tangling with his, our skin bare against one another.

He hadn't just removed his shirt, but all his clothes.

And his hot arousal was growing against my belly.

My throat worked to swallow. *Is this why he returned? For sex?* Because I wasn't sure I could give him that in my current state. My body would slick for him, of course. But I wouldn't enjoy it.

Does it matter? I thought bitterly. *Isn't this my job now? To fuck the Alpha when he wants it? To breed?*

A tear fell from my eye. Followed by another.

Only to be kissed away by Ander as he tilted my head back to meet his gaze. The purr-like rumble in his chest grew, surrounding us in a cloak of serenity that yearned to soothe away my pain.

His lips feathered across mine, not seeking, not dominating, just briefly touching. "I'm sorry," he whispered, apologizing for the second time.

Something told me he didn't utter apologies often.

"I won't leave you alone again," he promised.

Not that I believed him.

He only said that to make me feel better, to protect the child growing inside.

Actually, the only reason he did anything right now was for the baby.

My heart ached, the damn organ threatening to crack all over again. Fucking Maxim. He just had to target the food trucks. And stupid me for not questioning his directive.

I didn't miss my cave.

I didn't miss the humans I survived with either. The ones I once cared about had all died, teaching me to never grow attached again. Not loving another meant never mourning their inevitable loss.

But I did miss the simplicity of my former life.

The single drive to survive.

I didn't know how to handle my new existence. My place in Andorra Sector was to breed, nothing more, and I wasn't sure how to accept that.

Ander's lips brushed mine once more, drawing my focus back to him. "Katriana," he whispered, nuzzling my nose. "The pack relies on me to lead them. When you defied me by trying to run, it reflected poorly on my position in Andorra. My reaction to that perceived slight was harsh. However, part of me still believes it was necessary. I need you to understand our society and what it means to be mine."

But I'm not yours, I wanted to tell him.

Instead, I just blinked, my mouth refusing to move from the stoic line engraved into my features.

Was this to be my life? Breathing without thought. Existing without emotion. Stuck in a solitary state for eternity.

I shuddered at the very notion of such degradation. *This isn't me. This isn't who I am. This isn't who I want to be.*

But I didn't know who to be here. How to act. What to think. All I knew was how to sustain myself in the wild, and he'd taken everything from me.

No more cave.

No more Infected.

No more running.

I was safe here. Something I understood to be a gift, but

at what cost? My sanity? My body? My very soul?

Ander's chest vibrations amplified, his palm cupping my cheek as he gazed deeply into my eyes. "I need you to come back to me, kitten." He kissed me softly. "I miss your little claws."

My wolf snarled under my skin, not appreciating the feline reference. Or the insult to my *claws*.

"Mmm, there you are." He pressed me onto my back and slid over me to cage me beneath him. His rumble grew impossibly louder with each passing second, hitting a high note as his hips settled between my thighs.

So hot, I thought, spreading my legs wider to feel his cock up against my dampening flesh.

Just moments ago I didn't think responding to him like this would be possible.

My body proved otherwise.

Still, he made no move to seek gratification, instead going to his elbows on either side of my head, his golden eyes holding mine. "Your body appreciates me," he murmured. "But I want more from you than just your pussy." He pressed against me, causing me to arch beneath him on a moan. "Talk to me, Katriana."

And say what? I nearly growled.

Speaking created pain.

I'd suffered enough.

Yet my legs refused to move the way my mind directed them, the limbs lying limply beneath him rather than wrapping around his waist. Almost as if I'd severed the link between my brain and the rest of my body.

My arms were the same, refusing to move.

It *hurt* feeling so broken and trapped, unable to control anything, not even myself.

Another tear fell, desolation settling over me.

A sob threatened my throat, escaping on a cry that made me flinch.

And all the while, Ander purred, his heavy form holding mine, protecting me as I completely fell apart beneath him.

He didn't shush me. He didn't speak. He merely provided comfort in a way I never knew possible.

That damn rumble!

I hated it.

I loved it.

I craved it.

Vibrating, rhythmic, insanity, lulling me into a strange land of peace. It overwhelmed all my senses, forcing me to submit to the beauty of the sound reverberating in my skull.

I was dizzy from it.

Falling.

Loopy as fuck.

And so incredibly *hot*.

Ander had moved again, my head pressed to his chest, my thigh sliding between his. It happened in a blink, or maybe an hour, I couldn't say, my concept of time warping my understanding of reality.

This could all be a dream.

A beautiful one.

Ending in a nightmare.

I had no way of knowing, but that gorgeous, hypnotic echo settled everything within me. The aroma of pine filled my every breath. Alpha male heat bathed my skin. And a reverberation meant only for me swathed my heart.

Darkness came too quickly.

The sun long gone.

And when I awoke, I found myself alone, as always. Cold. Shivering in a bed that wasn't mine, a room I had no business lying within.

Had I ventured in here while I dreamed of Ander? Wishing he was here and inviting me into the solace of his arms?

What a cruel mind.

A wicked joke.

A crushing truth that stole my breath, only to be released on a scream so loud I was surprised the glass surrounding me didn't break.

I ripped at the shirt clothing me, throwing it on the ground, and moved to start on the blankets when a violent rumble shook me to my very core. Every part of me froze at the familiarity of that sound, my heart kicking up a notch.

"Ander?" I breathed, afraid to turn around.

But I didn't have to.

His palm traveled up my spine as he bent to kiss my shoulder. "I'm here. I was making us something to eat." He set a tray down beside me with his opposite hand.

My shoulders instantly relaxed. *He's here. Ander's here.* I leaned into him, seeking his familiar heat.

He sat next to me, his arm circling my shoulders as he brought me into his side and kissed the top of my head. "You need to eat something." Reaching around me, he plucked a piece of fruit from the tray and brought it to my lips. I tasted it first with my tongue, then allowed him to feed me the strawberry.

Another one touched my mouth as soon as I finished swallowing.

I opened, chewed, and swallowed again, only to have a third berry at my lips.

We continued the pattern for six more rounds before he switched to cheese. Then some sort of savory meat. And finally, he gave me a bottle of water that I chugged to rid my mouth of the salt.

The tray was still half-full, but I refused to part my mouth for him when he tried to taunt me into sampling a grape. So he popped it onto his tongue instead. I watched his Adam's apple bob as he ate. His purr never ceased, the sound wrapping me in a blanket of bliss as he continued to cradle me against him.

Safe, I thought. *Warm. Comfort.*

I closed my eyes, losing myself to his magnetic purr. A sigh escaped me, all my muscles relaxing, including my heart.

This wouldn't last.

I knew that.

But for the night, I accepted it and allowed myself to fall headfirst into a dream where I ran at Ander's side in wolf form, our paws creating a path together that was uniquely our own.

A fantasy.

Not our reality.

CHAPTER TWENTY

ANDER

SHE'S STILL NOT NESTING. I sent the message to Riley from my tablet. *It's been almost a week.*

Katriana sat across from me at the table, picking at her food. She still wasn't herself, but she seemed to be moving around on her own now.

The cautious energy swirling around her told me she was waiting for me to leave. Not because she wanted me to. On the contrary, she very much wanted me to remain, but she didn't trust me to stay. My promises did nothing, so I decided to demonstrate my vow rather than speak it.

My tablet dinged with Riley's response. *No shit.*

Thanks for the help, I shot back at her.

You dug your hole. Figure a way out of it. She accompanied the words with an avatar of her slapping me across the face.

Cute, I responded.

She sent me a photo of her middle finger in reply.

Anyone else, and I'd be reminding her of my position at the top. But I was in the little Omega's debt. Had she not yanked me out of my office, the results with Katriana could have been catastrophic. Fuck, they still weren't great.

As evidenced by the mostly silent female across from me.

I set my tablet down just as an incoming call sang across the panel. Dušan. Typically, I would excuse myself to take his call from the privacy of my office, but another idea crossed my mind.

Perhaps this would provide my Omega with the insight she required into my life.

I swiped across the tablet and transferred the conversation to my wrist device. A few clicks allowed me to bring up a translucent panel displaying the Ash Wolf Alpha's stoic expression.

"Dušan," I greeted.

"Ander," he returned, running his fingers through his dark locks. He did that a lot, I noticed. On anyone else, I'd call it a nervous tell. But Dušan didn't strike me as the nervous type. "I wanted to provide you with a brief update on the Omega. Is now a good time?"

He must have seen the kitchen behind me and my lack of a shirt. I opened my mouth to say yes, when Katriana stood. "I'll be in my room," she said softly.

"No, stay," I told her. "Please," I added to soften the demand I'd accidentally released.

Both of Dušan's eyebrows shot up.

Yeah, an Alpha issuing placative words wasn't common. "Don't start," I muttered at him, then focused on my Omega and held out my arm for her. She chewed her lower lip as she approached, her gaze darting between me and the screen.

Her damp auburn hair was draped in a thick wave over her right shoulder, the strands freshly combed from the shower we shared a half hour ago. One of my dress shirts hung on her petite frame, the ends skimming her knees.

Several outfits would be delivered for her tomorrow— something I should have done months ago. Which Riley, of course, had taken great pleasure in pointing out when I placed the order yesterday.

I'd accepted her criticism because it was deserved. But at some point, she'd need to give me a little credit for trying.

Dušan's eyes slid to my left as Katriana stopped at my side. "This is the Shadowlands Sector Alpha," I said softly, pulling her into my lap. "Dušan, this is my Katriana."

If he was surprised by the intimate introduction, he didn't show it. "Lovely to make your acquaintance, Katriana."

"You, too," she replied, clearing her throat. "Romania, right?"

Ah, Riley must have told her that. "What used to be Romania, yes," Dušan replied, his tone notably softer when addressing my female. His accent also seemed a bit more pronounced, confirming English wasn't his first language. It wasn't mine either. "I'm sorry to interrupt you and your Alpha, but I promised him an update today."

"Indeed you did," I agreed, drawing my fingers through Katriana's hair. I kissed her exposed pulse and locked gazes with the Alpha, my way of confirming that she was mine despite the message already being delivered loud and clear. I hadn't introduced them for his benefit, but for hers. She needed to see this part of my life to better understand me.

Still, I couldn't allow her to listen to all the business details. Not because I distrusted Katriana, but because I wanted to protect her from anything unpleasant. I knew this update was about his missing piece of the shipment, and if something violent had occurred, I wouldn't want her to hear the details.

"What's the sensitivity level of our topic?" I asked, knowing he would understand the code.

Dušan didn't miss a beat. "Green."

I nodded. Had he spoken any other color, I would have forwarded him to Elias. "Proceed," I said, wrapping my arms around my Omega.

"We found your tenth promised wolf, but there's a complication. I need to switch out the product for a better fit."

I frowned. "What kind of complication?" He'd claimed this was green, so the Ash Wolf couldn't be dead.

He considered me for a long moment before saying, "A

similar one to your current situation."

Now it was time for my eyebrows to lift because I immediately followed the reference. "Oh." He'd either mated the runaway Omega or intended to. "Well, right then. A replacement is acceptable." We hadn't laid claim to any specific Ash Wolf, just a set number. "How soon will you be transporting her?"

"Two days' time, unless you need her sooner?"

I shook my head. "Two days is perfect. We have a social gathering planned that evening to introduce your wolves to my pack. Perhaps Mad and Caspian can stay for the festivities before returning to you?" It was an olive branch on my part, a means of inviting our packs to mingle in a way they never had before. And the gleam in Dušan's pale blue irises confirmed he understood my intention.

If this deal went over favorably between our sectors, we could potentially trade more in the future.

"They would be honored to stay," he said after a beat. "Thank you, Ander."

"You as well, Dušan."

"And nice to meet you, Katriana," he added in that softer tone, his lips twitching at the corners into what almost appeared to be a smile. But it was gone before it fully formed, the feed disappearing a millisecond later as he disconnected the call.

I kept Katriana on my lap with one arm while using my opposite hand to drag icons across the screen with my index finger. Once I found the right one, I selected it and tapped out a message to Elias with an update.

Katriana watched with an intrigued expression. Finishing my task, I ran my thumb along the edge to bring up a live camera feed of the city. "This little device lets me see everything," I told her, flicking between the angles. I paused on a pair of wolves darting out of the building in the direction of the mountains. "Well, I guess Elias will see my message later." He and his Ash Wolf were apparently going out for a jog. "That's his new mate—Daciana. She's an Ash Wolf."

"Yes, Riley told me about your shipments." She tensed with the words, her attention leaving the screen. "I assume you'll want to meet them all soon."

"I already have," I replied. "And you'll be meeting them in two days at the social event I mentioned to Dušan." I originally organized it as a way to introduce all the Omegas and Alphas at once, including my Katriana, so that she may observe and see if she wanted another more than me.

But I now knew how foolish that would be.

Katriana was mine. She'd been mine from the moment I saw her on the feed, taking down my lab techs.

"Why?" she asked, looking back at me. "To torture me?"

I frowned at her. "You don't care for social events?"

"Not one where the father of my child is shopping for a new mate," she snapped, trying to push her way off my lap.

I clamped my arms around her, both stunned and thrilled by her anger. *There's my fire*, I thought, fighting a smile.

Then her words registered.

"Why the hell would you think I'm shopping for a new mate?" I demanded, my brow furrowing. "I don't need a new mate." *I have you.*

"What happens to me once the baby is born, Ander?" she countered, ignoring my question. "Do you rip him or her from my womb and give me to the next Alpha to breed? Is that my future here? My existence? The life you want me to live?"

"Katriana—"

"All because I tried to run?" she continued, laughing without humor, her shoulders falling. "But you were going to breed me anyway regardless, weren't you? So this was my fate all along. You just don't want me. So you'll mate one of the better Omegas who know how to please you, how to properly submit. And I'll… I'll just be a breeder." Her words had grown soft by the end, a whisper of a mumble that even my wolf senses struggled to hear.

"You're not a breeder," I corrected her. "You might not be my mate"—*yet*—"but you're more than a breeder, Katriana."

"How?" she whispered dejectedly, then shook her head. "Never mind. I just want to go lie down." She placed her palm over her still-flat belly. "I ate and now it's time to sleep. To keep your child healthy."

I frowned, not liking the way she phrased that. "*Our* child, Katriana."

She didn't say anything, pushing away from me.

I caught her around the waist and lifted her into the air, my chest rumbling against her on instinct. She was close to regressing, and I refused to allow it.

"We're moving forward, not backward," I told her, walking toward my room. "But if it's sleep you crave, it's sleep I'll give you."

With me right by her side.

I situated us both in my bed, hating that she hadn't felt comfortable enough to nest yet while also realizing a week wasn't long enough to cure her.

No, she required a hell of a lot more.

A gesture of some kind.

Not a claiming—she'd see that as a pitying mark at this point—but something grand.

Like a declaration of my acceptance.

Publicly.

I smiled against her hair, kissing the crown of her head as an idea formed. A solid plan of action, one that had to work. There were no other options.

Katriana Cardona was mine.

And I intended to keep her.

Forever.

CHAPTER TWENTY-ONE

KAT

THE FLOOR-LENGTH MIRROR revealed a stranger. I recognized my auburn tresses, but not the wavy style. My tattoos were all on display as well. And my eyes were the right color.

Yet the silky dress caressing my curves appeared meek. Delicate. *Feminine.*

I didn't wear dresses.

I preferred jeans and sweaters. Coats. Gloves. Hats. Weapons. Not strappy heels. How was I even supposed to walk in these?

"What's wrong?" Ander asked as he walked into the bathroom wearing a three-piece suit.

My eyes widened. I'd never seen one of these in person, only in magazines. Same went for the dress, but at least his attire I understood. Because wow, he looked amazing.

"Katriana?" he prompted.

I shook my head. "Yeah. Right. Nothing." *I just really want to rub all over your fine suit to see if it's as soft as it feels. That's all.*

But tonight wasn't about that.

Tonight was about meeting all the Alphas.

My future, apparently. Ander hadn't exactly said that, but I understood. Once I had his baby, one of the other males would take me to start the process all over again.

How many would I be forced to breed? Three? Five? Ten? Thirty? I shivered at the thought, recalling Riley's comment about the ratio of Alphas to Omegas in this sector.

Thirty truly wasn't all that off the mark.

And as I would live for... I frowned. "How long do wolves live for?" I wondered out loud, not actually sure of the answer. I knew shifters were immortal, at least in terms of disease and other human ailments. But surely there were ways for them to die.

He lifted a shoulder. "Until something kills us."

"And how does that happen?" I pressed.

His golden irises flared with unrestrained violence as he crowded me up against the bathroom sink, his massive palms falling to the counter on either side of my hips. "Why are you asking, Katriana?"

"C-curiosity," I breathed, trembling. "I-I don't know much about..." I swallowed. "N-never mind."

He grabbed my chin when I tried to drop my gaze and forced me to maintain his thunderous stare. My heart skipped several beats, my palms clammy.

Something about my question had set him off. I just didn't understand why.

"Anything that stops the heart for too long can kill a shifter," he finally said. "There are some Alphas in this sector who are close to five hundred years old—nearly five times my age—but look exactly as I do. I've met only a handful of wolves older than a millennium. They appeared a few years older, maybe forty by human standards, but their strength has only grown with age. My father being one of them."

"Your father?" I repeated in a whisper.

He dipped his chin. "Yes. He's a sector leader up in what

used to be Scandinavia."

"Which one?" Not that I would have heard of it, but I liked learning more about Ander. It humanized him a little.

"Norse Sector," he replied, releasing my chin to cup my cheek. "If you're thinking of trying to kill yourself, don't. It takes a lot to end a wolf's life, and you'll regret it in the end."

My jaw pretty much fell to the floor. "*What?*" Was that why he thought I wanted to know more about wolf life spans? My hand cracked across his face before I realized what I was doing, and I brought the offending palm to my mouth, covering it. "Ohhhh…" It came out muffled.

I hadn't meant to do that. Not at all. But the very idea that he thought I would be asking to kill myself had my blood igniting.

I hadn't survived this long just to hang a noose around my fucking neck!

Ander's lips actually curled, his golden gaze losing some of that furious intensity. "There's my kitten," he murmured, his touch moving from my cheek to my hand, exposing my mouth. He leaned in to kiss me softly, which was very much not the reaction I expected. "Mmm, you look amazing in this dress, by the way."

My brain sort of blinked off and on, short-circuiting from the last sixty seconds of nonsense. "You thought I wanted to kill myself?" And then changed the subject to talk about my dress? Yeah, no. "You think I'd do that after spending twenty-one years fighting for my life?"

He pulled back, his expression thoughtful. "Were you asking because you want to know how to kill me?"

"What? *No.*" I wanted to slap him all over again. "I asked because I know nothing about being a fucking wolf. I mean, I know there are sectors all over the world, that X-Clan Wolves are not the only kind of shifter out there, but no one has told me anything about being a wolf. Just expected me to accept it. To accept my place as a breeder." That last part was muttered, my fight fleeing on a sigh.

I would never kill myself.

But it was a bit of a relief to know that wolves could die, that I wouldn't be subjected to this for eternity.

Hopefully.

He gripped my nape, hard, tugging me back to look at him. "You are not a fucking breeder," he growled. "You are the mother of my future child. An Omega. And you're *mine*, Katriana." His mouth sealed over mine before I could protest that last statement, his tongue plundering and dominating and stealing the breath from my lungs.

All his kisses this week had been gentle.

But not this one.

He *demanded* reciprocation, his grasp tightening, his lips punishing.

It roused my wolf from her slumber within, exciting a throb between my legs that had been missing for weeks. I wrapped my arms around his neck, arching into him, taking what he gave and returning it in kind.

This I understood.

This I could handle.

And I rather liked that my heels made me that much taller.

The hand around my neck softened as his opposite palm fell to my ass, squeezing me against him. *Yes, yes. More of that, please.*

I felt alive.

Human.

Ready for anything.

"No," he said, ripping his mouth from mine. "I'll destroy you in this state." He released me so suddenly that I wobbled. "We have to go to the party, where I'll show you firsthand how our society works. Maybe that will help you understand."

My heart plummeted. *Right. The waiting Alphas and Omegas.*

He didn't give me a chance to reply, his hand finding mine and tugging me out of the bathroom at his side, his steps clipped as though angry.

Angry and aroused, my nose confirmed on a deep inhale. *Very, very aroused.*

That couldn't be good for a party with a bunch of Omegas.

Or maybe that was his intention.

My wolf threatened to growl, the need to mark him growing increasingly strong with every step toward the door. I didn't want to share him. The very notion of it left me wanting to break things.

So much better than caving in on myself in self-pity.

More invigorating.

Vivacious.

I inhaled once more, closing my eyes as his aroma seeped through my pores. My heart begged me to memorize his scent, to allow it to fuel me in preparation for whatever the night had in store.

Because I had no doubt tonight would well and truly shatter me once more.

Faced with my fate, I wouldn't have the opportunity to hide. It would become real. Watching him with other females, meeting the males vying for a space in my uterus, realizing just how powerless I was to everything in this new world. Everything would come to a head, and I couldn't handle much more.

My fragile heart slammed against my ribs, my feet tripping as Ander practically yanked me out the door. I opened my eyes only to study my steps, not wanting to fall because there was a chance I wouldn't be able to pick myself back up.

My vision began to blur.

Not ready. Not ready. Not ready.

The words repeated in my head as the elevator opened, then grew to a fever pitch in my ears as the doors closed, locking us in the metal contraption.

Ander hit a button.

The car began to move.

My knees threatened to buckle.

And then everything stopped with a slam of his fist against the controls.

I whimpered as he crowded me up against the wall, my hands fisting at my sides. "Please..." I didn't know what I was begging him to do or not to do. The word just sort of slipped free before my mind could catch up.

He cradled my face between his palms, his touch surprisingly gentle.

"Do you have any idea how hard this will be for me?" he asked softly. "And I only have myself to blame for it. When I failed to claim you, I never foresaw it as a punishment for us both. But it is, Katriana. The very idea of those Alphas seeing you tonight and even thinking for one second that you're available is enough to drive me mad. Enough to make me want to grab you and take you right back into my quarters, fuck you until you scream, and bite you so hard that you'll feel my imprint for months, not days."

My breath whooshed out of me, the ferocity of his statement rendering me speechless. Of all the things for him to say, I never anticipated that. He sounded remorseful and angry—not at me but at himself. And that thrilled a dark part of me, to realize I wasn't alone in my suffering. While the other part questioned the veracity of his words.

He had the power to harshly destroy me with a few well-woven sentences. That much I learned early on. But did he also possess the power to put me back together again?

"Oh, Katriana," he whispered, pressing his forehead to mine. "I can't let you walk in there without at least a part of me in you. They'll be able to smell our separation, which will only excite them more. You wanted a choice, and I planned to give you that choice. But faced with the reality of our situation, I can't. You're *mine*. And I will not share you."

His mouth claimed mine once more, his fingers sliding back into my hair while his opposite hand went to my hip to pull me against him. I clutched his jacket to keep from falling, my heart racing faster than before.

All his anger melted into arousal.

Pine.

Spice.

Man.

I moaned, my core throbbing to life. My dress hadn't allowed for undergarments, the silky fabric too close to my curves. Not that I'd been given any to wear anyway. It was a good thing the dress was black, or my slick might have ruined it.

"Ander," I whispered, my body taking over.

"Tell me to stop, kitten," he replied. "Tell me you're not ready."

Oh, but I was ready. "No," I said, needing this.

As fucked up as it was, I'd missed him—missed *this*. The

last few weeks, or however long it'd been, had numbed me from the world. I finally felt like myself again, even if for a fleeting moment. I wanted to fight him, to mark him, to take out all my frustrations on him, and then make him wear the result in front of everyone tonight.

My wolf clearly had taken over my mind. Yet rather than push her down, I embraced her, allowed her to drive my actions.

His belt practically fell apart in my hands, my nails leaving their mark along the leather before moving on to his button and the zipper. He bunched my dress up around my waist and hoisted me into the air as his growl called for a fresh surge of wetness to coat my inner thighs.

And then he was inside me, his thrust rattling the car as he roared in approval and slammed me against the wall.

There would be bruises, and I welcomed them. My backless gown left my skin exposed to the smooth metal surroundings, each push of his hips driving me higher and closer to a breaking point that would end in sobs.

My legs were around his waist, squeezing, begging him to fuck me harder.

Only, he slowed, his mouth catching mine as his tongue dove deep to rival the assault of his body below.

No, no, no. It wasn't right. I wanted harsh and violent. Not tender. Not soft. Not *slow*. I whined and he hushed me, kissing me again, forcing me to *feel* more than the joining of our bodies. He bathed me in intimacy and intent, worshiping me in the way only a male could. And I hated him for it.

Because it opened my heart.

Shattered a wall I didn't realize I'd erected.

And forced a tear from my eye.

"This," he whispered, gliding his cock along my inner walls. "This is mine." He plunged forward, hitting a spot that had me seeing stars for a moment before his teeth nipped my lower lip to draw me back. "And this," he continued, drawing out again. "This is also yours." He drove into me hard, causing my back to arch off the wall.

"No," I breathed.

"Yes," he affirmed. "There is no choice, Katriana. Our

souls already know each other. It's already done."

I shook my head back and forth, more tears falling. "No." It wasn't done. I could *feel* that it wasn't done. He hadn't bitten me. He hadn't claimed me properly. These were just words— words he could easily take away tomorrow. And probably would, just like he'd done before.

"You're not a fucking breeder," he growled, clearly aware of where my mind was heading. He must have read it from my body and the way I stiffened around him. "You're *my* Katriana. My Omega. Mine!" He punctuated the proclamation with a savage thrust that had me keening in his arms, my body convulsing madly around his thick girth.

Fuck, I was already coming, and he hadn't even knotted me yet.

His feral smile said that had been his intent, his golden eyes smoldering with male pride. "Your slick is coating my dick," he murmured. "Claiming me as yours for all the Omegas in that room to smell." He kissed me fiercely, his tongue owning every sound of pleasure escaping from my throat. "They'll all know I'm yours, kitten. And the Alphas will know you're mine."

He pulled out so quickly that I screamed, only to find myself on my knees with his cock in my mouth. Tasting myself on his bare skin had my thighs clenching all over again, bliss curling through my insides.

Fuck, I was addicted to this man, this *wolf*, this Alpha.

"I want to come in your pussy," he said, his fingers threading through my hair. "But then you would have to walk around with my cum dripping down your thighs all night. So consider this your choice, sweetheart. Do you want to swallow and carry my seed inside you or wander the party with damp legs?"

I was already going to be damp, thanks to the fucking against the wall.

But given how much semen I knew this man could spill, it would be a lot worse if I allowed him to come between my legs.

I sucked hard to demonstrate my answer and smiled when he groaned in response. "Fuck, you slay me," he marveled, his grip tightening, then loosening, and then tightening again. "I have a lot for you to take, Katriana. Be a good girl and swallow it all for me, baby."

The endearment caressed my senses, causing my heart to flutter with a glimmer of hope. I swallowed the sensation and focused on his mounting pleasure, reaching through the fabric of his pants to cup his balls. The front of his trousers was damp from my slick, my scent saturating him in the place that mattered most.

He was right.

Everyone would smell me on him.

That thought had me sucking him harder, needing him to mark me with his essence so everyone knew what we'd done here tonight. So that everyone knew I belonged to him.

In this, he could take all my choices from me.

I didn't want another Alpha.

I wanted *him*.

Because my wolf had already chosen for me—she recognized her mate. His rejection had spun me into a dejected web I didn't understand, but it made sense now.

He'd turned down my inner animal, leaving me wounded and confused and alone because I'd already chosen him. I only ran due to my fear of the unknown, my entire life until now fully consumed with the art of surviving. When faced with new circumstances, I hadn't known any other way to react but to escape and return home.

Only, this was my home now.

And so I needed to adapt.

To learn.

To embrace my wolf.

To claim my mate.

He growled above me, his shaft elongating in my mouth as he emptied his seed deep into my throat. I swallowed greedily, missing the taste of him, needing every drop he had to give.

And he was right—he had a lot saved for me.

It served as proof that he hadn't been with another, something I already knew based on his scent.

His grip loosened, his palm cupping my cheek in adoration

163

as I swallowed around him, taking every bit of his essence into me, just as he demanded.

He gave me a lazy smile, the kind that said he was both pleased and exhausted. I licked the final droplets from his head and sat back on my knees, waiting for him to say something.

Ander bent to lift me from the ground, my legs going around his waist once more as he slid his hardness through my folds, re-coating his skin in my arousal. "You sucked me clean," he explained softly. "And that's not acceptable. I want them all to know who my cock belongs to, Katriana. Who *I* belong to." He kissed me before I could reply, his tongue a brand against mine.

I relaxed in his arms.

Content with our mingled aromas.

The looming party didn't seem nearly as daunting now.

"I won't leave your side all night," he promised after he finished ravaging my mouth. "And if you want to leave at any time, just tell me you're tired, and we'll come straight back to our room, okay?"

Our room, I thought. "Is it our room?"

He pressed his forehead to mine. "Yes, Katriana. Everything I own is yours, making it ours."

I studied him, marveling at the handsome stranger holding me in his arms. What happened to the brute who kicked me out of his bed? The one who coldly informed me I wasn't his mate? Was this all for the baby? An act to pacify me until I gave birth?

Because he still hadn't truly claimed me.

Not in the way that counted.

But I couldn't find a single hint of deception in his gaze. I knew how to read people, had been doing it all my life. However, this man was an enigma. A dominant male wrapped up in a very soft, elegant suit.

I nodded, uncertain of what I was agreeing to, but agreeing nonetheless.

His lips curled as he disentangled my legs from his waist. "Careful when you zip up my pants, kitten. I'm still very hard for you, and will be until I can knot you again."

I shivered at the thought, my core spasming in response and dampening my intimate folds.

"Mmm, I do love that scent," he mused, fussing with the top of my dress while I cautiously drew up his trousers. As soon as I finished, he went to his knees and drew his tongue up my damp seam, a low growl rattling his chest.

Another wave of slick gushed out of me in reply to his Alpha call, my body trembling and ready. His teeth grazed my clit, sending me careening over the edge into unexpected oblivion as my legs gave out beneath me. His palm landed on my lower abdomen, holding me against the wall while I convulsed against his tongue.

This man! I thought. *Holy fuck, he's going to kill me.*

I barely recognized the words coming from my mouth, most of them gibberish wrapped around his name. My limbs were jelly by the time my orgasm finished, my skin hot and my brow covered in sweat.

How he did that, I didn't know.

But I wasn't complaining.

Never had I felt so languid and pleased. Well, maybe when we'd nested for a week. Yet something about this was freeing. Intensely intimate. Underlined in promises neither of us spoke out loud.

"*Now* we're ready for the meet and greet," he said, pulling my skirt down so the fabric danced along the floor again. Ander stood, his lips glistening with my arousal.

I went to my toes to kiss him, but he stopped me with a wicked grin. "Oh, no, Katriana. I want them to see."

He reached around me, pressing a button that restarted our descent.

CHAPTER TWENTY-TWO

ANDER

ALL EYES WERE ON KATRIANA. I couldn't blame them; she looked gorgeous in her silky black gown with her previously styled hair boasting a just-fucked vibe. I did my best to calm her auburn curls, but they had a mind of their own. Just like the Omega melting into my side.

I kissed the top of her head, my palm resting against her exposed lower back while we conversed with two of my oldest friends—Burje and Alyona.

At my request, most of the mated Alphas had attended without their Omegas. However, I'd specifically asked Burje to bring Alyona, as I suspected she and my intended would get along. Yet, while they seemed to be hitting it off, Katriana's eyes continued to drift to the males who weren't bothering to hide their intrigue.

She appeared to be surprised by the attention, but I wasn't.

She was an anomaly in so many ways; she just didn't realize it. A fact I felt responsible for and intended to rectify.

Her earlier comments about not understanding wolves, having been forced into this life without a proper introduction, struck me in the heart.

I'd failed her.

As my intended mate, I should have been the one to properly explain shifter life to her. I merely took for granted that she already knew, what with her father being an X-Clan Wolf, but then I discovered that she never actually met her father. I also wasn't used to having someone so green under my wing. Most shifters were born into this world, not genetically created in the lab.

Actually, the latter was quite rare. The technology of Andorra Sector far surpassed that of our brethren, denoting us as the only sector in X-Clan culture where werewolves could be created outside of procreation. However, most humans died during the change. Yet another reason everyone wanted to meet my Katriana—she was a rare survivor. Not just of the change, but of the Infected world as well.

"I, uh..." Katriana cleared her throat, her body curling into mine even more, seeking my strength. "I lived in the caves."

Alyona had just asked her about life outside the dome. Her hazel eyes went wide at Katriana's response. "But how? You were just a human and it's bitterly cold outside."

"Not as cold as back home," I interjected, grinning. I grew up with Alyona in my father's territory. Despite her Omega genetics, I'd never fancied her. Besides, her eyes were set on Burje from a very young age. The seven-foot-tall brute stood quietly beside her, the bottom of his beard brushing the top of her light blonde head.

"Back home?" Katriana repeated, glancing up at me.

"Scandinavia," I murmured. "Southern Norway, to be precise. Where Norse Sector is now."

She frowned at me. "If you grew up there, why are you in Andorra?"

"Because he was too powerful an Alpha to remain on as his father's Second," Elias said, joining our circle with

Daciana tucked into his side. "So he founded a new clan in Andorra just before the zombie apocalypse." My best friend loved that phrase.

I shook my head at him. "Before the Infection period," I corrected.

"Yeah, that," he agreed, taking a swig from his beer before focusing on Katriana. "Has he told you his stories about living in igloos yet?"

I rolled my eyes. "Fuck off, E." We both knew I didn't live in any fucking igloos. "Not even Winter Sector lives like that, and they're in the Arctic Circle."

He smirked. "Yeah, but you riding in a sleigh over the ice is a fun image."

"Remind me again why I tolerate you?"

"Because I'm awesome." Elias waggled his brows. "And I've kept this sector afloat for you while you've been off playing house with your pretty Omega. Who, by the way, I found in the forest."

"Yeah, yeah." I met his eyes over Katriana's head, thanking him without words. He gave a wink in reply, knowing I was grateful even if I didn't say it.

"You found her in the forest?" Daciana asked quietly, her demeanor far more relaxed than the first time I'd met her. Being with Elias had emboldened her, even made her glow a little. She gazed up at him with such reverence that my heart actually hurt.

Katriana didn't look at me like that.

But I wanted her to.

"Her human clan tried to steal one of our food shipments," Elias explained, focusing on my intended mate. "It didn't work out well for them, but Kat showed a knack for survival that the others in her group did not. So we rewarded her appropriately."

"By turning me into a wolf," Katriana replied, her shoulders stiffening. "Thanks for the *reward*."

His lips quirked up. "You're very welcome, Omega." His tone held a subtle warning that her sarcastic tone had not gone unnoticed by my Second. While he would likely entertain her disobedience in private, he couldn't afford to in this room.

Not when we were surrounded by Alphas where his position as lead commander could be called into question.

I cleared my throat and caught her chin to guide her blue gaze up to mine. "Do you want anything to drink, sweetheart?"

It was an invitation to leave the group, to give us a moment to speak privately. And I told her with my eyes to accept.

She nodded, swallowing.

I awarded her unspoken obedience with a tender kiss, then excused our presence with a nod and a smile before leading her to the far corner of the room near the drink stand.

"I'm sorry," she began, but I silenced her with my lips, threading my fingers through her hair and gently parting her lips with my tongue.

I wasn't angry and I wanted her to know that.

I also wanted everyone in the room to see us, to know how much I struggled to keep my hands off her, and to not question why we needed this moment alone.

She gripped the lapels of my jacket, pressing into me and aligning her soft curves to all the right places. I deepened our kiss, allowing her to taste the pleasure that still coated my tongue. She groaned in response, the sound one I cherished deep inside. While she—the human part—might not realize what was happening to her, I knew her wolf understood.

This was a public claiming.

A way of showing everyone in the room that I'd chosen her.

None of the available Omegas would approach me, not that any of them had tried. They knew from the second I walked in that I was off-limits, even if I didn't smell mated yet.

Unfortunately, this wouldn't be enough to deter all the Alphas. Particularly those who were already challenging my position.

Like Enzo.

I felt his stare from across the room, burning with the hatred he so poorly concealed. Artur wasn't much better, but he could at least maintain a stoic expression when the situation called for it.

Wrapping my palm around the back of Katriana's neck, I eased our lips apart and pressed my forehead to hers. "You're doing very well, sweetheart," I told her quietly, my words for her ears alone.

The chatter and soft music of the ballroom would drown out our voices, allowing us to speak privately. Even the wolves trying to hear us wouldn't be able to, not sequestered here in the corner away from the crowds.

"I wasn't thinking when I said that," she whispered. "It just came out."

"Don't let Elias's reprimand bother you." I nuzzled her nose. "He has a reputation to protect, as do I. Which is why the others probably assume I'm having a stern word with you." I cupped her face, holding her gaze and noting the confusion in her blue depths.

Right. Because she didn't understand our society or our rules.

I brushed my thumb over her mouth, my eyes following the movement.

"Shifters are higher on the food chain," I explained in a whisper. "We're powerful and superior to humans. And I'm not saying that to be cruel; it's merely a fact of life. So most see your change as a gift—one they feel you should be grateful for, as it elevated your status."

She swallowed, nibbling her lower lip. "And you? Do you think I should be grateful?"

"I do," I replied, refusing to hold back. "Without our gift, you'd be living in that cave or dead. Surely you can see the benefits of joining our world."

I gestured around the candlelit ballroom with my chin, touching on several expensive gold notes and the fresh buffet of gourmet food waiting to be devoured in the center of the floor. Some were already eating, having found seats at the round tables dotting the event space. Others were holding plates and nibbling on hors d'oeuvres. Everyone wore formal attire and most held drinks.

"It's a life of decadence," I continued softly. "A life most humans can only dream about, because even the mortal sectors live in poverty, much like your cave."

"There are human sectors?" she breathed, her eyes widening.

"Yes. Not in Europe, but in other areas of the world. I don't know much about that, as we don't trade with them, only other wolves. But just as there are other supernatural sectors, there are mortal ones, too. Everyone did what they had to do to survive the Infection. We chose to hide behind our science, hence the dome over our heads."

"But wolves are already immune."

"X-Clan Wolves are, yes, but not all wolves." I glanced at the group of timid Omegas from Shadowlands Sector. "Ash Wolves are not. So there's always the potential that one day the virus will mutate and begin to impact us. That's why we spend so much time and energy researching protective measures. Why we are constantly improving our technology in a world where it's truly not appreciated the way it once was."

"Before the Infection," she said, understanding bright in her eyes. "I've seen photos of things in magazines, similar to your monitors and watches, but not nearly as..."

"High-tech," I offered, knowing her familiarity with our resources would be limited. "Yes. We've enhanced our offerings over the years, found ways to develop our own electricity by using naturally reoccurring resources, and live much like we did a hundred years ago, only in a cleaner, safer environment."

"While everyone else suffers."

I lifted a shoulder. "As I said, we don't view humans as our equals. We never have. But we do allow them to exist on our lands, in our caves, when we could easily chase them off. And the resources you do access in the mountains, the fruits that grow in the spring that you harvest for the year, exist because we've ensured the land is fertile. We'll never invite them to live beneath our dome, but we have made their lives easier where we can."

I combed my fingers through her hair, tucking it behind her ear while she pinched her lips to the side. Her thoughts were clear on her face.

"You think I could do more, but what you're not

considering are all the wolves under my care. There are hundreds of us who live in this dome, all requiring resources of their own, and for much longer time periods than the average human. As I told you, we live a very long time." I released her hair and pressed my palm to her belly. "And we have our children to think about as well."

She dropped her gaze to my hand, her expression warming. "Our child."

"Yes. *Our* child." I pressed my forehead to hers, closing my eyes and breathing her in on a contented inhale. "You're going to be a beautiful mom, Katriana."

"Ander—"

A squeal interrupted our moment, Riley pouncing on us without any regard for our conversation. Jonas cast an apologetic glance my way while Riley engulfed Katriana in a hug.

"I've been so worried," she gushed, holding my female tightly in her arms. Her dyed-blue hair glinted beneath the light, matching the dress she wore. "You look amazing," she continued. "Smell good, too." That last part was said with a slight glare my way.

Yep. Still in the proverbial doghouse with the good doctor.

"Let's walk around the room and say hi to anyone you haven't met yet." Riley looped her arm through Katriana's, but Jonas stepped in her way with an arched brow.

No words.

But my lieutenant rarely needed them.

"What?" his Omega demanded. "You're both here. We'll be fine. Besides, someone has kept my new friend locked up for far too long and I want to show her off." Riley's gaze held a clear challenge as she looked pointedly at me.

My jaw ticked, part of me wanting to throttle the Omega for her clear disrespect. But the way Jonas watched her told me he'd be having a stern word with her later on my behalf, so I dropped it and instead focused on Katriana.

She appeared a bit dazed and uncertain, her gaze looking to me for answers. "Do you want to wander the room with Riley?" I asked her softly, brushing my knuckles over her cheek. "I won't be far."

Her tongue dampened her lower lip as she nodded slowly. "Yeah. I don't mind."

Riley grinned broadly at my companion and tugged her away.

"She still needs a drink, Riley," I said, my tone brooking no argument.

The feisty female cast me a warning glower over her shoulder but steered my intended toward the bar.

I blew out a breath and shook my head. "Your mate is a piece of work." And had she not helped Katriana over the last few months, I would have demanded she be put in her place. Publicly. As it was, I owed the bratty little Omega, so I was willing to let her behavior slide. For now.

"Don't worry. I'll reprimand her properly later." Jonas stared after his female, watching her hips sway as she walked.

"Something tells me she'll enjoy that reprimand," I murmured, noting the saucy little look she sent her mate.

"Oh, she will," he agreed, glancing at me with light blue irises the color of ice. Appropriate considering his Icelandic origins. "Things between you and Kat seem better."

"A bit," I agreed. *But we're not nearly where I want us to be,* I added to myself as she glanced at me with a glass of water in her hand, her gaze searching for approval. I gave her a reassuring smile. She didn't return it, instead turning back to Riley.

Yep. Definitely not where I wanted us to be.

"You and Riley had a rough start," I said, glancing at Jonas. "How did you fix it?"

He chuckled. "'Rough start' is putting it mildly. We literally crashed a plane."

"But you fixed it," I pressed.

"Yeah... yeah, we eventually did." He ran his fingers through his light blond strands while considering his mate. "Riley needed a purpose beyond being an Omega. She feared her genetics would define her, which was why she masqueraded as a Beta for so long. I had to prove to her that I saw more in her than the need to mate."

"Which is why you sought me out," I replied, recalling the day we met. "You wanted me to give her a job."

"Yes." He returned his focus to me. "Riley would never be happy barefoot and pregnant. She's not like Daciana or the Ash Wolf Omegas, who were bred to be submissive. She's more like your intended mate."

I read between the lines of that statement.

He was indirectly telling me to give Katriana a purpose outside of the bedroom. "Proving to her that I value more than just her body will help me win her over," I translated out loud.

"That's how it works with most women," Jonas replied, smirking. "Even the Ash Wolf Omegas. But our women need even more. Riley is happiest when she's in the labs. I would never take that from her."

So figure out what Katriana wants to do, and she'll be satisfied, I mused. "Thanks for the advice."

"You didn't really need it," Jonas remarked softly, clapping me on the shoulder. "You've already started down that path by putting her needs above your own. Just keep doing what you're doing."

My lips curled, amused. This was the most he'd said to me in one conversation probably ever, and it wasn't even that long a discussion. "Who knew you could be so talkative?" I teased.

He grunted. "You asked. I gave."

"I'll have to ask more often."

He gave me a look that matched his single-worded reply. "Don't."

"Noted." But we both knew I would if I needed the advice. The thing was, I didn't usually require it. Another anomaly surrounding Katriana—she made me uncertain about how to move forward, something that had never happened to me before.

I led this territory from the beginning without faltering. Yet this petite little redhead had me questioning everything. And I sort of adored her for the new experience.

"Want to grab—" Jonas's question was cut off by a yelp from across the room.

Tonic and Darren had cornered one of the new Omegas, their body language screaming dominance and unrestrained need.

"Shit." While I suspected something like this might happen, I'd really hoped it wouldn't.

"Good thing you put protocols in place," Jonas said, moving alongside me as I made a beeline for the two males. They growled, the sound reverberating through the room and resulting in several whimpers from the unmated Omegas all responding to an Alpha's call.

"Juveniles," I muttered, ready to string up the idiots by their innards, when I *felt* Katriana whine. My head whipped in her direction, finding her blocked in by Enzo and Artur. *Fuck.*

CHAPTER TWENTY-THREE

ANDER

RILEY PRACTICALLY FLEW INTO JONAS'S ARMS, her expression panicked. "Enzo shoved me away. I didn't know what—"

I was already moving, leaving the issue in the corner in favor of the other, more dangerous one stirring near the entrance of the room. Tonic and Darren were a diversion, and a shitty one at that. Just another reason why Enzo would never lead—he lacked a mind for strategy.

"On it," Elias said as he passed me, heading toward the two idiots crowding the poor Omega. He knew what to do. We'd discussed it at length prior to the party, preparing for every possible outcome.

Several other Alphas had already taken defensive stances, protecting the Omegas throughout the room. It created a palpable energy of authority that had many of the submissive females going to their knees on low moans, their slick permeating the air as growls sounded from those with less control.

Enzo's antics had awakened a potentially violent situation that would result in rutting and mindless pillaging throughout the ballroom.

Fortunately, I had countermeasures already in place to deal with this very situation.

As much as I wanted to kick his ass, it would only heighten the violent atmosphere and likely cause some of my well-meaning Alphas to subside to their animal tendencies. Omegas were notoriously unable to resist the call of an Alpha, which was why it fell on our shoulders to ensure that we controlled ourselves.

But once an Alpha lost himself to a rut, he couldn't pull back.

I shouldered my way between Enzo and Artur, not giving a fuck if I hurt them in the process, and pulled Katriana into my arms. Unlike many of the Omegas, she wasn't a trembling ball of need but a vibrating flame of fury.

"They just said—"

"Don't tell me," I whispered, my voice a plea. If she repeated their words and I found them as offensive as I expected, I'd lose my shit and kill them.

And then all hell would break loose.

I was the supreme Alpha in the room. Everyone looked to me for guidance, and if I started a fight, so would they.

And the Omegas would pay the ultimate price.

Katriana glowered up at me, then frowned at whatever she saw on my face. She nodded, then cupped my cheek. "I'm fine."

"Of course you're fine," Enzo snarled. "We didn't touch you."

"I'm going to strongly recommend you back away and leave, Enzo," I said in the quietest tone I could muster, my posture tightening with lethality. "Take Artur with you."

"We've done nothing wrong," the idiot argued. "You organized this event for the Alphas to meet all available Omegas, and this one is still available."

177

I turned slowly, placing Katriana firmly behind me. "This is why you'll never lead this sector," I informed him, my eyes capturing his in an Alpha stare meant to dominate. "You don't think before you act or speak."

He held my gaze, challenge lining his shoulders.

I stepped closer, allowing him to see how completely and utterly I would destroy him in this mood.

There would be no coming back.

No second chances.

I would kill him for this and be justified in my actions because of the chaos his asinine plan had stirred within this very room.

The growls and whines quieted around us, everyone focusing on the aggression threatening to unleash from their livid Sector Alpha—*me*.

"If you start this, I will finish it," I warned Enzo. "Just like I have the last two times you tried to remove me. Only this time, I won't be allowing you another chance. Do you understand?"

"Get them out of here," Elias shouted, calling on the Alphas strong enough to withhold their urges to usher the Omegas from the room.

I caught Enzo by the throat before he could look to his minions and finish what he'd ignited. His responding growl vibrated my hand, the sound not escaping because I crushed his vocal cords before it had the chance.

"I know what you're doing," I told him quietly. "But I'm always several steps ahead of you. Why do you think I allowed the mated Alphas to attend tonight?"

I knew I could trust them to remain in control. Only Burje, Elias, and Jonas brought their mates. Burje because he and Alyona were old friends and I wanted them to meet my Katriana. Elias because Daciana was an Ash Wolf and I thought her presence might comfort her fellow Omegas. And Jonas because I knew Riley could handle herself. All the others had attended without their mates, just in case they needed to step in to take an Omega under protection.

"Do the math," I encouraged him. "You know I have more than enough males here to handle and diffuse the situation."

There were twenty-two mated males in my territory.

Twenty of them were mingling at the party. The other two were with the mated Omegas, surrounded by Betas as a precaution. All Alphas took the security of their mates very seriously, and with the new additions, tensions had been high among the Alphas in Andorra Sector. Competitive drives were a funny thing.

Enzo clawed at my arm, his nails shredding my suit as he fought my hold.

I narrowed my gaze. "Drop your challenge and I'll release you."

He glowered just long enough to express his deep-seated hatred, then ever so slowly slid his eyes to the side.

I tightened my grip to let him know the feeling was mutual before shoving him roughly into the wall—just in case he thought to fake me out and charge at me.

But he didn't.

He folded over, his elbows on his knees while he wheezed out a series of curses.

"One of these days, you'll fall, Cain," Artur said conversationally. "And I can't wait to see it happen."

I smiled at the old bastard. "Okay. I'll be sure to wave at you on the way down." I folded my arms. "Now get out of my sight before I take that statement for the challenge we both know it to be."

He bristled but smartly retrieved his friend and left.

The rest of the room had partly cleared out, all the Omegas gone.

"They're safe," Elias confirmed from the middle of the room, his lip bleeding from whatever scuffle I missed in the corner.

A handful of younger Alphas were unconscious.

The rest all stood around, hands in their pockets, wearing irritated expressions.

Well, all but one. Mad—who I'd forgotten was attending tonight with Caspian—stood off to the side with a curious expression. Very different from his usual stoic one.

He would no doubt be reporting on the events of tonight

to Dušan. It was probably why he'd agreed to stay after the final Omega arrived earlier today, just to oversee tonight's meet and greet.

Well, thank fuck we'd handled it, or that could have impacted our future business partnership.

I blew out a breath and drew my fingers through my hair. "Right. That didn't go the way I intended," I informed everyone, not bothering to comment on the contingency plan I'd put in place. They all already knew, thanks to Elias and the team's quick cleanup of the incident.

Several Alphas grunted in agreement, but one stepped forward.

Samuel.

"Maybe not, but you proved a point," he said gruffly, surprising me. Samuel typically voted for team Enzo in meetings and had been adamantly against this deal with the Ash Wolves. "The Omegas are compatible."

"Genetics already proved that," Elias pointed out. "Or do you need to see my mate again?" The offer was meant to be a rhetorical slap across the face because his tone confirmed that he wouldn't bring Daciana anywhere near this room.

Samuel waved him off. "It's one thing to observe a mating between another Alpha and his Omega. Quite another to feel the pull."

Ah, so one of the females had intrigued him. Interesting. I'd have to find out which one. While the Alpha and I didn't often see eye to eye, I'd be willing to work with him on this if it meant having him on my side for once.

"Any other comments?" I asked the room. Since eighty percent of the council stood before me, it seemed like a good time to address other concerns. But most of them just appeared annoyed at having their evening spoiled.

"How do you plan to assign mating priority?" Samuel asked, arching a brow.

"I don't. The Omegas will." That proclamation grew a resounding rumble from the crowd that had Katriana clutching my jacket, her body pressing flush with mine. I reached an arm around to hold her to me, not caring at all how awkward it looked as I continued to address the council.

"We're doing this the old way—by courting. If you want an Omega to choose you to see her through the heat cycle, then I suggest you start wooing."

This was part of the deal I had with Dušan. He wanted his Omegas treated fairly. I agreed.

And the arched brow from Mad now told me he was very curious indeed to see if I planned to adhere to that requirement.

"Don't act so surprised and insulted," Elias snapped as the X-Clan Alphas grew even more agitated. "Ander told you this was part of the agreement. And we voted to see it through."

"But the Omegas are already here," Rajan protested from the back of the room. "Why do we have to play by Ash Wolf rules when we already have our part of the shipment?"

You mean aside from the fact that one of his lieutenants is standing in this fucking room listening to this conversation right now? I wanted to growl at him. *Think before you speak, idiot.*

Instead, I took a deep breath and replied, "Because if we don't, there will be no future shipments." I let that settle over them before adding, "If you like the offerings from tonight and want to win one over for yourself in the future, then I suggest you do this the way it was meant to be done. To keep our trading partner appeased."

That earned me a round of beautiful silence. Beautiful because it meant they wanted more Omegas. Which implied my arrangement—the very one they were arguing over for months—had worked.

Across the room, Elias's lips curled, his gaze telling me he'd drawn the same conclusion.

I'd finally found a way to appease the beasts of Andorra Sector.

"All right," Samuel said after several beats. "Courting it is."

Several of the males murmured agreement, and the female at my back noticeably relaxed.

"What about your Omega?" Rajan asked, stepping forward. "Are we allowed to court her since she's unmated?"

And there went the brief moment of serenity filling the room.

CHAPTER TWENTY-FOUR

KAT

EVERYTHING FROZE. My heart. Ander. The room. Even my lungs.

Are we allowed to court her since she's unmated?

Enzo and his lethal friend had told me all about their idea of courtship. While I suspected it didn't match Ander's interpretation of the word—since he'd said the Omegas would be choosing their mates—the two Alphas had thoroughly ruined my understanding of the term.

"In our day, an Omega of breeding age would be mounted by a room of Alphas like this, and whoever's seed took root first won the ability to claim his prize."

"Mmm, yes. But it seems Ander already won by that definition," the lethal one had mused, pressing his palm boldly against my abdomen. *"Yet he didn't claim her. Does that mean we can try again after the babe is born?"*

"Why wait that long? She'd lose the child during a rut with the right group of Alphas."

"Indeed she would." The lethal one had lifted his touch then, drifting upward to my breasts with the confidence of a male who knew he could do anything he wanted to me and win whatever fight I put up against him. I'd nearly screamed then, but a yelp from the side of the room had captured my focus. Followed by the growls and the very hungry gleam in Enzo's and his friend's eyes.

I grew cold again, thinking about their words and how they looked at me—like property, not a person.

Riley had warned me that there were those who might wish to take me from Ander. I had no doubt those two were on the list she mentioned. And the way they'd shoved her away as if she were nothing but a gnat in their way?

I grimaced and buried my head against Ander's back. His arm remained locked around me, holding me to him. But it seemed my movement had unlocked his ability to speak.

"No," he said, his voice holding a dominant note that caused my knees to shake. The urge to bow to him beneath that single word overwhelmed me, until I translated what he'd just said.

No. No what? Was it in response to my touching him?

"*I* am courting her," he added then, causing my lips to part. *What?*

"But by your own rules, we're all to court the available Omegas, and she's available." That voice matched the one from moments ago who asked if the Alphas could court me. I didn't know his name or what he looked like. But his tone was enough for me to know that I also didn't want to know him.

"Katriana is not an available Omega," Ander replied, his body vibrating against mine. "She is mine."

"Not yet," the voice pressed. "She's unclaimed."

"He's right," another spoke up. "She may carry your babe, Ander, but she's not yours. She's fair game."

"Assuming you want to challenge the Alpha of our sector, sure." That came from Elias. I recognized his lazy drawl.

"Wouldn't recommend that," someone else said, his voice

gruff and deep.

Conversation broke out throughout the room, the males divided on whether they should be given a chance to woo me or not and also split as to who demanded respect for Ander's wishes and who didn't.

I clutched onto his jacket, trembling.

I don't want them to court me, I thought. *I... I don't want any of this.*

Except maybe Ander.

No, there was no maybe about it. I *did* want Ander. Perhaps because his child grew inside me. Or because I didn't know anyone else. Or maybe it was as simple as my wolf recognizing his. I couldn't really say, but I knew with certainty that Ander was the only male for me.

"It's only fair for us all to have a chance to at least meet her, to test our compatibility."

"In my home clan, an Alpha recognized his mate and took her. End of."

"Why should we allow him his pick of the litter while the rest of us are left with scraps?"

"He'll have his child. Why does he need her, too?"

"What would you do, Ash Wolf?"

"Who the fuck cares?"

"Call it a passing curiosity. Ash Wolf?"

There was a pause before a low voice replied, "I believe this discussion is between you and your pack. What Shadowlands Sector would or would not do in this situation is irrelevant."

"Where did your Beta go?" Ander asked, a dangerous note lurking in his tone.

"You know how Betas are, Cain. He fled the second he sensed the growing aggression in the room."

"Don't change the subject," one of the Alphas countered. "You can't just claim the Omega for yourself, not when you expect us to court the others."

"Yeah, Cain. You can't hold us to rules without applying them to yourself as well."

"Do you all hear yourselves right now?" Elias interjected, his familiar voice carrying throughout the room. "You're acting like children."

"Says the freshly mated Alpha."

"Elias is right," another said, his voice gruff like the one who didn't recommend anyone challenge Ander. I suspected it might be Burje, but I hadn't heard him speak enough earlier to be certain. "Do you see how frightened you've made the poor girl? You're talking about her as if she doesn't have a choice."

"She doesn't," someone snarled. "Omegas submit. Or have you forgotten that, Burje?"

"Bet he lets Alyona dominate him" was one of the muttered replies.

Chuckles broke out, jeers following, until a growl quieted them all.

A growl that had my thighs clenching from the stark authority of the sound.

Oh, Ander…

"*Enough,*" my Alpha demanded, his anger vibrating through my hands to my chest.

I whimpered behind him, slick threatening to spill from my core. *Not now. Not now!*

"Let's take a vote," that cheeky voice said, a direct challenge in his tone. "Since you favor diplomacy and all."

"There's nothing to vote on," Ander replied. "Katriana is mine. She carries my child. I will be claiming her when the time is right."

"Ah, but did she choose you?" a new voice taunted, this one deep and causing all the hairs along my arms to dance. "Isn't that what he said, that the Omegas are choosing?"

Ander went rigid. "This is the way you show me gratitude for nearly a century of leadership. After working tirelessly to supply you with a fresh fleet of Omegas."

Silence met his proclamation.

"Fascinating," he replied, his arm releasing me to hang at his side. "You want my Omega to choose me publicly rather than trust my treatment of her." The words were spoken in a conversational tone that didn't match the tension riddling his form. "Shall I take that as the insult it is or allow it because you've all lost your fucking minds over the scent of fertile

Omega pussy?"

I flinched, his words harsh. But I also understood them.

Hierarchy was very important to the wolves, and his pack had just denounced him as their leader by not trusting his word. Ander was rightfully angry. And I sensed it wasn't just the lack of faith that pissed him off but also the very real threat lingering in the air.

He didn't want them to court me, because I was already his.

That much he'd proven tonight, both in the elevator and in this room. He hadn't so much as looked at another Omega, his eyes on me all night. Even now, I felt his claim all the way to my bones as his wolf prowled beneath the surface of his skin, lying in wait until his commander called him forth to seek justice for those who dared challenge his claim.

"This can all be solved by a few words from your intended," a gravelly voice offered. "Just have her tell the room her choice, and we can be done with this tomfoolery."

"So you, too, don't accept my word?" Ander asked, the underlying note of astonishment hitting me square in the gut. That suggestion had come from someone my Alpha had trusted. A friend.

It struck me then how much this display of distrust must bother him.

Almost one hundred years of leading, and they didn't believe he'd treated me fairly.

Maybe in the beginning, I would have agreed with them. He had taken me in a moment of weakness, but at no point did I not want him. Yes, my body had reacted without my mind's consent. Yet I would be lying if I said I hadn't wanted it that way. It served as a way to hold it against him later.

Except he'd broken me before I was given the chance to react.

Told me I wasn't his mate.

And that had hurt more than anything else he could have done to me, because I'd already chosen him by that point; I just hadn't realized it yet.

My wolf half was far simpler than my human side. She saw what she wanted and went after it, while my human mind constantly overanalyzed every situation.

But I recognized him as my mate even from the beginning, when my body wanted to submit before I understood what the hell I was doing.

"This isn't about what I think," the gruff voice finally replied. "The others in the room need some reassurance. Give them that and we can be on our way."

"By putting my intended mate on the spot and asking for her choice," Ander translated. "Something you would never subject any other Alpha to do, especially one in my position."

I frowned at his back. While I understood the implied insult of the situation, it wouldn't be very hard for me to speak up on his behalf to quiet the whole mess—just as the stranger had suggested.

But perhaps it was the principle of the matter that kept Ander from agreeing.

Or he's worried I won't choose him.

The thought struck me across the face, causing my lips to part in shock.

Oh my God. That was exactly why he continued to fight them. He thought I would reject him.

The elevator conversation came back to me in a rush, where I continued to say no while he professed that there wasn't a choice, that I already belonged to him.

My protests had nothing to do with his statements and everything to do with the fact that he hadn't yet claimed me— making the words untrue.

However, he'd just told this entire room of countless Alpha males that I was his intended. Had physically taken me before entering the room, ensuring everyone smelled us on one another. His intentions couldn't be more obvious. I just hadn't acknowledged them until now.

It was my acceptance of his wish to mate me that remained unclear.

"You're stalling," one of them accused.

"I'm not fucking stalling," he spit back. But I saw through his lie. "I'm enraged by this damn council undermining my power. *Again.* I'm the Alpha of this sector for a reason, and if you want to remove me from that position, then try. But I will not be questioned in this manner."

My knees wobbled as another wave of aggression left Ander, his fury palpable and demanding submission.

No, I said, forcing my legs to work. *No.*

I couldn't bow. Couldn't kneel. Not when he needed me. Not when I had something to say.

Releasing him, I took an unstable step back, my heel clacking loudly against the marble floor. I cringed as Ander turned, allowing me to see all the Alpha males beyond him.

At least sixty.

I knew there were more under the dome based on what Riley had explained regarding numbers. Perhaps only a certain sect of them were permitted to attend tonight's events. I'd have to ask Ander later. Along with about three thousand other questions rioting around in my mind.

Swallowing, I met his burning gaze. "Are you all right?" he asked softly, his tone far gentler than the one he used to address his Alphas.

"No," I admitted. "I'm not." I cleared my throat, trying to find my voice and the words I needed to say.

It would be so easy to throw his callous statement back at him right now. *You're not my mate.* A few weeks ago, I might have, just so he could see how it felt. But seeing the concern radiating from his eyes—and not just because of my admission to not being okay—I knew those words would hurt him even more than they had hurt me.

Because I'd be undermining him in front of his fellow Alphas.

Not to mention, denouncing him publicly—something he hadn't done to me. Actually, he'd done quite the opposite tonight.

So I straightened my spine to address the males in the room while doing my best to ignore their heated stares.

I cleared my throat and took a deep breath to ensure that my voice carried. "I choose Ander Cain."

CHAPTER TWENTY-FIVE

KAT

MY DECLARATION WAS CLEAR for everyone in the room, but only one Alpha needed my words.

The one standing before me with a shocked expression that confirmed all my suspicions. He thought I wouldn't claim him as he did me. Which also told me something very important about him: he didn't feel he deserved me.

Maybe he didn't after everything he'd done. However, being in this new world afforded me the opportunity to start over. To re-create myself. To become whoever I wanted to be within the parameters set by this sector.

His pack may have forced my fate.

But I determined my future and how I fit in their X-Clan world.

And I chose Ander Cain.

No other male in this room excited me the way he did,

something that became extremely obvious when they all started growling.

None of them had affected me, not until Ander issued a similar sound.

Just one look at him had my legs locking together, a fresh surge of arousal threatening to spill between my thighs.

Yet it was more than just lust.

Some foreign connection my human half couldn't define. My wolf understood it. A locking of souls that left me forever his, no matter the cost.

He grabbed me, pulling me into him for a kiss that branded me to my very soul. I wrapped my arms around him as my feet left the ground, his hands on my hips. He carried me from the room, leaving his wolves behind without a word.

Either my declaration had been enough to silence them or he just didn't care. Maybe both.

His tongue stroked mine.

His mouth a whispering caress.

His hands searing the skin at my waist.

I closed my eyes and gave myself to him completely. Everything I felt inside—pain, adoration, fear, confusion— became his as our mouths locked in a fiery passion that surpassed all our other interactions.

Because this one had *spirit*.

Our wolves were communicating on a whole new level, one not founded in desire but in something far more intense.

He *absorbed* me, taking the brunt of all my torment from the last few months and replacing the hurt with soothing caresses meant to heal. I could literally feel him piecing me back together, one fracture at a time.

He's touching my soul.

Such an intoxicating sensation, one I couldn't discern as reality from imagination. Whatever the cause, I jumped into it headfirst, accepting all that he could give and more.

"Put your legs around me," he said, balancing me against the wall as he hit a button for the elevator.

My dress bunched around my waist, exposing me to anyone nearby. *Let them see*, I thought. *Let them see what this Alpha does to me.*

Because I was soaking for him, my slick coating the front of his pants as I placed my core directly over his hardening length. *Mine.*

The elevator arrived, my back moving from one wall to the next while he somehow keyed in the code to take us up to his rooms.

I drew my teeth along his lower lip, biting him softly.

He growled in reply, causing me to arch wantonly against him, my body answering his call. "Ander…"

"I need to fuck you, Katriana," he groaned, dragging his mouth to my ear. "To hear you scream my name and make you come all over my cock before knotting you so deep that you'll feel me for days."

I shivered at the thought, anticipation thrumming through my veins. "Yes."

"It's going to hurt, baby."

"I know."

"But it'll feel good, too," he promised.

"I know," I repeated.

The world shifted around us as the elevator opened and he carried me directly to his penthouse and inside, the door slamming behind us with a kick from his foot.

His lips and tongue trailed up and down my neck.

His grip tightened and loosened.

His cock strained against the zipper.

So much heat. Vivacity. Pleasure. Yet too many clothes.

I was tearing at his suit before my mind caught up, his chuckle of amusement doing things to the sensitive spot between my legs.

He tossed me onto the center of his bed, prowling over me with his jacket partially off and his shirt askew. "Grab the headboard," he told me. "And don't let go unless I give you permission."

My lip curled in a snarl, my fingers not approving of the demand. Yet I found myself obeying and curling them around the sleek metal poles behind me.

"Good Omega," he praised, placing his palm at my throat before dragging it down to the V-neck of my dress.

"Katriana," I snapped at him. If he did the whole

191

"Omega" thing during sex again, I'd fucking kill him.

His mouth quirked at the side. "Katriana," he agreed, then gripped my dress and ripped it right down the middle.

I jolted in surprise, my body left completely naked beneath him as the silk parted around me. He deftly unbuckled and removed my shoes next, then paused to study every inch of my exposed form.

"Beautiful," he mused before bending to take one of my straining nipples between his teeth. I nearly released the headboard, but the warning glimmer in his eyes stopped me.

His name left my lips as a curse, my core pulsing with need as my damp walls contracted around nothing but air.

I craved friction.

Required *him*.

His cock.

His deep, addictive thrusts.

This time I moaned his name, trembling beneath his skilled mouth as he switched his attention to my other breast. "You chose me," he marveled softly, his golden irises finding mine.

"There was never a choice," I replied, arching my hips. "We both know that."

He studied me for a moment, the heat of his breath teasing my damp nipple. "You didn't want a choice. Not really."

"Maybe," I agreed, my grip tightening. "Or maybe you made the inevitable choice for me, saving me the time it would take to draw the same conclusion."

"That we were made for each other," he translated before sucking my taut peak deep into his mouth.

"Yesss," I hissed.

Fuck, this was hotter than usual.

Because for the first time, my wolf and human parts were aligned and married in their decision.

"My wolf knows you," I marveled, shaking my head. "It doesn't make any sense, but I *feel* the truth inside me."

"Soul mates," he murmured, laving at my breast before licking a damp path downward to the place I desired him most. "We're soul mates, Katriana," he said against my clit.

"Yes, yes," I panted. I never believed in such a thing,

mostly because I never contemplated the notion of it. Why would I when I expected to die at a young age? Romance wasn't a novelty I could enjoy, so I chose not to consider it.

However, Andorra Sector offered me a whole new experience, one I'd spat in the face of out of annoyance. I wanted to make my own fate, not have it fall into my lap. Yet given the option, I'd be crazy to reject this—immortality, a strong mate, children, a world where I didn't live in fear and wonder which day would be my last.

A bleak comparison, but my reality.

Ander Cain was my soul mate.

Was that why he lived so long without taking an Omega? It had to be more than just the shortage, as he existed before Andorra Sector came to fruition. Was he waiting for me all this time?

His teeth skimmed my sensitive folds, his tongue piercing my channel and temporarily sending me to the moon and back. Only, he released me a second later to settle back on his knees.

I opened my mouth to protest, but his fingers silenced me. My throat grew dry as he slowly unfastened his tie and unbuttoned his shirt to reveal the flat planes of his chest. The little hairs along his lower abdomen taunted my instincts, causing me to almost release the headboard again. I wanted to run my tongue over him, memorize every muscular divot of his stomach before venturing lower.

"You look hungry," he said, a grin in his voice.

"I am," I admitted. "But not for food."

He cocked his head to the side. "I fed you in the elevator, kitten. You can't possibly need more already. Unless my offering wasn't enough?"

"Not enough." I squirmed as his shirt and jacket and tie all fell to the floor. "God, I need you to fuck me, Ander."

His hand paused on his belt. "Yeah? You want me inside that pretty little cunt, baby?"

"This better be the pain you mentioned," I said, squeezing my thighs together in search of necessary friction. "*Because you are killing me.*"

Both of his palms landed on my knees, tugging them apart

to expose me—*all of me*—to his gaze. "Don't move."

I growled in response, fire igniting in my blood and curling in my lower belly. My arousal permeated the air, slick gushing out of me in welcome, begging him to do his job. "*Ander.*"

"Katriana." He merely sat there, watching as every hair along my arms and legs stood on end. "You're very wet."

No shit, I wanted to shout. But a whimper escaped me instead.

"I love you like this," he said, returning to his task—*fucking finally*—of removing his belt. "Wet. Needy. Edging on defiant. Tell me how badly you want to release that headboard and finger yourself into oblivion right now, Katriana."

"It won't work," I admitted, gritting my teeth. "Not good enough."

He chuckled. "You're right. It would only torment you more." He leaned down to kiss my sensitive bud, laving the swollen nub and causing me to vibrate almost violently in response. "Such a good kitten," he whispered. "Mmm, I want you to purr for me."

I was about to tell him I couldn't when he proved me wrong by latching onto my clit and sucking so hard he literally shoved me over the edge into oblivion. The scream I released hurt my ears but paled in comparison to the agony splitting my abdomen in two.

Despite the ecstasy spiraling through my belly, the orgasm didn't satisfy me in the slightest. If anything, it left me that much hotter, that much more in *need*. "Ander," I cried out, tears threatening my eyes.

My fingers ached from holding on to the headboard, my thighs shaking from the restraint it took to keep them open.

Fuck, it hurt.

So, so much.

If he didn't fuck me soon, I'd break. Die. Shatter without him.

A sob tore through my chest, the pleasure-pain still vibrating through my pussy, my channel searching for the intrusion I required. "Ander, please."

"Shh, I'm here," he whispered, his mouth sealing over mine as his cock slid inside me with unerring accuracy. I hadn't even felt him finish disrobing, too lost to the sensations assaulting my being.

But, oh, it felt good. Right. Amazing. Every drive forward, the way he hit me deeper each time, touching that point inside me that evoked stars behind my eyes.

And his lips. Perfect. Kissable. Mesmerizing.

He fucked my mouth with his tongue, dominating me in every way. I whimpered, my hands needing to touch him, and somehow he knew. "Wrap your arms around me, baby," he said softly, laving my lower lip before plunging in deep to steal my breath.

I gripped him harder than I had the headboard, holding on with all my strength as he picked up his pace to a brutal speed that slammed me into the bed.

More, more, more, my wolf chanted. She wanted him to bite me. To sink his canines into my flesh and claim me the way he should have months ago.

But he continued to kiss me instead, his body owning mine in a completely different manner. He didn't give me time to complain, or the space I needed to contemplate it, because every punch of his hips against mine drove me higher into an orgasmic state that threatened to shatter my concept of reality.

I panted.

Clawed at his back.

Screamed his name.

Became absolutely wild in my craving.

And he maintained complete control, guiding us both to the precipice at his own speed.

I begged. He gave. I trembled. He pushed. I sighed in frustration. He groaned in anticipation.

Give and take.

Back and forth.

Harder and faster.

His knot growing.

There, I thought, coming apart on a wave of euphoria that painted the world in black, leaving me breathless as he tumbled with me over the rapturous cliff.

Some part of me realized this sort of fucking would have killed a mortal, or at least left her in serious pain.

But I welcomed the throbbing, content with the pang of his violence shivering across my skin. It made me feel alive. Owned. Completely possessed by my Alpha. *Claimed.*

"You didn't bite me," I managed on a breath, his seed still spilling into me with his pulsating knot.

"Not yet," he whispered, nuzzling my throat. "But I will."

"When?" I demanded, eliciting a chuckle from him.

"Soon," he promised. "I want to show you something first."

I frowned. What could he possibly want to show me? "What is it?"

"You'll see," he replied, nibbling my pulse. "Trust me."

CHAPTER TWENTY-SIX

ANDER

MY WRIST BUZZED as I handed Katriana another pillow. Seeing Elias's name, I hit ignore and focused intently on my intended mate.

She'd gone into nesting mode about four hours ago. When I tried to help, she pushed me away with a growl. So I'd switched tactics and started handing her things from all over my condo, including the pillow from the couch.

Which she tossed on the floor with a scowl.

Okay...

I went back to my closet, searched through my dirty laundry for more shirts, and brought them to her as an offering.

She sniffed them, then grabbed one with a sigh and added it to her masterpiece. The way she paced told me she wanted more, so I went in search of additional bedding in my closets, handing her everything I could find.

Then I started on clean clothes and flipped the device on my wrist to Off when it vibrated again. Whatever Elias needed, he could wait. Katriana's nesting was far more important. It meant she felt alive again, healed, and I intended to be here for her every step of the way.

She plucked a pair of jeans from my hands, her fingers tracing the fabric reverently. Folding them, she set them on my nightstand, then snatched the cotton shirt I'd draped over my arm, and added it to her creation.

Hands on her bare hips, she cocked her head to the side and breathed deeply in satisfaction. I stood still, waiting. One of her palms drifted to her abdomen, the protective gesture warming my heart. "Yes," she whispered. "Yes, this will do."

She slid into her nest, wiggling around to find the perfect spot, then looked at me expectantly.

Yeah, I wasn't about to turn down that blatant invitation from my very naked Omega.

I joined her without a word, staring into her eyes as she studied me with the wolf in her gaze. She palmed my cheek, her thumb tracing my bottom lip. "Thank you for helping."

"You did most of the work." I wrapped my palm around the back of her neck. "I just supplied the material."

"It's weird," she whispered. "The instinct to burrow, I mean."

"Omegas feel protected when they *burrow*," I explained softly, using her term. "And pregnant females become very protective of their nests in the later stages of their pregnancy."

"They do?"

I nodded. "Yes. And you'll be even fiercer when the babe is born. I bet you won't even let me hold our child without a debate." I grinned at the thought, drawing her in for a slow kiss that quickly heated as her tongue slid into my mouth.

Hearing her tell the entire room two nights ago that she'd chosen me had liberated something deep inside. I wanted to claim her more than ever, but I also needed it to be right.

Which gave me an idea.

One I would act upon just as soon as we christened this new nest.

I moved over her, settling between her already damp thighs. No mating call required. Katriana was always ready for me.

She moaned as I entered her fully, my hips setting a languorous pace. I wanted to savor her. Devour her. Memorize every single moan. And do it all over again just to see what I could do to change her reactions.

Fast pumping made her pant.

Slow, shallow strokes resulted in mewls for more.

Severe thrusts elicited gasps and curses tied to my name.

And when I cupped her ass and angled her hips upward to receive me even deeper, she cried out.

Mmm, that was my favorite response from her. Not pain, but exquisite pleasure.

I captured her mouth, kissing her reverently, as I drove into her.

"Ander, Ander, Ander," she chanted against my lips. I knew what she craved and I gave it to her, because I yearned for it, too. The rapturous release, our joined passion flowing from us both, as my knot clung to her. She milked me dry, our nest fully christened by the time we finished, leaving us gratified and sighing beneath the sheets.

I rolled over, bringing her on top of me to relax with her head against my chest, the aroma of sex surrounding us both in an intoxicating cloud of ecstasy.

"I may never move again," she mused, drawing lazy patterns across my skin. "So I hope you're comfortable."

Amusement bubbled in my chest. "We'll need to eat at some point."

She reached between us, drawing a finger between her folds and bringing the mixture of our arousals to her lips.

"Fuck, Katriana," I groaned as she sucked the juices from her skin. My shaft reacted, my half-hard state quickly elongating to a full-on erection once more. "You're going to kill me, woman."

Her lips curled. "Good thing wolves don't die easily." She crawled upward, straddling my hips and leaning down to introduce some of that exotic flavor to my mouth.

Only, an intruding scent had me yanking her under me as

a warning growl left my mouth. "You're lucky I value you as my Second, Elias."

He snorted. "You're not answering your comm."

I pulled back the blanket enough to be able to glare at him in the doorway. "Because I'm busy, jackass."

"And so was I when Jonas came knocking on my door. Apparently, you're ignoring him, too." The irritation in his tone rivaled my own. "You know I wouldn't bother you if it wasn't important."

"What is it?" I demanded.

"Someone broke into the storage lockers and stole a dozen vials of X-Clan serum."

Okay, that was enough to clear me from my protective thoughts. I rolled off Katriana and sat up while she curled herself around my leg, hiding beneath the blankets.

"By the look on your face, you already know who did it," I said, noting the tense lines of his mouth.

He nodded. "Security feeds showed Caspian breaking in the night of the meet and greet."

"Shit," I muttered, rubbing my hand over my face. "I knew something was off about his absence and Mad staying behind." It just hadn't felt right. "I even commented on it."

"Yeah, I know. But everyone was too focused on your intended to think straight," Elias replied. "You should have seen them after you left with her." He shook his head. "The only good part was Samuel finally coming to his senses. He told the Alphas that courtship was the right route, one that requires respect should we want to acquire more Omegas."

"A brief win only to be soiled by Caspian's foolishness." I sighed, shaking my head. "I can only guess what Enzo and Artur are saying now."

"They want blood."

"Of course they do. How else would they consider handling the situation?" The damn brutes lacked the ability to strategize and think outside the box. "Let me guess—he wants to conduct an air raid of the Ash Wolves?"

"No. He wants to kill all the Omegas because he's convinced they're all spies."

My entire body went cold. "*What?*"

"Now you see why I interrupted your little nesting time?"

"Why the fuck didn't you lead with that information?" I demanded, leaving the comfort of my bed and stalking toward my bathroom to grab a robe. Elias had seen me naked countless times. Shifter life and all that. But I needed to wear something before I started making calls.

"I've hidden them all behind a wall of trustworthy Alphas," Elias said, leaning against my door frame, the picture of ease.

"And Daciana?"

"She's with them and trying to help calm the girls down. One of Enzo's idiots tried to take the slaying order into his own hands and got ahold of the newest Omega—Narcisa. Samuel, of all people, stumbled upon them and slit the other Alpha's throat."

"Who was it?"

"Tonic."

I shook my head. "Tell me he's dead."

"Nope." Elias's lips popped on the end. "It was a superficial wound that knocked him out. But I've got him locked up in the dungeon, awaiting your order."

"No wonder you kept calling."

"And I would have been up here sooner to drag your ass out had I not been busy handling the chaos unfolding in *your* sector."

"That's why you're my Second," I said out loud, while mentally acknowledging that I owed him big-time.

"Indeed I am." He arched a brow. "So where do you want to start?"

"I need to talk to Dušan," I replied, switching my watch comm back on. "Stealing our serum doesn't make any sense. If he wanted it, he would have requested it as part of our trade." And never once had the Ash Wolf Alpha mentioned our ability to create X-Clan Wolves.

I started toward the door, then remembered the Omega I'd just left in the sheets, and turned back around to peek into our nest. "Do you need anything, kitten? Food? Water? A bath?" I could pour her one while I spoke to Dušan.

She stretched her arms over her head, her athletic form on

full display. "How long will you be?"

"I'm not leaving." I leaned down to kiss her on the nose. "I can call the Shadowlands Sector Alpha from here."

"Oh." She frowned. "But what about the Omegas?"

"I trust that Elias is keeping them safe," I said, glancing at my Second. His responding nod confirmed my suspicion. He wouldn't leave his mate somewhere unprotected if he didn't absolutely trust the men he put in charge. "Once I talk to Dušan, I'll address the others. This will blow over quickly."

Because I knew in my gut that Dušan hadn't done this.

Enzo and Artur were just looking for ways to thwart my success, and taking the Omegas out of the equation would accomplish that.

But what they didn't consider was the fallout with the Alphas who wanted the Ash Wolf Omegas. I was willing to bet more of my council wanted those females alive rather than dead for something they hadn't done. Not to mention how much work went into acquiring them.

"Some juice, maybe?" Katriana asked.

I gave her a smile. "I'll be right back."

Elias followed me into the living area and the kitchen, his grin spreading from ear to ear. "Say what you want to say," I told him, opening the refrigerator. The orange juice sat on the second shelf beside a plate of freshly cut cheese and meats. I grabbed both and set them on the counter before retrieving a glass.

"Domestication looks good on you, Ander." He popped a hip against the wall, waggling his brows.

I scoffed. "You can do better than that."

"Nah, I really can't because I'm just as lost to Daciana as you are to Katriana." He smiled a little. "It feels good, doesn't it?"

I finished pouring the glass for Katriana and considered his words. "Yeah," I admitted. "Yeah, it does." After putting the container away, I sent a message to Dušan to provide him with a two-minute warning regarding my need to speak to him. "Stay here," I told Elias. "I'll be right back."

Katriana was sitting up in the bed when I returned, a sheet drawn up to her chest. I set the tray and juice on the nightstand, then leaned down to kiss the top of her head. "This won't take me long. How about you eat and shower, then maybe we can go for a run?"

My wolf was itching for an excuse to get out and stretch. Mostly because I wanted to rip apart two certain Alphas and a little exercise would help with that. It would also allow me to fulfill the plan I had in mind regarding our mating.

She hadn't seen me in wolf form yet, nor had we bonded properly.

Once I fixed that, I would claim her.

And we could spend the night fucking under the stars.

"A run?" she repeated, her eyes widening. "Like, outside?"

I chuckled. "Yeah, kitten. Outside."

"In the fresh air?"

"Where else would we go?" I asked, amused by her questions until it hit me *why* she was asking. "Oh. Because you've not been allowed out." Shit. I was an idiot. "We're going to change that," I promised her, more solemn now. "We'll go for a run tonight. Outside. In the snow. Together. Okay?"

Her entire expression brightened. "Really? As wolves?"

"Yes."

She dropped the sheet and went up onto her knees to throw her arms around my neck just as my wrist buzzed with a reply from Dušan. I pulled her into a quick kiss, adoring the way she grinned so excitedly at me. "Let me handle this, then we can go. But eat first. You'll need strength for the shift."

She nodded enthusiastically. "Okay. Yes. I'll eat."

I dropped a kiss against her lips. "Good. I'll be in the living room with Elias, so come out when you're ready. Don't forget your new clothes in the closet. And wear boots." We would have to walk to the edge of the sector in human form, then we could shift and go for a real run.

My wolf vibrated beneath my skin, anxious for freedom. It'd been weeks since I'd shifted, longer than ever before. But remaining here with my intended had superseded my own needs. Now that she appeared to be feeling better, I could introduce her to the way things would be between us going forward.

203

Starting with an evening prowl through the mountainside. After I dealt with Dušan.

Leaving her, I rejoined Elias, who had collapsed into one of my recliner chairs. "This smells new," he remarked.

"Yeah. Katriana destroyed the old one."

He laughed. "Right. I forgot about that."

"No, you didn't," I accused, sitting across from him. "It's why you mentioned the new scent, which we both know isn't even new anymore considering I replaced it all nearly three months ago."

He winked at me. "This is why you're Sector Alpha, Cain. You always see through me."

"Yeah, yeah." I selected Dušan's name on my device and hit Dial. "Let's get this over with."

CHAPTER TWENTY-SEVEN

KAT

MY LIPS PURSED TO THE SIDE. *I need to cut my hair.* The length had reached the middle of my back, causing my red locks to tangle too easily. But I couldn't find any scissors or knives to work with in Ander's bathroom. He had to keep them somewhere since his black strands were chopped close to his ears and I'd yet to see him wear it any longer.

Leaving my hair down to air-dry after my shower, I started looking through my new clothes for something appropriate to wear. He'd literally filled half his closet with outfits just for me.

Jeans. Sweaters. Boots. Long-sleeved shirts. Stretchy pants. Dresses. All varying sizes meant to accommodate my stages of pregnancy.

My cheeks warmed at the thoughtfulness as I grabbed a pair of jeans and a black sweater. Undergarments weren't something I wore growing up—clothes were scarce—so I ignored the drawer of panties and bras. Something told me I wouldn't be a fan of them. I did, however, grab some socks for my boots.

I was in the middle of lacing them up when Ander's voice sounded all around me.

"Wolves of Andorra Sector, good evening. As you may have heard, we recently experienced a breach in our security when one of our visiting Ash Wolves stole twelve vials of X-Clan serum. After a long discussion with the Shadowlands Sector Alpha, I believe the issue will be sorted swiftly and efficiently. He has assured me this was not an act coordinated under his leadership, but by a rogue wolf, and that wolf will be punished accordingly."

I stepped out of the closet, searching for him, frowning. "How are you doing that?" I whispered, glancing all around the empty bathroom. He wasn't in the bedroom either.

"Some of you have called for revenge in a most unacceptable manner. The Ash Wolf Omegas are officially part of Andorra Sector and officially under my protection. Anyone found attempting to harm or kill one of the females will be dealt with swiftly and brought to justice under the fullest extent of our law."

I peeked into the living room to find him seated at the dining room table with Elias across from him. The latter brushed his finger over his lips, indicating for me to remain quiet, while Ander glanced at me with a warm look before refocusing on a translucent screen.

"This matter is not up for debate, nor will it be addressed by the Alpha council. Negotiations with Shadowlands Sector requires a certain amount of respect and faith, and I am choosing to accept Dušan's verbal promise to rectify the situation on his end. Stealing from us was not okay. He acknowledges that and has apologized on behalf of his brethren. I will keep you all apprised of the situation as I learn more. For now, note that any violence within our sector will not be tolerated." He stared down at the screen with a look so fierce the hairs along my arms danced.

Oh, I never wanted to be on the receiving end of that

expression.

It'd probably bring me to my knees in a second. Hell, he wasn't even looking at me and I wanted to bow.

This was the Alpha of Andorra Sector. The male everyone trusted to lead. And he'd just issued an edict. One would have to be a fool to disobey him.

"Enjoy the rest of your evening," he concluded, selecting a button and leaning back in his chair. He arched a brow at Elias. "Satisfied?"

"It's not me you need to be asking, Cain." He pushed away from the table and stood to his full height—one that rivaled Ander's. "I'm going to keep guards on the Omegas. I don't trust Enzo and Artur, or any of his minions, to adhere to your command."

Ander nodded. "This only increases our need to see the females mated. They'll be in danger until they have an Alpha to protect them."

"I'll talk to the males who have expressed interest, see how our Omegas are feeling as well. Since you're insistent on the courtship principles and all that." He winked at me with those words and started toward the foyer. "Enjoy your run. I'll hold down the fort."

"You're a good Second," Ander called out over his shoulder.

"I know" was the reply, just before the front door slammed.

Ander chuckled and moved a few screens around before hitting some button that caused them all to vanish into thin air. He refocused on me with a hungry gleam, his gold irises tracing my form. "You look beautiful, future mate," he murmured, standing and sauntering toward me to twirl his finger around one of my damp locks of hair. "I need to find you a hat."

"And scissors," I told him. "I want to cut my hair."

He tugged on the strand, his lips curling. "I can help you with that after our run, if you want."

"Really?"

He pulled me in for a kiss, his lips warm against mine. "Of course."

"I'd like that."

"Me, too." He nuzzled my cheek before releasing me. "Let me throw on something more appropriate than this robe and we'll go."

"Okay." I busied myself by examining the table while he changed. There was absolutely nothing unique about it. Just wood. No buttons. No fancy hidden panels. Just a standard dining area. "So how do the screens appear?" I wondered out loud, searching his chair next.

"My watch," Ander replied, having already returned in a pair of jeans and a fitted gray sweater. I recognized the pants as the ones I'd put on the nightstand. He must have grabbed a wool top from the closet, as well as the shoes and socks.

He held out his wrist, showing me the device.

"It looks like an old-fashioned timepiece, but click this button here"—he pressed his thumb against the right side of the clock face—"and a screen pops up that scans my retinas for activation. Now I have complete access to all my systems, just like I do on my tablet or my computer in the office." He spun the images through the air around us, showing me multiple screens.

"And you used this to speak to everyone in Andorra Sector?"

He nodded. "Yes. The entire city is connected via technology. Every home, every room, has a frequency I can override in the case of an emergency. I don't use it often, but I considered the threat level against our Omegas to be worthy of a public broadcast." Ander closed all the screens with a flick of his wrist and pressed his palm to my lower back, nudging me toward the main hallway that led to the door.

"Do you think it'll stop them?" I asked in the foyer.

"No." His lips flattened. "But my men will."

"And then what happens?"

"And then I deal with a problem that's been festering for far too long," he replied, opening the front door.

"Enzo and the lethal one," I guessed, pausing next to the elevator.

"Lethal one," he repeated, selecting a button on the pad. "Oh, you mean Artur. I suppose he is the deadlier of the two, but Enzo has the bigger mouth. He's been trying to take my position for decades. Never wins."

"And Artur?"

"He hasn't tried to challenge me." He guided me into the elevator as the doors opened, then pressed a series of buttons. "Four. One. Seven. Three. Hash key, or pound sign. That takes you to the bottom floor."

I blinked at him. "What?"

"That's the code, in case you want to step outside for fresh air in the future. Or you could go up to the roof. There's a little seating area up there, but it's really cold in the winter. It'll improve in a month or two as we get into the spring months." The metal slats slid to the side to reveal a large marble-floored area while he spoke. "This way, kitten."

"You're showing me how to leave," I marveled, glancing up at him. "I thought I wasn't allowed to leave?"

"I told you not to try to *escape* again," he clarified. "But you're not a prisoner, Katriana. I should have made that clear. I also should have taken you out for a run long ago, and for that, I apologize. There are a lot of things I've failed to explain, and that ends now."

Two guards bowed as we approached the exit. They opened a set of glass doors with a flourish as Ander thanked them by name. I barely heard him, my focus on the snow dotting the sidewalks and the fresh breeze infiltrating my lungs.

Air. I inhaled deeply, my eyes closing in contentment as the elements swirled around me. Oh, how I missed the fresh flavors and scents of the outside world.

I twirled on the sidewalk, my boots helping me to maintain traction in the light layer of white flakes. Someone must have recently shoveled, because the snow in the nearby trees and bushes was well over a foot tall. No, more. It nearly reached my knees.

I dipped my hands into the icy goodness and allowed it to freeze my skin as Ander tugged a hat over my head. Startled, I glanced at him. "Where'd that come from?"

"I had it tucked into my back pocket with these." He handed me a pair of gloves.

"What about you?" I asked, allowing him to slide the wool over my fingers and hands.

"Fur," he murmured, winking.

I frowned at him. "I have fur, too."

"That you do," he agreed. "How about you hold my hand to keep it warm while we walk, then we'll both change into something warmer." He threaded his fingers through mine and tugged me to his side. "There's a lot more snow up in the mountains. Let's go play."

Warmth caressed my insides. *Play.* "I like the sound of that."

"Good." He slid his opposite hand into his jeans and started walking down the sidewalk.

I maintained his quick pace, taking in the scenery as we ventured through the heart of Andorra Sector.

All the wintry elements glistened beneath the moon, most of the lights in the city either off or on a dim setting. Or maybe it was the windows that blocked out the luminescent glows within. Either way, it painted a beautiful night with snow and moonlight and various types of fir trees mingling between the buildings.

"It's really gorgeous here," I admitted, truly seeing his home for the first time. Glimpses of the sector were available from the outside, but witnessing the magic from the street provided a very different experience.

"It is," he agreed. "But my favorite view is from the mountains." He nodded his chin toward one of the summits outside the dome. I'd never hiked that one but was familiar with the location because I'd woken up to that view every day from my cave.

"Is that where we're going?" I asked, awed.

"Yep." His wolf seemed to grin down at me through his golden eyes. "You said you were up for a run."

"Yeah, I thought you meant inside the dome."

"What would be the fun in that?" he asked, guiding me down a narrow path between buildings. It opened into a courtyard, and beyond it, a glass wall. "There are areas inside that we can run in, if you prefer. But most of us venture into the surrounding woods."

Is that safe? I wanted to ask. Then I realized how ridiculous that sounded. What could an X-Clan Wolf possibly have to fear? They were the apex predators in this area, maybe even in the entire world. Humans were too weak to put up a fight, and the shifters were immune to the Infected. Why not roam around freely?

The only threat I could think of was the Ash Wolves, and they lived too far away to be a problem.

"Is this okay?" Ander asked, pausing midway through the field to study me.

"Yeah. Yeah, it's more than okay." The idea of running in the mountains actually excited me. "But I might need some help with, uh, shifting." I hadn't shifted since before—

Wait...

I palmed my belly and met his amused gaze. "Can I shift while pregnant?"

His amusement fled, his lips curling down at the corners. "I really have failed you, haven't I?"

"What?" I glanced down. "I just meant—"

He caught my chin to guide my focus back up to him. "You really know nothing about being an X-Clan Wolf, and I just left you for weeks to live on your own without any explanation. If anyone should be chagrined by that, it's me. I made a lot of assumptions about your knowledge because of your father."

"My father?" I repeated, my brow furrowing. "But I never met my father."

"Yes, although your mother did."

"I don't think she knew him well." I chewed my cheek, considering how to phrase this. "She never said much about him, other than to claim he cared about me. But I suspect he never knew I existed. I think he either left or died before she could tell him she was pregnant."

Her words had always seemed to be the kinds of things a mother said to her curious child, not wanting to cause harm or hurt feelings. But as I grew older, she rarely mentioned him. If he cared so much about me, she'd have continued with the mantra to ensure I believed her, not dropped the act.

"It's a cruel world out there," I added with a shrug. "She

probably didn't even expect to be able to carry me to term."
Not because she didn't want me, just a result of the hand fate
had given us.

"So you had no idea your father was a wolf?" he asked.

I gaped at him. "*What?*"

"I'll take that as a no," he muttered, running his fingers
through his hair. "Shit, I thought you knew. That's why you're
an Omega. Well, that's our theory, anyway. His genetics
triggered something in yours that made you predisposed to
submission."

My mouth worked, but sound failed me. Not that I knew
what to say.

My dad was a wolf?!

"It also explains how you've survived this long," he
continued softly. "You were part wolf. With our intervention,
you evolved into a full X-Clan Omega." He palmed my cheek.
"This was not the venue I would have chosen for this
conversation. If you want to go back to talk more, we can run
another night."

"N-no," I stammered, blinking rapidly. "I-I want to run."
No. I *needed* to run. To do something other than stand here,
frozen, unable to process. To shut off my brain. To escape
the insanity clawing at my thoughts. "Please," I whispered.
"Let's run."

He nodded, his hand in mine all that propelled me
forward.

My dad was a wolf.

Did my mom know?

Where did he go?

Is he in Andorra Sector now? Still alive? Would I ever meet him?

The questions were all firing at once, my legs moving on
autopilot to follow Ander through the snow. It felt like only
seconds had passed by when he stopped, the dome at least
half a mile behind us.

"Are you sure about this, Katriana?" he asked softly,
brushing his knuckles across my jaw. "You look shell-
shocked."

"Yeah, you just told me my father was a wolf." How did
he expect me to react? With rainbows and smiles? I nearly

212

laughed at the notion.

"I thought you knew," he murmured.

"How the hell would I know something like that?" I demanded, my voice leaving me on a higher pitch than I intended.

"You're right," he replied, shaking his head. "I made all these assumptions about how much you understood based on that detail, without ever actually asking you. I'm sorry, Katriana. I'm not turning out to be a very worthy mate." His brow came down, his hand falling from my face. "I need to make it up to you. And I think I know how."

I frowned at him. "How?"

"By teaching you everything you need to know about being a wolf." He tugged off his sweater, letting it drop to the wintry ground. "Get undressed. We'll start with how to shift."

CHAPTER TWENTY-EIGHT

ANDER

KATRIANA STOOD GLORIOUSLY naked before me, her arms wrapped around her shivering form. "I-it's n-not w-working."

Yes, I could see that. Most wolves were born, our ability to shift an innate part of our mental state. But Katriana seemed unable to call upon her wolf, despite the beast prowling beneath the surface.

I circled her, my bare feet protesting with each step against the snowy earth. But my intended had my complete focus. "I can call to your wolf, but if you fight me on it, it'll hurt."

"Has to b-be b-better than th-this." She waved down to where she stood on my sweater, her legs locked together in a way to keep warm.

Our genetics helped us fight the cold better than a human, but without our fur, we very much felt the icy elements.

"When I do this, you'll start the change, regardless of if you're ready or not," I warned.

"L-like, force the sh-shift?"

I nodded. "Yes."

"H-how?"

"With a growl," I said, stopping in front of her. "Omegas are built to satisfy an Alpha's cravings. It allows me to control your form. If I want you as a wolf, I can call to that part of your nature, and then I can just as easily make you human again."

"O-oh," she mouthed, the sound lost to the chatter of her teeth.

I moved closer, wrapping my palm around the back of her neck and pulling her into my warmth. She could have every ounce of my heat if it helped her to stop shaking.

Dropping my lips to her ear, I softly added, "And if I want you wet and ready to receive my cock, I can do that, too. Even now, in the snow."

"You've d-done that."

I nodded. "Yes. A mating call is the most natural. But I also have the ability to help provoke your shift. Perhaps it'll help you learn where your connection is hiding."

"Y-yes," she said, nuzzling my chest. "H-help me."

I kissed the top of her head and closed my eyes. "I promise to only do this to you when you ask me to," I said. "For shifting, I mean." The mating call I would absolutely use on her because we both enjoyed the reward of that.

Wrapping my arms around her, I allowed my wolf to surface, our thoughts joining as one to create a low growl in my chest. Katriana shivered in response, a soft sound spilling from her lips as I deepened the vibration, demanding her animal side come out to play.

She moaned, her body beginning to shake. "I… I feel her…"

"Follow the call, baby," I whispered, releasing her. "Let your wolf take over. She'll guide you through the change."

I took a step back, watching as Katriana fell to her knees, her limbs already transforming. A beautiful smile broke out across her face, followed by a sigh as she gave in to the shift.

It'd been too long since her last change, something I blamed myself for. I should have been mentoring her from the beginning.

Blowing out a breath, I pushed the guilt to the side. I could either wallow in it or do something about it, and I'd always been the proactive sort. We'd make up for lost time, and I'd show Katriana everything she needed to know about our life.

She released a soft little mewl as the final phases of her shift settled across her spine, red fur sprouting across every inch of her pale skin. I drew my fingers through her red coat, enjoying the silky quality. She leaned into my touch, a faint grumble of approval following my caress.

"You're gorgeous, Katriana," I said softly, crouching beside her and allowing my wolf full rein. He practically leapt from my skin, nearly a century of practice allowing me to shift between forms with ease.

It still hurt in parts. That would never go away. But I learned to numb the pain in my youth. It was mainly my jaw that ached with the way it restructured to form my snout.

The rest was easy.

Just a restructuring from bipedalism to all fours.

I shook out my black coat and stretched, my joints popping from disuse. Wolves were meant to change a few times a week at a minimum, which meant Katriana had to be cramping even more than I was. Or maybe not, considering she'd spent most of her life in human form. Maybe it would be the opposite for her.

After extending my back legs one more time, I turned to face my mate and found her blue eyes trained on my body. Admiration poured from her gaze, pleasing my wolf immensely.

Yeah, I was a lot bigger than her. Stronger, too. Hence my Alpha status.

I nudged her with my muzzle and cocked my head to the side, indicating that I wanted her to follow.

She gave an adorable little yip in reply that I translated as permission to proceed. I took off up the mountain at a leisurely pace, sensing her presence near my hind legs and using that as a gauge for how hard to push her. Her smaller size suggested she wouldn't be able to move as fast as me, but I had a feeling she could keep up where it counted.

Katriana proved me right as she picked up her speed to match mine along the way, practically running by my side near the end when I moved into a full sprint. She must have taken that as the challenge it was because she started racing me, her legs moving at an incredible pace for one so new... until she tumbled into a snow mound.

I quickly rolled to a stop and went back to help her out of it, grabbing her scruff with my teeth and yanking her back onto the safer path.

She snarled—her way of pouting—and I licked her muzzle in reply, telling her it was okay. It happened to all of us. And honestly, I was astounded by her agility when she hadn't spent much time in this form. She'd be quite the wolf once she grew into her fur a little more.

With a head butt, I guided her toward the edge of the mountain, wanting to show her the view. I watched to ensure her footing stayed on the path this time, preferring not to lose my intended mate over the cliff.

If she noticed, she didn't react. Instead, she remained glued to my side and lay down beside me when I sat in my favorite spot.

Her fur stood on edge when she followed my focus to the valley below. We were nowhere near the highest vantage point, but we were high enough to take in the breathtaking night scene painted before us beneath the moon.

This was where I went when I needed to be alone to think. Never had I allowed anyone to join me. But it felt right having Katriana by my side, her presence a warmth that soothed my wolf. I leaned down to tug on her ear affectionately, then licked the side of her face. She snorted in reply, so I did it again. Then pinned her when she tried to squirm away.

Releasing a low growl of warning, I held her in place with one massive paw against her scruff and licked her a final time. Then nuzzled her neck.

She grumbled a bit in reply, yet I felt the way her body relaxed beneath my attentions. The human part of her didn't understand, but her wolf did. Eventually, she returned the affection with a few licks of her own before snuggling into me on a sigh.

We lay like that for a while with the stars dancing overhead, time pacing as it always did, until a rim of light began to dawn on the horizon. After releasing a lazy yawn, I poked her with my nose to indicate we should get back. She rolled onto her back in protest, and I lightly nipped her throat in reply.

As much as I wanted to stay here all day, this wasn't an ideal place to claim her. It would require shifting back, and my poor mate would freeze. So we'd find another place on my mountain, one where she could stay in her clothes. Or maybe we'd build a fire to keep warm.

Regardless, it would be somewhere out here, where we could be alone with just our wolves and nature.

She eventually stood, stretching in a similar manner to me. Then she followed me down the path at a much slower pace, neither of us wanting to leave the outdoors behind. Our wolves craved the fresh air. It was something I'd accidentally kept from her for too long.

Once we were by our clothes, I shifted back into my human form and smiled down at her. "I think we should do this every night."

She panted in agreement, then sat to observe me as I drew on my jeans.

"You're going to have to shift back," I teased her.

She cocked her head to the side, making an adorable expression of confusion.

"I know you can understand me, kitten."

She growled as if to remind me of her wolf status.

I smirked. "Still a kitten to me, baby."

With a determined noise, she initiated the shift on her own, causing my heart to swell with pride. It seemed taunting her—

My senses piqued, cutting off my thoughts and scattering my focus to our surroundings. Something didn't smell right. I sniffed, sensing the cause. "Stop," I demanded, referring to her transformation back to human form.

But of course, she couldn't halt the shift; she was too

young and inexperienced. All it would do was hurt her more.

I swallowed the growl building in my chest, not able to use it on her. Not when I knew it would only worsen our situation.

We'd have to do this another way.

"Hurry up," I whispered, earning me a snort.

She hadn't picked up on the approaching danger yet. Given her mid-change status, I could understand. I quickly laced up my shoes, my attention drifting to every corner.

They're surrounding us, I realized, picking up on the subtle traces in the wind. *Seven. No, eight.*

"As soon as you're done, I need you to run," I said in as low a voice as I could. "Grab your sweater and shoes and go."

She was almost back with me, enough for me to see the confusion etched into her features.

But I couldn't focus on her.

Not right now.

Not with the approaching males.

"Ander—"

"Shh." My wolf form heard better than my human one, but I could still *hear* their boots crushing into the snow. The subtle brush of fabric and fur. Some were on two legs, others on four.

I rolled my neck, preparing for a fight. There was only one reason they would surround me—to take me down as a unit.

Because Enzo wasn't strong enough on his own.

Katriana threw on her sweater, then tripped as she went to grab her boots.

I caught her elbow, prepared to steady her when a crack pierced the air.

I barely registered her scream, my stomach suddenly on fire as I fell to my knees in surprise.

Nine, I thought numbly. *There were nine.*

One of them had stayed back with a sniper rifle.

Smart play, I acknowledged, blinking in surprise at the blood pouring from my abdomen.

It all happened so quickly, yet I processed each move in slow motion. The way Katriana fell to my side, her palm pressing to my skin. My sharp inhale that hurt far more than it should. A curse on the wind. Growls. The quickening of steps over the snow.

I shook my head, trying to clear it.

Katriana needed to run. To get out of here. To call for Elias.

Then I felt her fingers on my wrist, lifting my hand and pressing the button I showed her only hours below. "Work, dammit, work!"

I blinked down, confused as the screens flew upward.

"Contact Elias," she demanded. "Now, Ander!"

No. The screens weren't the way to alert my Second. Nor did I want the idiots approaching us to have access to them.

I closed them with a trained tilt of my wrist, then brushed my thumb along the hidden panel at the side of my band. A subtle buzz told me the alarm had been sent. It was up to Elias to respond.

And I didn't care to rely on others.

"Put your shoes on," I said. "*Run.*" I couldn't fight with her here. I needed her safe. Back at headquarters.

But it was too late.

One moment, we were alone.

And the next, there were eight X-Clan shifters forming a ring around us.

With Enzo and Artur at the helm, their expressions victorious.

"Well, well. It seems I'll get to watch your downfall after all," Artur mused. "And I think we'll start by taking your pretty little mate."

CHAPTER TWENTY-NINE

KAT

RUN! some part of me shouted. But I couldn't. My legs refused to move. My exhale frosted in the air before me. My blood froze in my veins.

Eight males. All with weapons.

My lone protector shot.

And I stood in the snow in nothing but a sweater.

Even if I could run, I stood no chance. These males were stronger and faster, and I suspected they wanted to chase me. The two in wolf form would be on top of me in a few steps, likely wounding me on the way down.

No. Fleeing wouldn't work at all.

I only had one option here—to fight. But I needed to be smart about it, to play my cards right. And pray like hell that Ander recovered from his bullet wound.

He'd told me wolves were hard to kill, and I assumed they

healed faster than humans. The question was, how much faster?

"Try," he said, replying to Artur's threat. It came out harsh, his palm pressed to the wound on his abdomen as he remained steady on his knees. The heat of his body poured across my exposed legs, thawing me from my frozen state.

Enzo cocked a gun and aimed at Ander's head. "Oh, we'll more than try."

Ander's lips curled into a taunting grin. "Pull that trigger and you'll never be Sector Alpha."

"He's not the one who wants the position," Artur said, placing his hand over Enzo's gun. "I will be challenging you. After we finish breaking your Omega." He glanced at Enzo. "Don't shoot him in the head. I need him alive and alert enough to watch. But if he tries to fight, shoot him in the legs or the groin."

Enzo's lips curled. "Gladly."

Ander's jaw ticked. "I never took you for a coward, Artur. Eight-on-one is hardly a way to prove you possess the power to rule."

"We'll see how you feel after I finish with your little mate, hmm?" His cold black eyes focused on me, energy growing around him as he held my stare, demanding I submit.

He'd done this to me at the party as well, tested my backbone and mettle with a few subtle advances.

I refused to kneel for him.

But I could give him an inkling of my fear to lull him into a sense of superiority.

If there was one thing I knew about men, it was their frequent habit of underestimating my size and knowledge. He had a gun strapped to his hip—one I knew how to use, thanks to my mother—and a knife in his boot, if the way his jeans fit around his ankles was any indication.

His buddies in human form were all similarly dressed.

If I could steal even one of their guns, I'd be in a much better position.

"Touch her, and I'll kill you." Ander uttered the words in a low tone, his body vibrating with intensity beside mine. He certainly wasn't acting like a man who'd just been shot.

"Oh, I plan to do a lot more than touch her," Artur said, taking a step toward me. "I'm going to claim her as mine. Just as soon as I deal with that child of yours growing inside her."

My blood ran cold all over again.

"No," I snarled, the word falling from my lips on instinct alone. I curved a protective hand over my belly and stared the Alpha down. "Fuck off."

His eyebrows rose as some of the other males chuckled. "My, but you are a feisty one. No wonder Ander took a liking to you." He shifted his gaze to Enzo. "I'm going to enjoy fucking that disobedience right out of her."

Enzo nodded, leering at me while still pointing his gun at Ander. "Well, you know how broken Omegas can be after the loss of a child. It'll be easy to mold her into the proper version from there."

Artur smiled. "Yes."

Ander lunged, only to be tackled from behind by two males and a wolf, another crack going through the air that made him howl in pain. Enzo clocked him across the face, and a brawl began, painting the ground in blood.

Shit! I hadn't expected him to do that. I needed to think quickly, to use the distraction to—

Hands around my neck caused me to shriek, but the sound didn't leave as the palm cut off my airway. A hard body hit my back, another at my front, growls vibrating me on all sides.

Not vicious growls.

But the mating call.

Oh God, no...

My body began to warm, my wolf cowering in a corner as slick began to permeate the air.

No!

I refused to let them do this to me. *Think, dammit, think!* I'd been able to fight Ander in the beginning. I could certainly thwart these monsters now.

Oh, but they were growling far more aggressively. He hadn't made that deep a sound, my body reacting to him regardless of the mating instinct.

"Katriana!" he called out, something broken in his voice.

But I couldn't see him.

Couldn't think beyond that *growl*.

Stop, stop, stop!

"Should have claimed your mate," someone said, the voice penetrating the cloud of confusion rioting through my mind. "Then she wouldn't be begging for a new Alpha to fuck her raw."

Lips on my neck. Lips that didn't belong.

A growl that was too deep. *Not Ander.*

Warmth pressed against my lower belly, my sweater gone.

Hot male.

Needy male.

Not the right male.

More growls—one I recognized. I reached for *him*, needing *him*.

"We're going to take good care of her for you, Ander. Don't worry. She'll come, even while we make her bleed inside."

Snarls filled the air.

A pained howl.

My own joining the chorus.

Because I didn't want this. I knew, deep down, none of this was right. Ander had warned me that Omegas couldn't resist the call of an Alpha, and now I knew what he meant. I felt myself falling to all fours, my body resembling a puppet on a string while my mind rebelled every step of the way.

This wasn't right.

This wasn't my fate.

This wasn't how I chose to survive.

Submitting to Ander came naturally. This—the male lining up behind me—wasn't natural at all.

He thrust forward and I rolled, my back hitting the icy ground. "No!" I screamed, scrambling as far away from the intoxicating cloud as I could until my back hit the leg of another male.

They had me surrounded.

They were laughing.

Chuckling.

Enjoying my torment.

Growing excited by the second.

I registered them all in one sweep of my gaze, my mind focusing just enough to take in the scene of a bloody Ander being held by four men. The others all prowling toward me. Two of them without pants.

Enzo and Artur.

They appeared part amused, part crazed, their erections telling me exactly what they had in mind as more growls graced the air. None of them right. None of them *mine*.

These animals wanted to *hurt* me. Kill *my* child.

Not happening.

Not with me lying down to take it.

They could take their damn growls and shove them up their asses.

My wolf had given up, her need to submit keeping me on my knees. But the human in me dominated now. The one who had put up with far too much shit over the years to allow this to happen.

I wasn't an ordinary Omega, but a made one.

And I would die before I let them touch the life growing inside me.

The hairs along my arms danced, my soul coming to life beneath my skin. "I will not submit," I hissed, forcing myself into a crouch, prepared to fight until my last breath. "You'll have to kill me first."

Enzo stroked his cock lazily, his gaze gleaming. "Oh, breaking you is going to be a true delight, little red."

Artur didn't appear nearly as amused, his growl intensifying.

I smiled. "What's the problem, Alpha?" I taunted, cocking my head. "Having performance issues?" I studied him, watching as the four approached from all angles. "It certainly says a lot that you have to growl to get your girl in the mood. All Ander has to do is look at me to soak my thighs."

Artur snarled. "Grab her and hold her down. If it's a dry fuck she wants, it's a dry fuck she'll get." His grin was positively evil. "Besides, I always did favor blood as a lubricant."

I jumped to the side as his two goons made a grab for me. Then I swept a leg out beneath the one in a manner he

225

wasn't expecting. His gun went flying and I dove for it.

Only to find an arm wrapped tightly around my waist.

Fuck! I squirmed, trying to kick him off me, but his grip only strengthened.

And then Artur was in my face, his fist connecting with my jaw so harshly I saw stars.

Ander made a noise that reminded me of murder, drawing me back to the surroundings a few aching seconds later.

Artur caught my chin, squeezing so hard I swore I heard the bone crack. "I'm going to fuck every hole, over and over again, then bite you right on your fucking pussy to claim you as mine. And that'll just be an appetizer for our future together. Everyone in this fucking sector is dying for Omega cunt, and I'm a sharing sort of man. Which is why I invited Enzo to help me break you."

His words should have provoked fear in my heart.

But all I could do was laugh humorously.

"What kind of Alpha shares?" I asked.

That earned me another punch to the jaw.

This time I tasted blood.

And spit it out into his face.

He grabbed me by the throat, squeezing until black dots sprouted through my vision. "I'm going to fucking *own* you, you little cunt."

No, I thought. *No. Because I'm not yours to own.*

My back hit the snow again, a heavy body collapsing over mine as hands gripped my shoulders from above to hold me down. I struggled to comprehend who was where, my consciousness wavering.

Until a palm on my belly began to press down at the same time my thighs were spread.

Fire licked up my spine, going directly to my brain and blasting me back into reality.

Artur studied his hand in maniacal fascination while positioning himself between my thighs. His brown-haired buddy was above my head, watching with a keen smile.

Neither focused on my face.

Neither paying any attention to my free hands. Holding my shoulders down only kept my torso immobile. Not my arms.

And a gun positioned at the hip right next to my head.

I didn't think. I reacted, reaching for the pistol and aiming it at the monster between my thighs.

Two rounds into his chest sent him flying backward, while the guy above me startled too slowly to stop me from sending a bullet directly upward into his head.

Shouts rang out around me, but my predator drive had initiated.

I aimed.

I fired.

I didn't think twice.

Until my gun ran out of bullets.

Then I pounced on one of my victims, grabbing a blade, and began slicing my way through the assholes on the ground while chaos unfolded around me.

Blood.

Guts.

Brains.

I reveled in the violence. Screaming obscenities. Swearing murder. Living in a sea of carnage.

I had Artur's hair in my fist, my blade working through his neck, sawing savagely at his flesh. Ander said it took a lot to kill a wolf, that it required the heart to stop beating for too long a time.

Well, let's see you survive this.

I wanted Artur *dead.*

Gone.

Destroyed!

He tried to take my child from me.

He tried to *rape* me.

He hurt my mate.

My family.

Me.

No more. I wanted his death, his blood, his life, in my fucking hands. And I snarled in triumph as I finished the task, throwing his head into the snow with a growl that came from my wounded wolf.

Someone said my name.

I ignored it, moving on to my next victim—the one who held me down and watched with such morbid fascination. Well, he didn't seem all that excited now, not with my dagger digging into his fucking throat.

A macabre energy settled over me, driving my actions, calming my spirit, as he, too, lost his head.

But as I moved on to victim number three, I found myself wrapped up in sturdy arms.

I snarled.

Fought.

Lashed out.

Yet my new aggressor stole the blade from my fingertips and relocated my hand to his head. I tugged at his hair and screamed, angry and consumed with the need for vengeance. A warm vibration was the only reply, one that gave me pause.

I liked that sound.

Soothing.

Purr-like.

Mine.

I pressed my face into the familiar scent surrounding me, licked the skin beneath my mouth, and trailed my lips upward to a masculine throat. Mmm, this one I didn't want to slice. Instead, I tasted him, luxuriating in the familiar male.

My male.

I nibbled him. Nuzzled him. Climbed him. Wrapped my arms around him. Kissed him.

He growled into my mouth, his fingers threading through my hair as he pressed me against something spiny. *Tree trunk*, some part of my mind registered. *Yes, yes.*

I clawed at him.

Both of us covered in blood, ice, and unmentionable things. But I didn't care. "Mine," I breathed, arching into him. "Mine. Mine."

"Yours," he agreed, pressing his jean-clad hips into the tender space between my thighs.

I drew my hands downward, wanting to remove the barrier, when new scents tickled my nose. My arms tightened around him, my eyes scouring for the intrusion.

"Jesus fucking Christ," a male voice breathed.

Elias.

I blinked. *What happened?*

No, I knew what happened.

I killed a lot of wolves.

But how?

Wait… Ander! I immediately ran my hands over him for a different reason, searching for his wounds, terror gripping me by the throat. "Are you okay?"

He chuckled against my throat, nipping my pulse. "Yeah, baby. I'll heal."

"It's not funny!" I shrieked, trying to shove him back enough to look at his abdomen where he'd been shot.

And, oh my God, there were more wounds.

At least three that I could see just from my vantage point.

"Why the hell are you standing?" I demanded, trying to pull myself from his arms. "You need a doctor. We need Riley!"

"I'm fine," he replied, wrapping his palm around the back of my neck. "Look at me." I couldn't. I was too busy trying to see the full extent of the damage. He tightened his grip. "Katriana. Look at me."

The demanding growl in his tone had my gaze flying upward.

Smoldering gold irises held mine, reminding me of the sun on a hot day.

"I'm fine," he promised, then pressed his bulge against my sensitive folds. "If I wasn't, I wouldn't be ready to fuck you right now."

"Oh." I licked my lips. "But they shot you."

"Yeah, and it fucking hurt. But I told you, wolves are hard to kill. Especially one as powerful as me. Why do you think he needed four Alphas to hold me down?"

"I hate to break this up, but what the fuck?" Elias demanded, coming to stand beside us. "Why does it look like someone took a butter knife to Artur's throat?"

"Katriana beheaded him," Ander replied without breaking my gaze. "And it was one of the most beautiful acts of violence I've ever witnessed."

"And the others?" Elias asked.

Ander released my neck to lightly stroke his knuckles across my aching jaw. "A violent collaboration between me, Katriana, and some unknown sniper up in the hills."

"That'd be me," a deep voice announced with a grunt. I whipped my gaze toward the voice just in time to see a redheaded Alpha drop another male to the ground. "Well, once I took this asshole down, anyway." He kicked the body toward Ander, then dropped a rifle next to him. "He was using that to help from a distance. I decided to take over after I broke his neck."

I blinked at him.

His voice was familiar. He'd been at the party the other night asking about courtship. Not the one who wanted to court me, but the other Omegas.

"Samuel," Ander said, his surprise evident in his tone and his expression. "You shot Enzo."

"I did," he admitted. "And Darren, too." He kicked the guy at his feet. "But this idiot only has a broken neck. Figured I might need him as a witness to corroborate my story." He lifted a shoulder. "Although, once you realize my relation to the girl, that might be a moot point."

That stirred a frown from both me and Ander.

But it was Elias who spoke. "What relation?"

Samuel looked around us to where Ander's Second stood in the snow with his arms crossed, eyes narrowed. "Well, she's my niece."

CHAPTER THIRTY

ANDER

"YOUR *WHAT?*" I demanded, shock rippling inside me.

"My niece," he replied calmly. "She's my sister's daughter."

Katriana froze in my arms, her lips hanging open.

"And you're just telling me this now?" I snapped.

"I didn't realize it until the other night, as that was my first time seeing your intended mate. But I recognized her immediately. And then you were a little busy after that point." He slid his hands into his pockets. "I did, however, file a report with Ceres. He's running blood samples to prove what I already know. But she's definitely Marianna's daughter."

"That's my mother's name," she whispered.

"I didn't know you had a sister," Elias said, echoing my thoughts. "Was she a Beta?"

"No." And I knew before he continued exactly what kind

of wolf his sister was; the truth lurked in his eyes. "She was an Omega."

"You hid an Omega from the council." I shifted my hold on Katriana, her body beginning to shake against mine. "She needs a jacket."

Elias handed me his before I even finished, and I wrapped it around her shoulders before helping her to her feet. Our clothes were ruined, her boots somewhere beneath the carnage.

"We should continue this discussion somewhere warmer," I said, glancing around the scene. Several other wolves had arrived with Elias, all of them standing at attention with stoic expressions.

I ran my fingers through my hair, blowing out a breath.

They needed me to go into Alpha mode, to provide an explanation, deliver an edict, *something*, to help them feel secure about the bloodbath on the ground.

The entire sector was probably aware by now of what happened out here as well.

Great. Nothing like starting a day in style, covered in blood and bullet wounds. My fucking stomach cramped from the necessary healing. My thigh throbbed from the cheap shot Enzo had hit me with during my initial attack. My heart pounded for my intended mate and what she almost went through. And my wolf wanted to rage through the massacre site to guarantee that no one lived.

"My mother was a wolf?" Katriana whispered, staring at Samuel. "Not my father?"

"Your father was human," he replied. "Your mother had intended to try to mate him, actually. Except he didn't survive the trip to Andorra."

"The trip?" I repeated.

"Marianna was never part of Andorra Sector. She lived on her own after the Infected outbreak, choosing human company over wolves. When she fell in love, she reached out to me about joining us here, with the hope that you would allow her to turn her intended into an X-Clan Wolf. Only, he died before she had the chance."

Meaning he wasn't hiding an Omega at all, just

withholding details about his sister's status. "And when she arrived?"

"I created suppressants in the lab to help her mask her scent," he admitted. As one of my more accomplished researchers, that task wouldn't have been difficult for him. And it wasn't like I patrolled the whereabouts of my wolves in the mountains. "I knew what would happen to her and her child, should they be discovered. Someone would have forced the mating bond on Marianna, and—"

"Her child would have likely been killed by the claiming Alpha," I finished for him. Because the baby was the product of an Omega with another male. A *human* male. The insult alone would warrant the child's death.

He dipped his chin in acknowledgment. "I'll accept the punishment for hiding her, but I will never apologize for it."

Elias and I shared a long look. He knew I couldn't deliver a verdict on this information now. Not after everything that'd gone down today. There were too many other pressing matters.

"How is that possible?" Katriana asked, drawing my attention back to my first priority—warming up my shivering mate. "Omegas require an Alpha to mate, right?"

"Yes, Omegas require an Alpha for the mating bond. And they need a rutting Alpha to help them through estrus, or the process is quite painful," I explained softly. "But an Omega can technically procreate with others, the child is just much less likely to survive."

"And humans can be predisposed to our genetic markers," Samuel added. "Which, from what your mother told me, your father possessed all the inclinations of an Alpha. Had he been provided the X-Clan serum, he would have likely turned into an Alpha wolf."

Katriana shook her head, her denial palpable. "But my mom died. This can't be right."

"Your mother was shot in the head by one of the idiot humans in that cave," Samuel said softly. "She might have survived it had she not suppressed her wolf nature all those years. But she couldn't risk being caught in animal form."

"Suppressing our wolves makes us inherently weaker," I

agreed, kissing the top of her head. "It makes sense."

"Wh-why didn't she tell me any of this?" she whispered, more to herself than to us, but Samuel replied anyway.

"I can't answer that for her. But I do know you meant the world to her. She risked everything to remain here because she knew you'd be safest in Andorra."

"How was I safe here?" she demanded. "I lived in a cave where I nearly starved to death countless times. I was kidnapped by wolves. Forcibly changed. Impregnated. Almost fucking raped by these assholes. And now I'm covered in blood, freezing, and you're calling me *safe*?" She started to laugh. Only, the laughs turned into sobs, and I pulled her into my arms to console her.

"We'll discuss this more later," I said, looking pointedly at Samuel. "I expect you to be waiting in my office."

He agreed with a silent nod, his face giving nothing away.

"What do you want to do about the bodies?" Elias asked me, gesturing to the field.

I considered my options, noting the two breathing males. One was Darren—who apparently had taken up a hobby of sniping from the trees.

The other was Walton, a newbie Alpha appointee to the council.

Allowing them to live would actually be a fate worse than death. They'd have nowhere to run, forced to exist as rogues.

Fitting, in my opinion.

"One minute," I said, responding to Elias's hanging question regarding the bodies.

Kissing Katriana on the temple, I pulled her into my side as I moved through the field in search of the heads I needed.

Enzo's was still attached to his body.

Artur's, not so much.

"Will you be okay if I release you for a minute, kitten?" I asked softly. She was sniffling, but not really crying, her shock seeming to have melted into a colder emotion as she stared down at Artur's remains.

Katriana nodded mutely, then watched as I pulled a knife off one of the corpses and sawed through Enzo's neck in the same way she had done to Artur.

When I finished, I grabbed him by the hair and went to retrieve his buddy's head. Only, it wasn't where I'd spied it a few minutes ago. Because Katriana had picked it up.

She met my gaze with a determined one of her own. "Tell me I get to burn it."

Hmm, this side of her I liked a hell of a lot more than the broken parts. My lips curled in approval. "We can light the entire field on fire, if you want."

"Not the field. Just the bodies."

I nodded. "Just the bodies." My gaze shifted to my Second, his expression telling me he already knew what I wanted.

"You heard your Alpha," he said, addressing the still-silent army he'd brought with him. "Pick up the remains and carry them to the center square. Time for a barbecue."

"But leave Darren and Walton. They're hereby excommunicated and can figure out how to survive on their own." I spit on their remains. "And you know what? Tonic can share their fate. Toss him out on his ass; let him help his friends." As he hadn't been part of this merry little gathering, I assumed he was still in lockup.

"Consider it done," Elias replied.

"Good." I started toward the dome with Katriana by my side.

She said nothing of the snow beneath our feet.

She didn't even shiver.

I felt her determination growing with every step, her anger fueling her movements. My feisty female had finally returned. I only wished it'd been under better circumstances.

A guard met us at the entryway, the male bowed so low I thought he might be kissing the snow.

He must have sensed our aggression.

The violence.

The anger.

The very real need to put my people in their place to keep this from ever happening again.

My fury grew with every step, fueled by Katriana's own emotion.

They'd threatened our child. Her body. My claim. My

leadership. And I could not allow that to go without some sort of consequence.

Andorra Sector would bow before their Alpha. They would beg me to remain. They would fucking respect my position.

A crowd had gathered in the square, Elias having sent out an announcement of an emergency sector meeting.

Many of the wolves gasped upon my arrival, noting the dried blood coating my form and Katriana's exposed legs.

We looked like we'd survived hell.

I still had two wounds healing in my torso.

Katriana's hair was a nest atop her head.

And we both carried the heads of the two males responsible.

I threw mine into the center of the square, a small river flowing to our left drowning out the sound of Enzo's skull hitting the cobblestone. Katriana threw Artur's remains down with a little more force, his face bouncing off the ground upon impact and causing several bystanders to jump back.

"Is there anyone else?" I demanded, ensuring my voice carried to the crowd, echoing off the surrounding residential buildings. They were five or six stories tall, forming a reasonable sound chamber for a demonstration such as this one.

Only the subtle flow of streaming water along the side of the square answered me.

Then the other bodies began to arrive.

One by one, Elias's men dumped the remains into a pile worthy of a bonfire.

I didn't light it. Not yet. Because I wanted to make sure no one else wanted to join it first.

I stared everyone down around us, not missing a single set of eyes as I forced the crowd to their knees beneath a wave of power radiating from my chest on a deep, guttural sound. It was the kind of growl that demanded submission from everyone, regardless of rank. "This is *my* sector," I said, furious that anyone had even considered challenging me in such a way. "If you don't want to fall to my command, speak now and leave."

More silence.

More kneeling.

Even Elias fell beneath the wave of my energy. Either as a sign of respect or because I was truly emitting that much dominance. Perhaps a mixture of both.

It didn't matter.

I craved obedience. Needed the acknowledgment of my position at the top. Required their *respect*.

I growled again for emphasis, my fury unleashing in a whip across the crowd. My people *dared* to try to take my future heir. My intended mate. My position.

How dare they question my rule, my wolf snarled. *After everything I've given.*

Whimpers echoed in the crowd, the sound music to my ears.

Until I heard it from the one female I never wanted to hear whine outside of the bedroom.

My intended mate.

Katriana had fallen to her knees beneath my outburst of dominance, her shoulders shaking as she lowered herself until her forehead hit the ground.

No, my wolf snarled. That was not the right position. Not for my mate.

I squatted before her, drawing my fingers into her dark red strands, then gently pulled upward. "No, Katriana," I whispered, forcing her tear-filled gaze to meet mine. "You never bow to me here." In the bedroom, yes. In front of the sector, no. "Stand up, sweetheart. Please."

She blinked, her throat working to swallow.

I gave her a subtle tug, helping to draw her upright and into my arms while everyone else remained in a subservient position around us.

"You're my mate," I told her, cupping her cheek. "Your position is by my side."

Her lips parted, and I knew what she was thinking. Could see it in her gaze. *Doubt.*

I reacted before she could even speak the words, using my hold in her hair to yank her head to the side, and sank my teeth into her neck.

Claiming her.

Marking her as mine for *everyone* to see.

But most importantly, for her to feel.

She gasped against me, her hands clutching my shoulders as our link snapped into place, finalizing our bond.

Like an arrow from my heart to hers, lacing us together for life. Branding her soul with my name, and mine with hers.

Never had I felt more complete.

More alive.

More fulfilled.

And as her blood touched my tongue, ambrosia filled me inside.

My mate.

My Katriana.

My life.

Mine.

CHAPTER THIRTY-ONE

KAT

Tears poured from my eyes, not of pain but of joy.

Ander Cain had finally claimed me.

Marked me as his.

In front of the entire damn sector.

And now all I wanted was to drag him back to his room and reward him properly with my very willing body.

He finally released me on a growl, only I didn't give him a chance to speak before I yanked his head down to claim his mouth. I tasted my blood, and a violent part of me desired to sample his essence as well.

So I bit down hard on his lower lip, causing him to snarl against me.

And then he groaned as I sucked on the wound, taking him into my mouth and swallowing his decadent blood.

"Fuck," he breathed, lifting me with one palm against my

ass. I wrapped my legs around him, needing him. *Now.*

The bonfire could wait.

Hell, they could burn the damn bodies without me.

All I wanted—*required*—was my mate to claim me in every way. "Take me," I demanded. "*Brand* me."

A wall hit my back.

Some side of a building I hadn't even noticed. Nor had I felt him walking. But he'd moved us out of the courtyard and into an alleyway, hiding me in some nook.

They were all still there. I *felt* their presence, their awe, their overwhelming curiosity in watching an Alpha rut his Omega.

It should have bothered me. I should have demanded privacy.

Oh, I should have done a lot of things.

Said other things.

Screamed.

Fought.

Mmm, no. This was where I needed to be, with my mate.

I ripped the button from his jeans.

Tore down the zipper.

And rubbed my slick all over his cock.

"You're fucking perfect," Ander marveled, slamming into me in a harsh thrust. "Fucking everything I could have ever dreamed of."

"Harder," I demanded, digging my heels into his firm ass. "Make me yours, Ander Cain."

We were filthy.

Murderous.

Angry.

Covered in the remains of our enemies.

Animals.

Mates.

And I wanted every fucking inch of him inside me, drilling me until I screamed.

His lips crashed into mine, our essences mingling in our mouths as his tongue fought for dominance. I fought back, making him work for it, needing him to force my submission in the best way.

He wanted me at his side.

I wanted to be there.

But in this, I required his protection, his strength, his absolute supremacy. He gave me everything I wanted, his hands on my hips, holding me harshly as he fucked me into oblivion. I bit him. He bit me. I licked him. He licked me. I screamed. He growled. I raked my nails down his back, and he slammed me harder into the wall.

Violent.

Punishing.

Amazing.

I panted, crying out, and hugged him to me with a ferocity no one stood a chance at breaking. Not even him.

"You're mine," I whispered, awed, arching against him. "My Alpha."

"My Omega."

"My mate."

"My love," he replied reverently, his lips trailing down my neck to the place he'd bitten me to lap at the wound. "I love you, Katriana Cardona."

Five words.

Sealing my heart to the fate I'd finally accepted.

"I love you, too, Ander Cain," I said, taking his mouth once more with my own as his pace slowed to a different kind of fucking.

Soothing.

Soft.

Worshiping.

My eyes began to water, my heart beating rapidly in my chest. What had begun as an intense need to claim had morphed into an emotional dance underlined in intimacy, our souls joining in matrimony while our bodies moved as one.

This was love.

Our wolves marrying each other for life.

No one would ever be able to come between us.

And we would forever work as a team, to raise our child, to lead, to be whoever we needed to be—together.

Ander licked a path to my ear, his breath sending a shiver down my spine. "You're mine, Katriana." His knot exploded out of him, affixing itself to my inner channel as he spilled deep inside me on a soft groan meant for my ears alone.

"And you're mine," I returned, climaxing around him and shuddering in rapture.

My body warmed all over, the snow falling around us hardly registering. It wasn't until he shifted that I felt the scrapes against my back from the building—where he'd made me bleed, just like I requested.

Only, it wasn't painful.

Just us.

Our way of being together.

Everything in this world happened for a reason, and I now understood my fate. My reason for being.

I was a part wolf turned whole, my existence tied to a male who needed me in his world to help him lead. Not to submit. Not to crawl at his feet. But to function as a partner in my own unique way.

"I want to learn more about your world," I whispered. "How everything works."

"You want to help me survive," he surmised.

I nodded. "Just as you've helped me."

He brushed his lips against mine. "You already have, more than you know." He kissed me again, slower now, his knot still pulsing inside me. "You give me purpose, Katriana. I didn't realize it was missing until I met you."

His tongue slid into my mouth, dancing lazily with mine while our bodies came down from our high, his knot slowly releasing me.

Ander dipped his head to my neck, nuzzling his mark. "Does it hurt?"

I shook my head. "Not as badly as you refusing to claim me."

He flinched. "I should have bitten you the day I first met you. I knew immediately that you were mine. It was why I took you to my den."

"I'm glad you didn't," I admitted, drawing my palms up and down his back while he held me effortlessly against the wall. "It meant more to me now. Today. Like a reward for everything we've been through. Fate's way of ensuring we both deserved it." It sounded ridiculous, but the gleam in his gaze told me he understood.

"Shall we celebrate with a bonfire?" he asked softly, dropping his forehead to mine.

"Watch our enemies burn?" Because they were *our* enemies, not just his. Anyone who threatened my mate threatened me. Forever and always. We were a team.

He nodded. "Yes."

Somehow I knew his answer wasn't just in response to my question but also to my thoughts. He couldn't exactly read my mind, just as I couldn't read his. Yet I *felt* him inside me. His emotions vibrating along some invisible string that tied our hearts together to beat in synchronization. It was the most fulfilling sensation, sensing his adoration and protective energy. His dominance. His innate need to worship me. His warmth.

I nuzzled into him on a sigh, content. "Anywhere you go, I will go."

"You can run every now and then," he replied, smiling against my hair before kissing the top of my head. "I wouldn't mind chasing you. Just be prepared for the consequences."

"Consequences like you fucking me?"

"Absolutely," he replied, pulling out of me and steadying me on my feet before drawing up his zipper. As I'd popped off the button, it was the best he could do. Which left him in a pair of sexy jeans slung low on his hips. No shoes. If his feet were cold, he didn't comment. I suspected his wolf kept him regulated.

He laced our fingers together and drew my hand up to his lips, pressing a kiss to my wrist. "Bonfire or shower?"

"Bonfire," I said. "I need to watch the bastards burn."

He grinned, approval radiating from him. "Me, too."

"But after, we can shower. Maybe you can finally show me how to properly use it."

His eyebrow lifted. "You don't know how to work the shower?"

"Have you not noticed all the puddles after I spend time in your bathroom?"

"I thought you were just being a brat."

I snorted. "Yeah, no. Your shower and I are not friends. I

grew up using lakes, remember?"

He studied me for a long moment, then threw his head back and laughed, the sound one I didn't usually hear from him. So full of joy and wonder and outright amusement. "Oh, Katriana. The life we're going to share together."

He lifted me up into his arms, carrying me like the grooms carried their brides in those magazines my mother had kept.

My heart gave a pang at the memory.

She was a wolf.

But I never knew.

It made me wonder what other secrets she had kept and if I would ever find them. Maybe I wasn't meant to know.

Or maybe, this was the fate she'd always intended for me.

Mated to an Alpha male. Protected. In love. And finally creating a proper family of my own.

Not a bad life.

No, I thought as Elias held a torch to the pile of corpses. *No, I'd even go as far as to call this life an amazing one.*

I relaxed against Ander.

Smiling.

While I watched the remains of our enemies go up in flames.

Long live Andorra Sector, I mused. *And remember, if you fuck with me or my mate, we'll destroy you. The end.*

EPILOGUE

ANDER

One Year Later

"HOW ARE THINGS IN SHADOWLANDS SECTOR?" I asked, relaxing into my home office chair.

Katriana had helped me turn one of the many unused bedrooms into a meeting space that served me better than our dining room table had. I hadn't really needed one before, but her sexual needs during her second and third trimester had made leaving my penthouse almost impossible.

She was better now that our son had been born. But I rather liked keeping them close, so I chose to remain here.

Dušan smiled. "Things have improved since I handled the serum issue."

Yes, it'd taken him some time to sort all that out. I didn't ask for the specifics but understood they involved his new mate and the Ash Wolves' susceptibility to the virus that created the Infected.

It was the primary genetic difference between us—X-Clan Wolves weren't impacted by the Infected at all. But Ash Wolves could contract the disease, which created a rather lethal hybrid. Hence the reason we'd put certain measures in place to protect the Ash Wolves who had mated members of Andorra Sector. It'd been part of Dušan's requirements. Not that we needed it. We would have protected the females anyway.

"I'm glad that's been taken care of," I replied, referring to the serum issue. "I'm hoping that means another trade deal is in our future."

"That's exactly why I called," he drawled. "Well, that, and to ask what the hell is going on up in Winter Sector."

I grunted. "That's a fucking mess, is what it is." My father called the other day to give me a rundown of the situation.

"We're hearing rumors about a revolution," Dušan said, leaning against a tree and running his fingers through his dark hair. "Seems the infamous Queen of Mirrors has her hands full."

"Doesn't she always?" I asked. Winter Sector up in the Arctic Circle was a notorious Beta circle with only one Alpha—a female—and her three Omega male consorts. She cruelly refused to mate any of them, forcing them all to vie for her attention.

Such a vile, harsh woman.

Many hated her, mostly because she held on to the prized male Omegas, which were even rarer than Omega females in our world. Granted, Alpha females were just as rare. Hence her supposed royal status.

"I'm rooting for Norse Sector to take them down," the Shadowlands Sector Alpha admitted. "Be sure to pass the message along to your father."

"Or you could tell him yourself since apparently you've opened trade deals with him, too," I suggested.

The Alpha's lips quirked. "So he did tell you about that."

"As you already noted, he is my father," I replied, matching his amusement. "One of these days, you'll stop trying to play games with me."

Dušan smirked. "Yeah, maybe. But not any day soon."

"Of course not. That'd be boring." I cocked a brow. "Now tell me what you want to trade."

All traces of joking disappeared into his serious mask as we dove into a discussion on what his sector needed and what he was willing to offer in return. I gave nothing away, listening to his terms and noting what I liked and disliked about each one. When he finished, I nodded. "I'll take it to my council and be in touch."

He blew out a breath, a glimmer of respect shining in his gaze. "Good. I like that about you, Cain. You strive for diplomacy in a world where dictators can easily rule."

"Case in point, Winter Sector," I drawled.

"Exactly."

"I'll be in touch soon," I promised, sensing movement in the doorway.

Dušan signed off in his usual fashion without a goodbye just as my mate walked in with our son glued to her hip. He had his fingers wrapped around her red hair, tugging in the way he seemed to favor.

Like father, like son.

I, too, enjoyed pulling my mate's hair.

Just in a slightly different fashion.

His growing mane of auburn hair glinted in the light, his gold irises looking around my office while his little nose twitched. He probably wondered what voice he'd overheard with his enhanced hearing and was scenting for anything out of place.

"Everything all right with Dušan?" Katriana asked, her face glowing with maternal warmth. She really did wear motherhood well. I couldn't wait to give her another baby. But I knew she wanted to wait, at least for a year or two.

Which meant being careful during her heat cycle.

Something I did not enjoy. And neither did she.

"Ander?" she prompted, giving me a knowing smile.

"Dušan and his people are fine," I replied. "I suspect he's found a way to combat the Infected, but he didn't confirm it. I hope for the safety of his sector that he has."

"Me, too," she murmured. "I had no idea Ash Wolves weren't immune."

"I had heard rumors, but our trade last year confirmed it when he told me to put security measures in place for the Omegas." I lifted a shoulder. "Hopefully, he'll pass on whatever he learned to our scientists so we can better protect his former wolves."

Katriana nodded. "Yes, I hope so, too." She nibbled her lower lip, considering me for a second. "Samuel called. He asked to come over later for dinner."

"Again?" The damn Alpha seemed to love my son as much as I did. I supposed he felt a familial obligation of sorts, what with being Katriana's estranged uncle.

She hadn't really gotten over her mother being a wolf and never mentioning it. I couldn't really blame her. Hell, I hadn't exactly forgiven Samuel for not telling *me* as his Sector Alpha. He claimed not to realize it until the Omega and Alpha gathering that night—which had been why he'd seconded my opinion on the courting. I'd thought he was interested in an Omega, but no. It'd been his niece he cared about.

What a fucked-up way of showing it.

"I know he's not your favorite person, but he's good with Quim," she murmured, kissing our son on the head. He cooed happily in response, adoring his mother's attention. "Isn't he, baby boy?" she asked him. "You love your Uncle Sammy, don't you?"

I smirked. "I really hope he calls him that when he learns to speak." Because Samuel would hate it.

"Oh, it's happening," she replied. "Trust me."

"Have I told you today how much I love you?"

"Hmm, only twice," she said, leaning against the door. "And you haven't tried to knot me in about six hours, so I may need some convincing soon."

My lips quirked up. "Yeah?" I pushed away from my desk to prowl toward her. "What about some convincing now?"

"Your son might have something to say about that."

"We'll give him a bottle and put him to bed."

"Yes, because that worked so well last time," she deadpanned.

I crowded her against the door, leaning in to kiss her, much to the annoyance of Quim—who let out a little growl of displeasure that had me chuckling. "Our little Alpha is already testing his father's limits." I bopped the little one on the nose, smiling at him. "Good luck, little wolf."

He tried to bite at my finger in response, another of those noises coming from him.

"So protective of your mother," I mused, proud. "You'll make a fine Alpha someday."

"And I'm going to be surrounded by testosterone," Katriana muttered.

"We could always try for a girl next time," I offered.

"Don't even think about it," she snapped, pointing her finger at me. "I am nowhere near ready. And you owe me at least a year of orgasms first."

I laughed outright. "Only a year?"

"I'd ask for a decade, but we both know you'll demand another baby before then."

"Damn right," I agreed, following her as she started down the hallway toward our room. I knew that walk. The sway of her hips. The intent of her scent. She was going to give me what I wanted, assuming our little Quim agreed to take a nap.

And he'd better.

Because as my mate had said, I owed her a year of orgasms.

No, I owed her so much more.

A life of pleasure. With a little bit of pain. And a whole world of happiness.

I watched in astute reverence as she laid our baby boy in his nest in the corner of our room, my heart filling with adoration for them both.

My existence was complete.

My world a work of perfection.

Quim quieted as Katriana hummed, her own version of a purr sending him into his dreams much like mine did to her.

But when she turned, I knew sleep was the last activity on her mind.

"Take me to bed, mate," she demanded.

I smiled, wrapping my hand around the back of her neck. "That sounded an awful lot like a command, Omega. What

249

should I do about that?"

"Remind me who my Alpha is?" she suggested, blinking innocently up at me.

"Mmm, that I can do," I replied, taking her mouth in a punishing kiss before pulling her dress up and over her head. "Now get on that mattress and spread your legs for me." She took a step back, but I snagged her by the waist, yanking her to me once more. "And, Katriana?"

She swallowed, her eyes taking on that dazed appearance I loved. "Yes?"

"You'd better be fucking wet for me," I said, nipping her lower lip. Then released her with a swat against her ass.

She crawled up onto the bed, then glanced demurely over her shoulder. "Ander?"

I arched a brow, inviting her to speak.

"I'm always wet for you," she said, smiling as I groaned.

My female.

Topping from the bottom.

Well, if that was the way she wanted to play, then that was exactly what we would do. Because I lived and breathed for this woman.

My mate.

My eternity.

My partner for life.

I removed my clothes, watching as she spread her legs just the way I asked, her slick coating her creamy thighs.

Mine, I thought, stepping toward her. *Forever mine.*

THE X-CLAN UNIVERSE CONTINUES WITH WINTER'S ARROW

True love is a myth.
A trick.
A way to subdue the heroine and take everything from her.

Winter Snow

My "true love" conspired with my stepmother to have me killed and stole my throne.

But they failed.

I've been in hiding and refining my vengeance. I'm no longer the damsel they mistook me for once upon a time. I'm coming for them. And my kingdom, too.

Who needs dwarves when you have wolves?
Who needs blades when you have arrows?

My name used to be Snow. Now they call me the Winter's Arrow. Because I'm here to destroy them all.

Kazek Flor

I'm not a prince but an Alpha. And I take what I want, when I want it. So when I found an Omega princess dying in the woods, I took her and made her mine.

I'll train her. Embolden her. Help her seek the vengeance she is owed. Then, together, we'll take down Winter Sector and the wicked Queen of Mirrors.

Run fast, little wolves.
Your former princess is about to rise with me by her side.
And we're thirsting for your blood.

Author's Note: This is a standalone Snow White retelling and based in the X-Clan Omegaverse universe.

X-CLAN: THE EXPERIMENT

Daciana

I'm an offering. A test. A pawn in an agreement I know little about.

Fly to Andorra Sector.
Allow them to experiment.
Mate an X-Clan Wolf Alpha.
Hope for the best.

Those are my orders. My fate. My current existence. There's nowhere to run, and the moon is a clock I can't ignore. One of these Alphas will claim me, assuming our genetics are a match. And if not, well, that's a fate worse than death.

Tick tock.
Make a choice.
Your future depends on it.

Elias

The pretty little blonde wolf has seen too much pain for her young years.

It makes me want to fix her.
To adore her.
To show her there can be good in this world.
But our future is wrapped up in an experiment.

Either she's compatible or she's not. The moon will determine our fate, or perhaps my inner wolf will decide it for us. Because with each passing moment, it becomes harder not to claim the female who I know in my heart is very much mine.

Run, run, little one.
And don't look back.
For if I catch you,
I just may bite.

Note: This is a standalone novella featuring characters from *Andorra Sector*, Book One of the X-Clan Series. It has Omegaverse elements and features a happily-ever-after ending.

ACKNOWLEDGMENTS

This entire idea wouldn't exist without Erin Bedford and the Zombie 2099 Project. I'm so thankful for being included and enjoyed working with the other authors in this collection. Who knew the apocalypse could be so entertaining?

As always, I owe my husband a debt of gratitude for all of his support and love and for ensuring I eat when on a deadline. Thank you for being a partner in life. I love you.

This book wouldn't have been possible without my alpha/beta team: Katie, Allison, Jean, and Diane. Thank you all so much for reading and helping me keep Ander in line.

Thank you, Bethany, for fixing all my commas. I still hate them and the rules dictating their placement. One of these days, I'll read the CMOS rules. Or maybe I'll leave that up to you. ;) Thank you for everything!

Louise & Diane: You both keep me afloat when I need it most. I can't thank you enough for all your help in the background and for running my world while I leave it to play with the voices. You both mean so much to me!

Chas & Kathy: Thank you for all your PR assistance and for organizing my life. You help me in countless ways, and I'm forever grateful.

Famous Owls: Thank you for being such an important part of my team and for always making me smile. You all rock!

Specials thanks to my ARC team and Enticing Journey Book Promotions for your support on this project.

And to the readers: Thank you for taking a chance on Ander and Kat. It's a new world, which is always scary for me to share, but I'm loving the voices inside. I can't wait to play with Kazek and Winter.

Until next time… xx

ABOUT THE AUTHOR

USA Today Bestselling Author Lexi C. Foss is a writer lost in the IT world. She lives in Atlanta, Georgia, with her husband and their furry children. When not writing, she's busy crossing items off her travel bucket list. Many of the places she's visited can be seen in her writing, including the mythical world of Hydria, which is based on Hydra in the Greek islands. She's quirky, consumes way too much coffee, and loves to swim. Cheers!

ALSO BY LEXI C. FOSS

Made in the USA
Monee, IL
11 June 2024

59620915R00163